PERIL AT THE PELLICANO HOTEL

ADRIANA LICIO

The Home Travellers
Press

Peril at the Pellicano Hotel

Book 4 in the *An Italian Village Mystery* series
By Adriana Licio

Edition I
Copyright 2019 © Adriana Licio
ISBN: 978-88-32249-08-8

Cover by Wicked Smart Design
Editing by Alison Jack

CONTENTS

1

ARRIVALS

The rain had been hammering furiously against the car windows all through their journey, the wipers working at full speed, so discovering that the hotel didn't have a proper garage didn't improve Erminia Spilimbergo's mood. Instead, there was just a simple outdoor car park awaiting them.

"I guess the entrance is beyond the palms over there." She pointed her small curved finger, its nail ruby-red lacquered, at the white building on the other side of a screen of vegetation.

"You're right, Mother, but I can't get any closer than this as the nearest parking places have been taken."

"I guess we'd better wait in the car for a few minutes until it stops raining."

"It's been going on like this for a whole hour, not too sure it will stop in a hurry."

"Of course it will, Francesco!"

Francesco suspected even the weather wouldn't dare to contradict his mother. Instead of replying, he tried to park the car between two pine trees, however ridiculously tight the space was with little room to manoeuvre.

"Go more to the right, then re-align the car and try again," she said, turning her head and looking over her shoulder.

He knew better than to do otherwise. Despite the fact that Erminia Spilimbergo could not drive, she had her own theory on the best way to execute every aspect of the skill, just as she had on almost everything else in life.

"I hope the hotel won't be too damp, it's absurdly close to the sea."

"I'm sure they will have some form of heating. In fact, I asked them."

"It's not the same as staying in a drier place, but at least it won't be as bad as in Portugal." Their accommodation in Porto had had no form of heating whatsoever, despite it being the end of October when they had stayed. Coming from Udine, they'd never imagined a home without a heating system, so they hadn't thought to check with the owner of the accommodation. It hadn't been that cold, to tell the truth, but Francesco had had to put up with his mother complaining incessantly for the entire two weeks of their stay to research the area. He'd learned his lesson.

The minutes passed by, and if anything, the rain got more violent, the wind stronger.

"I hope those precarious branches won't break and hit our car," Erminia said, looking at the pine trees separating the neighbouring car parking spaces and being shaken up by the wind.

"Mother, maybe we should make a break for the hotel." Francesco nervously pushed a pair of rather thick glasses up his aquiline nose, then scratched the black curls protruding all over his large head.

"You should have cut your hair before we set off."

"Mother!"

"And don't scratch your head as if you were a monkey." Then she smiled at him with an unexpected tenderness, as if he were a little child. "Let's wait here a few more minutes. No point getting cold, only to discover the hotel is colder than the car."

He sighed heavily in resignation as the minutes ticked slowly by.

A red and white Fiat 500 entered the car park and the driver parked easily in the space beside them without any manoeuvring. Two women got out, both laughing loudly as one tried to keep an umbrella open while the other pulled a couple of wheeled cases from the boot. The taller figure stopped beside Francesco's dark blue car. Chuckling, she couldn't resist peering in through the fogged windows, only to meet eyes with Erminia.

"Oh my goodness," she cried, still chuckling. "You were right, Valentina, it's the two of them. Erminia, what are you doing sitting there like a dummy? The hotel is just in front of you."

The wind howled and turned the woman's umbrella inside out. From the warmth of her car, Erminia tightened her thin lips and rolled her index finger horizontally to say, "We'll join you later." Undaunted, the new arrival opened the car door, indifferent to the rain and the cold hitting the older woman in the face.

"Come on, we've come to the rescue. I'll shelter you under my umbrella." She let go of the door handle and, with an energetic flick of the wrist, managed to turn the umbrella the right way out.

Erminia hesitated.

"Come on, you can't enjoy a retreat in the hotel car park." And with that, the tall woman opened the car door even more and stretched out her hand, determined not to take no for an answer, even from the formidable Erminia.

Erminia took the woman's hand and clumsily got out of the car, doing up the top button of her coat and pressing her bag against her body to protect the precious leather from the torrent of water.

"Francesco, fetch the luggage. Valentina will shelter you with her umbrella," the tall woman commanded.

Splashing in the water accumulating on the ground, the two women reached the hotel porch, which only partially sheltered them from the rain and not at all from the wind.

"There's the main door," said the tall woman, pushing a lock of dark brown hair from her expressive face. "We're safe!"

"My feet are completely soaked, Vittoria," Erminia blurted out. Her beige court shoes had not provided her any protection. "And I hope the water won't stain them."

Behind them, Valentina passed in front of the entrance and dropped her bag under the portico. Fighting to keep her small umbrella open, she then crossed the hotel terrace, passing the white bar tables getting drenched by the storm, and stopped only when she reached the low parapet. Just below her small, thin figure, the black sea was roaring, its waves furiously pounding against the rocks and flying up into the air, drenching the wall and parapet she was facing. She raised her dark eyes. The sea seemed to have eaten up the beach she had seen in the hotel's promotional pictures. Beyond the mass of water on her right, she recognised the dark mountains through which she and Vittoria had been driving a few minutes before: powerful rocky walls falling directly into the sea, the road suspended a hundred metres above the waves, half way up the vertical mass. The frailty of human beings in the face of the unleashed power of nature made her shudder, while at the same time she was mesmerised by its raw beauty.

Raising her hood and closing her useless umbrella, she shut her eyes and breathed in the smell of the wild sea, feeling the mixture of rain and spray on her face. She passed her tongue over her lips. They were slightly salty, as if drenched by tears...

A light tap on her shoulder made her jump. A tall man was sheltering her with a more robust umbrella. The waves crashing against the rocks below were so loud she could hardly hear what he was saying.

The man raised his shoulders, and then dropped them. His soft smile barely hidden by his thin moustache, he invited her to accompany him inside with a movement of his head. Valentina nodded meekly and he gently embraced her small figure with his arm as they moved towards the hotel.

As they entered, a plump blonde woman with a huge smile on her face came towards them.

"Valentina dear, I'm so happy to see you…"

"Hello, Annika," she replied, hugging the woman. "Feels so good to be here all together again." Her eyes lingered momentarily on the man beside her before moving around the rest of the hall. Erminia, at the reception desk, was already complaining about how cold the hall was.

"Vittoria is waiting for you over by the lifts. As for me, I'd better help Stefano. He's having a tough time with Erminia." Annika's pretty face softened into a grin. "Dump your luggage in your room and we'll be waiting for you in the hotel bar."

Valentina followed her gaze to the end of the hall. There was already loud laughter coming from the bar.

"That's our Guido. I guess he's entertaining Simone with his jokes – and his love of drink. Off you go, now."

As Valentina rejoined her sister, Annika looked at the man who had accompanied her in.

"She is charming, isn't she, Alberto?"

"Of course, you know what I think."

Then why did you let her go? Men are so strange.

"Well, your criteria for assigning the rooms are, of course, all wrong." Erminia was still pestering the receptionist, Stefano. "There's no way we're going to accept a room at the corner of the building. I know it will be dreadfully cold."

"But madam, the central ones have already been allocated, and I can assure you, you will find your room pleasantly warm."

"No! There are more rooms in the other wing of the building."

"But the heating hasn't been switched on in those. We only turned the heating on in this wing…"

"How thoughtless of you! What about other guests?"

"There are no other guests, except your group and two others. This wing will accommodate you all." Stefano was evidently trying with all his might to keep his cool. On the very first week of opening, customers were already complaining. What would it be like by the time the August rush came around, when everyone seemed to think their neighbours had a better room, the air conditioning was too cold or not cold enough, their balcony was too small, their view not as good as...?

Annika sighed and sidled up to Francesco. As tall as he was, he just stood meekly behind his mother, not wanting to get involved, as he had done for his entire life.

"Erminia, dear, have you even looked at your room?" she asked gently.

"No, but I have seen where it is. I don't like corners, especially on days like this. This man does not seem to understand how unreasonable it is to expect me to pay a lot of money for a cold room."

Stefano rolled his eyes.

"My fault, I suggested you have that room," Annika explained. "I thought you'd prefer a larger one as you're sharing with your son." Erminia was gearing up to protest some more, but Annika cut her short. "As I was wrong, you can have my room – a central one – and I'll be more than happy to take yours. I had set my heart on the corner room with its wonderful views, but then decided it would be too selfish of me." She smiled. "Maybe you would like to inspect both rooms before making your final choice. And Francesco, you can have a say, too."

"I'll be happy where Mother is happy," he said, trying to sound as if the issue was too trivial to bother him.

Annika turned towards the desk, rolling her eyes up to the ceiling. "Please, Stefano, hand me the keys to both rooms. I'll let you know who's staying where when I come down. For now, I'll accompany them."

"If Mrs Spilimbergo decides to take your room, I'll send the cleaner up straight away. She will also help you to move your luggage into the corner room."

Erminia did not change her mind. She picked Annika's room, and the latter was only slightly bothered at having to move the stuff she had unpacked that morning to make herself comfortable in her home for the next week. Dropping her luggage in her new room, she caught sight of the mountains from the balcony to the side and the sea from the one straight ahead. As dreadful a day as it was, the view was impressive.

But no time to admire it now. I'd better join the others downstairs.

∼

FROM THE BAR, THE SOUND OF MEN LAUGHING AND CHATTERING greeted Annika, a sign that at least some of the guests were having a good time.

And men are so much easier to deal with than women. At least, some women…

Guido was telling stories in his husky voice with his barely contained energy, and Alberto and Simone were enjoying his tales. Annika looked at the drinks: three tumblers containing a transparent liquid with a 'fly' in each, the fly being a coffee bean, leaving no doubt the liquid was Sambuca, an aniseed-flavoured liqueur and Guido's favourite drink when he was in Italy.

"So, Guido, you're already leading the other guests astray with your bad habits," Annika said as she approached them.

"Come on, it's only a little Sambuca, and these two men are so appreciative now…"

Annika shook her head, smiling. "How about your rooms? Are you happy?"

The three men nodded.

"Excellent," Alberto assured her. A single word from him was enough.

"You couldn't have chosen a better place," Simone said, flushing slightly.

"The place is amazing," Guido said. "A pity about the weather, but the road here is impressive. I can't wait for the wind to calm down a little so I can fly my baby."

"A new drone?" Simone asked him.

Guido nodded enthusiastically. "But mainly a new camera. Shooting from this one is a dream."

"Is it responsible for the videos I viewed on your blog recently?" Simone asked with admiration. "The Dolomites, Abruzzo National Park and some motor races?"

"Exactly, how do you like them?"

"It's another way of looking at the world. One more step in the evolution of photography."

Guido was used to having all the attention focused on himself, but he was generous enough never to forget about the people around him. "And how about our plans, Annika? Have we all arrived?" he asked.

"We're only waiting for Giò, my friend who lives locally and helped me to organise all this. We're supposed to be meeting at 7pm to share our goals for this week, but it's still only 6.30. The four who are upstairs will be coming down soon so we can have a little fun time."

"That means we can have one more Sambuca in the meantime," and Guido emptied his tumbler with a gulp and a laugh.

"Silly boy!" Annika cried.

"It will help me feel more comfortable when everyone's here. I always feel intimidated by meetings."

Alberto smiled at him. "You've never seemed shy to me."

"I try to conceal it the best I can."

"Wish I could," said Simone.

"Then you'd better finish your glass and have one more with me," Guido encouraged him.

"Oh no, don't ruin him too," Annika said. "I will allow you more drinks only after dinner. For now, we wait for Giò."

2

A WRITERS' RETREAT

A tall figure was fighting to get into the hotel, pushing the door with her back to keep it open as she was holding a large tray in her arms. The tray was wrapped up to protect it against the rain that was pouring down more heavily than ever.

Stefano, the receptionist, went to help and offered to take the tray as the woman removed her coat. Then Annika came forward.

"Giò, you should have called me. I would have come out to the car park to help."

"No point in the two of us getting drenched. One's enough." Giò exchanged her coat for the tray. "Have they all arrived?"

"Yes, they're all here," and Annika pointed to the bar. "The late comers are still in their rooms, refreshing. Or should I say, warming up a little? Whatever. In any case, I asked them to join us for a short meeting at 7pm, just before dinner. But now, come along, I can't wait to introduce you to them."

Annika led Giò into the bar, where the three men were waiting.

"This is Giò, an internationally acclaimed travel writer who's been helping me to organise this retreat in Maratea."

Giò's thin face turned pinkish. "Well, in fact, I don't actually call myself a travel writer as I only write travel guides. I'd love to write real travel books."

Guido looked at the tray she was holding. "What's this? Have you prepared a surprise for us?"

Giò glanced around. Alberto looked like a perfect gentleman, probably a bit younger than he seemed, but definitely not her type. Simone was clearly a shy guy looking to hide in the background. And then there was Guido with his cheeky, teasing grin. He was not good-looking – not in a conventional way, at least – but...

No, she wasn't looking for a man. At all. It had only been six months since her partner of 10 years had ruined everything shortly before their wedding, so she was not looking for more trouble. But, just in case, she decided to take the question at face value and ignore any implicit deeper meaning.

"These are bocconotti, a special cake made with sour cherries that is Maratea's speciality. I thought I'd bring some for you as a welcome gift."

"Did you bake them yourself?"

"In fact, I did," Giò lied. Unfortunately, Annika, who knew all about her friend's culinary talents – or lack thereof – let the cat out of the bag.

"Giò's granny is the best chef in town. She baked them for us."

Giò blushed. "Well, she helped me..."

Guido guffawed, unconvinced. Annika stretched her lips in an apologetic grin.

"Well, that was nice of you, Giò, I'm sure we will all appreciate them. Shall we have a taste now?"

"No, Granny says they're best after dinner," Giò replied instinctively, turning red an instant after the words left her mouth.

Everyone burst out laughing.

"So, great chef, take a seat here." Guido invited Giò to sit next to him. "Are you drinking? There's a nice Sambuca here. I made it with my own fair hands before coming over…"

"I don't like Sambuca," Giò replied. "A glass of red will do me."

"Red? You're a passionate but refined type, then?"

"They're coming," said Simone, pointing to the long corridor as the other four guests joined them.

"Since we have the bar all to ourselves," said Annika, "I'm tempted to hold our first meeting here instead of in the meeting room. After all, it will mostly be an informal chat to update each other on the progress we have made since our last meeting."

The guests all nodded in approval. The bar facing the rain-beaten terrace was warm and cosy, and they could sit on the sofas around a little table with their drinks. It all felt like being on holiday with close friends.

"First of all, I want to introduce you to Giò Brando. She's joining our group for this, our second meeting, taking the place of Margherita Durante."

"That hideous woman!" Erminia growled, shaking her head in disapproval, the loose skin on her neck wobbling. She patted Francesco on the back as if to protect him from an evil spirit.

"Mother!" he begged, trying to preserve some dignity. Experience had taught him it was useless to challenge her over-developed maternal instinct, but he still made an attempt every now and again.

"Margherita was what I call a bad mistake," Guido agreed, nodding.

"Well, it wasn't Annika's fault. How could she have known?" Simone's voice trailed off, his freckled cheeks reddening once more, his light-blue eyes sinking in the floor.

"None of us has ever blamed it on her," snapped Vittoria. "But Margherita Durante was certainly the worst thing that could have happened to our group."

"Who was she?" Giò asked. She already knew she was taking the place of someone who had left the group, but she hadn't known that something had gone terribly wrong with her predecessor.

"Evil in person," Vittoria said drily, no hint of humour in her words. And the others all silently nodded in agreement – all except for Guido, who seemed to be somewhat indifferent to the subject.

"Well, we're not here to speak of her." Annika's voice was upbeat. She always tended to look on the bright side. "I told her she had to leave the group, and we've found a positive replacement in Giò. She is a heck of a talented writer."

"And an exquisite chef, too," Guido added mockingly.

"Oh, please!" Giò pretended to slap him on the arm.

Annika carried on, ignoring their little altercation. "Now, if you don't mind, I'd like to suggest we take it in turns to tell the others whether our writing resolutions have changed since last time, what we have achieved so far and what we are hoping to get from this meeting."

The room went silent.

"Do you want me to start?" asked Annika.

"Yes please, you're such a natural icebreaker," Valentina said, gently laying her head with its mass of black curls on her crossed arms. She moved as gracefully as a kitten. Annika told them how she had kept up with her resolution to spend less time on social networks and had cut down to one blog post per week, thus getting more time to write her book on ancient traditions in Western Sweden.

"And I hope to use this week and my stay in Maratea to finish the first draft," she concluded. "Knowing that I was to be accountable to you today has kept me focused all these months."

Everyone clapped their hands enthusiastically. Erminia and her son then told the group about their book on the 16th century paintings found in churches and small towns that were unknown to the tourist masses. A couple of times, Francesco tried to contribute, but the flood of words from his mother drowned him out.

"I think Francesco should say something of his own. Please, Erminia, let him speak," Annika said softly.

They all looked at him expectantly.

"Well, in fact," he blabbered, "in fact, ahem, I think Mother said it all."

"Maybe you want to tell us how you organise your work. What happens after the visits? Do you take notes and use them in your books? How do you share the work between the two of you?"

Francesco turned bright red. "Well, we don't really split our work. We visit places together, and then she writes and I read…"

"And at other times he writes and I read. It really depends on which one of us a particular piece of art has spoken to the most. We don't plan things, as in 'I'm going to write chapters 1 to 10, then he's going to write chapters 11 to 20'. Rather, we keep exchanging pieces and thoughts, and it would be hard at the end of the process to say who's done what."

Francesco nodded in relief as his mother smiled at him.

"That's beautiful, provided you manage to keep the right equilibrium and both of you feel their creative side has not been curtailed, but is free to come out in the final product," Annika commented. Both mother and son assured her that was exactly how the creative process worked for them.

"Well, that's not always so easy when you work together," Vittoria said. "For example, in our recent book on the Balkan countries, Valentina alerted me to the fact I was the one stirring and shaping the project."

"Which was not what you intended, of course," Valentina added.

"No, certainly. But if two people want to give a book a sense of unity, they unavoidably end up with one supplying the greater input, direction, animus, while the other follows on."

"And how's this awareness going to shape your future projects?" Annika asked.

As Simone looked at Annika, Giò spotted the admiration in

his eyes. Annika could be so soft and gentle, but at the same time assertive. Hadn't she helped Giò to find the critical issues in her own writing?

Vittoria laughed. "We decided it was time to do some solo work beside the common project."

"And what's that?"

"We're going to try some fiction – sweet romances and horror. Each to her own project."

"Can't wait to read Valentina's sweet romances," Erminia said, smiling softly at the younger woman. She liked Valentina far better than her curt sister.

"Oh no," Valentina corrected her, "I'll be the one writing horror stories."

Clapping and cheers followed her words.

"There's a roaring fire behind that quiet exterior," Giò heard Guido whispering to Alberto with a meaningful wink.

"I know," the other replied wryly, caressing his thin moustache.

Then came Guido's turn to introduce his work. He started off by cracking a couple of jokes to make them all laugh.

"I'm not good – yet – with words, so I hope you won't mind that I brought some photos along. That's the best way I could think of to introduce you to my project."

He bent down to retrieve a black carrying case from the floor beside him, extracted about a dozen A3 shots and placed them on the table. Without a hint of false modesty, he spoke.

"As you know, apart from Giò who's just joined us, I'm quite good at taking photographs. Almost as good as you are at baking, Giò."

Giò opened her mouth to protest, but no sound came out. All the others chuckled – the story of her pretending to be a great chef had reached those in the group who hadn't been present when she'd arrived.

"I'm sorry, Giò." He looked at her from behind his curtain of curly red hair. "I promise, no more jokes about your bocconotti."

"Now go ahead, Guido," Vittoria prompted. "What are those pictures about? They're splendid."

"These are some of my Iran shots. The country, believe me, is beautiful beyond expectation. I got thousands of photos, and videos, but now I need to compile them – well a selection of them – into a book about Iran. But mostly, I need to write the text. It's not really a story, but neither do I want something too didactic."

"Is that the tough part for you?" Alberto asked.

"Yes, to the point that I've considered hiring someone to write it. But then again, I've spent such a long time in the country, I'm the only one who can write the text to accompany these pictures. For my presentation today, I've picked a few pictures for each chapter – one or two for each topic I want to cover."

One by one, he took each photograph and explained what he had found in the country that had made him think. An entertaining man, good for a laugh and a joke, Guido was serious about his work. A fire was burning behind his hazel eyes. Small head movements highlighted some of his words. He was standing up and his hands, arms, whole body moved around, at times gently, at times more energetically. Used to international audiences, where words could not always be understood, he had learned to use his body language to express his inner feelings.

"This is Iran on a sunny winter's day." He was pointing to a picture of the Aladaglar rainbow mountains featuring incredible streaks of colour, from red to green, copper to purple, embraced by a soft light. Then it was the amazing frescoes and decorations of the Vank Cathedral, the artisans on them designing carpets, painting colourful plates or engraving the metal of teapots and silver cutlery. The hectic bazaar with lights coming through holes in the ceiling; the stunning red of the Allahverdi Khan Bridge, its image reflected on the waters below; mosques and palaces that seemed more like embroidered patterns than real buildings, so rich were the details of their decorations.

Giò was enraptured by his flow of words. She had never visited Iran, but she was enjoying Guido's stories about its hospitable people, ready to share the little they had and curious to meet foreigners and hear their views on their country. Only when he said, "And with this one I'm done," and put all the pictures back into his folder, only when she heard the others enthusiastically clapping and congratulating him, only then did Giò face the rather uncomfortable realisation that she'd better keep her feelings in check from now on. This Guido fellow was a bit too intriguing.

"And what do you expect from this retreat?" Annika asked, sounding as if she had enjoyed his presentation as much as Giò had.

"I'm planning to write the whole book."

"Wow!"

"Well, I won't have much time later, so I'd better use my time here to do the best I can. And you see, it's not a real book. I don't need tons of text as I would for a novel. And I would love some feedback from you all during our evening meetings."

"Guido is referring to our habit," Annika explained to Giò, "of presenting a piece of our writing at the end of the day and discussing it. It's not a 'critical review'; we just express our feelings as everyday readers would, and suggest improvements only if we really feel we have some constructive feedback to give."

Giò was nodding vigorously in agreement. "I've been in a few writers' groups where you were meant to spot faults in someone else's work, regardless of whether you felt your criticism was constructive. We all ended up rewriting passages that were fine as they were, leading to ugly pieces of work much worse than the originals."

The people around her nodded too, as if to say, "I've been there."

"That's why I decided I'd show my work only to you guys,"

Guido said. "I trust you. Well, most of you…" His gaze rested on Erminia and he gave a teasing grimace. They all laughed.

"Awful boy, I've always admired your work. In fact, I've told Francesco he should start by gaining inspiration from pictures and photos, as you do."

"I was just kidding." Guido winked at her and went to hug her as if she was his mummy as well as Francesco's.

"And now you, Alberto," Annika continued as the laughter died down.

"Most difficult to follow Guido," he said with his gentle smile. "I think we should save him for last in future."

"That's a good idea," said Annika with a smile. "But your project is very interesting too."

"Well, since our first meeting, I've been continuing with the idea that emerged there. I've focused on it, made a field trip every other weekend, and I can confirm I'm writing a guide on wines produced in Piedmont, but I'm only considering family-run businesses where the quality of the product isn't compromised by the market. Niche producers of the best quality. I'd love it to be a guide not only for experts, but for those who want to explore the region beyond its wineries. So I will include a few itineraries to allow readers to discover small villages and local traditions."

After Alberto had finished, Annika sent an encouraging look towards Simone. As usual, he turned red and lowered his eyes to the floor, but he spoke nonetheless.

"Well, I'm still writing my trilogy. Last time we met, I had my first book ready to go. I published it, but then I got stuck on the second book, and frankly I haven't done much since. But now I have an outline and plenty of ideas, and I am determined to go ahead."

"You had some doubts because you were writing in a completely new genre, weren't you?"

"Yes, this is my first trilogy in YA fantasy."

"And you launched your first book?" Once more, Annika tried to encourage him.

"Yes, I did."

Annika shook her head. *There's no way I can get this guy to speak.*

"You had so many doubts about that first book. I remember you had to let Alberto read it, and he encouraged you to go on."

"I'm very grateful to him," Simone said in earnest. "All the credit belongs to Alberto."

"You're impossible!" Annika burst out. "What Simone is finding it so difficult to tell you is that his first book was a huge success. Readers loved it and the book ended up in the Italian bestsellers list. Now, they're all asking for a second book."

"Wow!" Giò cried. "That must feel awesome, Simone."

"In fact, I'm not too sure I can write a second book as good." He shook his head, and Giò could tell he wasn't putting on an act.

"Simone is the archetype of the insecure artist." Annika smiled at him. "He doesn't realise how inspiring his success is for the rest of us."

"I'm OK, I'm just happy we're meeting again and hope I can get some help with book two. Believe me, I don't know who wrote that first book, and if it was me, what happened to me while I was writing it?"

Questions and answers followed, then it was the turn of Giò, who felt a little intimidated as all eyes looked at her.

"Well, nothing much for me, really. I've just finished writing an ordinary travel guide to Scotland, and you know how it is… since it's a guide, all my personal bits will be left out. Which is a pity, as I believe it's there, in your own impressions, encounters with people you've never met before, misadventures, unlikely modes of transport to places in the middle of nowhere… well, I believe that's where the real essence of the place lies."

"And Giò has showed me some of the leftovers," said Annika. "Like a man on Rannoch Moor who'd become so friendly with a deer, the animal would come to him whenever he called it while beating a pot with an iron spoon. Or how she got lost on the moor and how black it can get after sunset if you happen to linger outdoors..."

"Well, Annika suggested I write a memoir of *My Scotland*. I'm not sure where I should start, but before I'm commissioned for another tourist guide, I'd love to work on my own project. For once!"

The group clapped their hands, stamped their feet, Guido whistled, and even Francesco hoorayed loudly – looking to Erminia for approval first.

"Do you think this hotel is only here for you?" an angry voice shouted from the corridor.

Startled, they all turned. A sturdy woman in her late sixties stood in the doorway, her square face lined with deep wrinkles around her eyes and lips and crossing her cheeks.

"I do apologise," Annika cried in dismay. "We thought we were the only guests in the hotel."

"Well, as it happens, you aren't."

"As I said, I apologise. On the other hand, it's not yet 8pm and this is a bar, so I wouldn't expect total silence..."

"I know already how this is going to end up, with all of you getting drunk and shouting and vomiting throughout the night."

"My boy would never do such a thing," Erminia growled.

"Do you mean that pudding-head beside you? Well wasn't he whistling loudly just now? As soon as his mummy goes to sleep, he'll be turning to the most dishonourable activities. I know his kind: well-behaved Mama's boy in the morning and drugged-up hooligan in the evening."

Before Erminia could let fly at the woman, Annika intervened again.

"You're totally mistaken. We're a group of authors, and we've come here for a writing retreat. We won't be up late into the night for the simple reason we've got lots of work to do during the day. Besides..."

ADRIANA LICIO

Annika was cut short by the woman's incredulous question.

"Authors? You? And what's your publishing house?"

"We're all indie authors."

"Indie what?"

"Independent authors."

"You mean self-published rubbish. You're the ones dumping all sorts of junk on the market – things a publishing house would never bother with; a rejected and frustrated lot stealing money from unsuspecting readers."

"How dare you!" Vittoria cried.

"As someone with a career of 40+ years in real writing, yes I do dare to say what I think of you useless scribblers. But be warned: at the first hint of noise, I won't hesitate to call the police."

"There are no police in Maratea," Giò said, grinning.

"There are always police, even in a forgotten little backwater such as this."

"No police, just carabinieri."

"Then I won't hesitate to call the carabinieri, or the fire brigade, or whoever is in charge of the damned place as soon as I see you crawling drunkenly across the floor." With that, she turned her back on them and walked through the corridor, supporting herself with a stick. They heard her addressing the receptionist.

"How can you tolerate the noise those people are making, not respecting the peace of the other guests? I'm going to write an awful review on TripAdvisor."

"But Mrs Galli, it's only 8pm, and they are in the bar. We took care to place you as far from the bar as possible – you certainly wouldn't have been disturbed in your room."

"But they're staying in the same wing as I am, and I won't tolerate any noise."

"Curfew starts at 11pm, but I'm sure they will be quiet and peaceful long before then."

"With those dishonest faces? I expect it will be a long night. I wish you had told me when I booked that I would be sharing a roof with a bunch of drunks."

"I don't think…"

"I don't care what you think. All I hope is that you will finally serve my dinner. It's a disgrace that the restaurant doesn't open till 8pm."

"I feel for you, Giovanni," whispered Stefano as she hobbled off towards the restaurant, thinking of the waiter who would soon be attending to her.

3

ALAMUT

Having been pushed along the alleys of Maratea by strong gusts of wind, unable to keep her umbrella open, Agnese Brando, Gio's older sister, was very happy to reach her shop. Opening the heavy wooden shutters was difficult as the wind was constantly pushing them closed again, and she had to hold her bag as well as the useless umbrella. Her rather plump figure wasn't much help, either, when she had to get down on her knees to keep hold of everything, but somehow she finally managed to get in.

She massaged her frozen hands and decided she would not bother to put the rattan sofa outside, as was her habit on sunny days. It would be at risk of flying away, along with the outdoor decorations.

I don't expect many customers will be coming in today anyway. Should I do some bookkeeping?

This was not her favourite task, but it had to be done, and the quiet shop would allow her to get it finished. She sighed, made sure all the lights were on, switched on the radio for company, wiped the counters with a cloth and cleaning spray, swept the floors, and then met her gaze in the mirror.

You can't put it off any longer, can you?

She glanced around. For once, everything looked tidy and in its proper place – no new stock; no jewellery to arrange…

Come on, Agnese, let's make this as pleasant as possible, she thought. Filling the kettle with hot water, she then took her time choosing a candle. She lit it – Fig Tree by Dyptique, so cosy – and inhaled the refreshing perfume, conjuring up visions of greenery and early summer.

Fetching lemon and ginger for her tea, she was ready. She took a huge pile of invoices and started to enter details and numbers on the computer. Barely 10 minutes had passed before the door opened and a drenched figure staggered into the shop. As she removed her hood, Agnese recognised the slightly overweight figure and short pixie haircut with side bangs, the eyeliner and blue eyeshadow enhancing expressive brown eyes. Angelica had been a customer of hers for a long time.

"Thank goodness you're open!" the woman said, searching for an umbrella stand. "I'm sorry I've made such a mess." She pointed at the streaks of water on the floor.

"Hello, Angelica, and don't you worry. I always say that if the floor stays clean for too long, it's not a good sign for my shop."

The woman flashed her a big smile and her embarrassment faded away. "That's a nice way to put it."

"You're drenched, such a pity we should be having this kind of weather in April." Agnese thought about her sister. Poor Giò was feeling awful as guests were coming from all over Italy for a writers' retreat and had been expecting sunny days, walks on the beach, coffee breaks by the swimming pool. "So how are you? I haven't seen you for a while."

"Isn't it strange how it's possible not to bump into each other for so long in a small place like Maratea?"

Agnese nodded. "I guess it's something to do with our daily routines. For me, it's home-shop-home, and having two kids, I seem to find little time for anything else."

"Routine, you're right. That's exactly what's killing me."

Angelica's tone was so distraught that Agnese didn't think this was general chit-chat. Having learned to stay silent at times like this, she tilted her head to reassure the woman in front of her that all her attention was on her and she'd be happy to listen.

"Don't you think life in Maratea is very dull?" Angelica's generous cheeks puffed out as she heaved a melancholy sigh. "There's no excitement, no new things to discover, just one dreary day after another."

"It certainly is a small town…"

"It's not only that. I can speak to you openly because you've never been like them, but I do feel a lot of people here are too jealous or petty. There's never anything good going on, anything to look forward to. Does it make sense to live one's life wishing the days away?"

"I confess," Agnese smiled, "that days seem to fly by for me. It seems only a short time ago I was cuddling Luca as a tiny baby in my arms, and now he's taller than me."

"Oh, I know, it's different when you have kids. I didn't mind it so much when Lidia and Nicola were with me, but now they've left for university, these last two years have made me wonder if I've totally messed up my life…"

"Is something wrong between you and Rolando?"

The woman sighed heavily again. "You noticed that too?"

Agnese hadn't noticed anything at all. She hadn't seen Rolando for ages, either, but when a wife is as deeply dissatisfied as Angelica, the first question to ask is generally how her married life is going. Again, Agnese opted for silence.

"Mind you, I feel rather guilty. Rolando's a good man, and I do feel affection for him, but to him it's no problem if our life goes on as it is for another 25 years. He's such an… how should I put it? Such an unambitious, contented man. He works his office hours, collects DVD and cinema magazines. He takes me to the cinema most Saturdays and for lunch on Sunday at his favourite restaurant. A week in Sardinia in the summer, and another one in the Alps in winter. And that's exactly what my life will look like for the next 30 years."

And with that, she burst into quiet sobbing.

"Oh, you poor love." Agnese reached out and gently stroked her back.

"He doesn't realise how important it is to give meaning to one's life, to *do* things. When we got married, he insisted we'd live in Maratea as he had been offered a job here. And I've spent the best years of my life in this dreadful place."

"It's not that dreadful!" Agnese wouldn't want to live anywhere else.

"How can you say that? We could be living in Rome – there's so much going on there. People dress up, go to theatres, cinemas, film festivals. There's always something new, one must feel more connected to real life living there."

Agnese wondered what Angelica meant by *real life*. But maybe it was better to start with the smaller things.

"I'm sure you can persuade Rolando to spend a weekend in Rome every now and then. Nando and I do that; at times, it's nice to visit cities and see what's going on in the wider world. I understand that. Here in Maratea, we're a bit protected from the great waves of change."

"Not protected, we're suffocated. And the people? They're so banal. They never ask the big questions about life, never strive to do their best. They're just mediocre and satisfied."

"I think people are the same wherever you go," Agnese spoke as if to herself. "I don't think places affect people – inwardly, I mean. And most people living in cities wouldn't have time to fit the big questions into their frantic daily lives. Possibly less so than people here."

"Oh no, Agnese, you're wrong. There's a different level of sensitivity in the city – so many exhibitions, places where people can meet. And I'm fed up with my colleagues at the post office, they're happy to just gossip about each other. That's all they care about."

"Have you shared how you feel with Rolando?"

"I tried, but he doesn't understand. He thinks it's just a whim. He's not aware of my needs, nor does he care."

Agnese looked outside. The rain was still rattling furiously against the glass door. It was unlikely another customer would turn up as long as it continued.

"There's only one way I know of to help you."

"And what's that?" Angelica said after blowing her nose loudly into a handkerchief Agnese had handed her.

"I'll give you a perfume session to discover the right fragrance for you now. That will help you see what you're meant to do."

"That's lovely." Angelica smiled all of a sudden, as happy as a kid in a sweet shop. "I knew you were the only person in this stupid town I could talk to."

Agnese reached for the 'Back Soon' sign on the door, switched on a lamp in an alcove that contained an ebony counter and invited Angelica to sit in front of her. She then opened a drawer next to her legs and, one by one, carefully selected eight different candles.

"Please smell each one of these and choose your favourite. Don't overthink it, just concentrate on which one resonates the most with how you feel today."

"This is so exciting, Agnese. Are you like a Tarot card reader, but with perfumes?"

Agnese shook her head with a soft smile. "No Tarot, and no chatting, please. Just concentrate on each perfume."

Angelica smelled every single candle. With a shake of the head, she pushed away a few she didn't like, then concentrated on the three that were left.

"This one." She finally pointed to a powdery amber-scented candle with touches of burnt labdanum. "It's so comforting and conjures up the beauty of an Oriental night, telling stories around a campfire."

Agnese nodded, took all the candles away, and placed on the

desk eight bottles, each one containing a different perfume accord. She dipped a thin paper strip, or *touche*, in each one and asked Angelica to smell them carefully and make her choice. By this time, the woman was so absorbed with what was going on that she didn't even try to speak. With one hand cupping her pretty, chubby face, she smelled each paper strip, her perfectly made-up eyes closed to concentrate on the scent, then she made her choice without any hesitation.

"Definitely this one."

"A mix of flowers: osmanthus, rose and jasmine."

"That must be a secret garden," Angelica said, her long lashes batting over her dark eyes in excitement.

This woman does not lack imagination, Agnese thought. Selecting eight new bottles, she had Angelica make her third choice. This time, she chose the cosy, resinous essence of benzoin.

"You're definitely in love with the Orient," Agnese said.

"Indeed, I wish I could live the *One Thousand and One Nights*," Angelica joked.

"We'll see what the essences think of your choices," said Agnese, searching through a pile of cardboard tables for the one representing the Oriental family. On one side of the card, a number of perfumes were listed, but she turned it face down so that she and Angelica could no longer read the names.

"What now?" Angelica cried, clasping her hands.

"You've made your choices, now we have to see what Chance suggests for you." Agnese handed her a red and gold spinning top. "It's up to you," she encouraged her.

"Oh my, how exciting." Angelica's fingers gave the wooden top an energetic twist. It spun across the table in a frenzied rush, moving to the right, then to the left, then it flickered as if undecided, and finally it stopped. Agnese pinned the position and turned the table face up.

"Alamut! That's just too perfect for you."

"Alamut? What kind of word is that?"

"It's not a word, nor a name; it's a whole universe," Agnese said as she crossed over to one of her cabinets on the other side of the shop. She came back with a hexagonal red bottle.

"How pretty!"

"Close your eyes and hold out your wrist."

Agnese sprayed Angelica's wrist with two gentle jets, then sprayed more of the perfume in the air, creating a little cloud of essence just above the woman's head. As the essence reached her nostrils, Angelica recognised it.

"That's the *One Thousand and One Nights*!" And she opened her eyes, almost wondering if Agnese's shop had turned into a sultanate.

"This is a beautiful creation by Lorenzo Villoresi, called Alamut after a place he visited in Iran. Everything he smelled there – in magic gardens, harsh mountains and night camps – is captured in this perfume. You may want to use it any time you feel a little low."

"You're a magician! Thanks so much, Agnese."

Angelica paid, declined Agnese's offer of a bag and put the precious bottle of perfume directly into her own bag, which had dried a little from the rain. Encasing Agnese in her plump arms, she hugged her in gratitude, then left the shop.

Agnese sniffed the cloud of perfume Angelica had left behind.

Not too sure what difference a perfume can make, other than cheering her up, but it definitely smelled good on her.

4

THE PARTY-POOPER

"Let's go in with our hands over our mouths and not speak a word, just keep looking at her," Guido suggested to the group on the threshold of the restaurant. But Mrs Galli didn't even raise her eyes from the book she was reading. The waiter, Giovanni, signalled for them to follow him to the other side of the room, as far away as possible from the older woman, and sit next to a table where two other guests were seated.

"I hope they will be nicer than her, or we'd be better off having dinner in our rooms," Vittoria said.

"Dr Siringa," Giò said, recognising one of the two men sitting at the table.

"Hello, Giò, how are you doing?" The man stood up. "Are you one of the few brave enough to come out in this awful weather?"

"In actual fact, I'm staying here for the next week, taking part in a writers' retreat."

"How lovely! May I introduce you to a colleague of mine? Dr Lorenzo Gimondi is the MD – medical doctor – in Capitello."

Giò and the doctor shook hands, and he gave her a half-smile.

"How are patients in your neck of the woods?" Giò asked

courteously. Capitello was a village a few kilometres away from Maratea.

"Better than they would have me believe," the man muttered, the sarcasm glittering in his eyes. Just then, the waiter came over with two dishes of spaghetti and seafood.

"I'd better leave you to enjoy your dinner. It's been a pleasure," Giò said, nodding towards the piping hot dishes.

When she returned to her companions, they were standing, looking out at the sea below the large arched windows. Outside lamps illuminated the dark mass of water, rolling violently below them.

"I didn't realise the restaurant would be just above the sea," Simone said.

"In fact, it isn't," Giò explained. "Normally you'd see a path amongst the rocks, leading to the Anginarra Beach on the other side of the hotel. But the stormy sea has devoured it all; the beaches have disappeared under the waves. It's impressive."

They stood silently, listening to the howling wind and the waves crashing against the rocks and walls.

"So, what can I offer you tonight?" the waiter asked, bringing their attention back into the room.

"Would you suggest something special for our guests?" said Giò without looking at the menu.

"We have some delicious antipasti," Giovanni had evidently been hoping to do just that, "mixed seafood, marinated anchovies, and a few warm specialities directly from our chef."

"I think we might share some of those," said Giò, looking at the expressions of approval on the faces around her.

"If you like seafood, we've got a good selection for our linguine allo scoglio."

"I think that and the antipasti might be enough. We'll decide later if we're having a second course."

"Good idea!" Erminia laughed, her loose skin dancing, her lack of chin making her look like a seal. "Let's not stuff ourselves, we need to conserve a little energy for our first writing sprint after dinner."

Giovanni hovered, unconvinced.

"Yes?" Giò encouraged him.

"We have some paranza... it'd be a pity if your guests didn't try it," he murmured sheepishly.

"Oh my goodness," Giò laughed, "I'm afraid we can't say no to such a treat."

"What's paranza?" Alberto asked.

"It's a mixture of small deep-fried fish, caught yesterday, I guess, as no one could have gone fishing today," explained Giò. "The fish are no longer as small as they used to be, because of the need to ensure they can reproduce and thrive, but it's still an excellent approximation."

Giovanni agreed, nodding. "It includes anchovies, shrimp, red mullet, squid, and it's simply divine! "

"Sounds heavenly to me." Guido jumped up. "And can we get some wine to accompany our food?"

"May I suggest a Grottino di Roccanova?" Alberto said. "It's from Basilicata and I've always been curious to try it."

Giovanni approved of his choice and left.

"Rather than yoga," Erminia said, "we should have a Jane Fonda workout tomorrow morning. I've a feeling we're likely to have put on a few kilos by the end of the week."

The wine tasted and approved, the jolly company soon forgot about the abusive lady on the other side of the restaurant as chit-chat and jokes filled the air. The arrival of the antipasto was celebrated with some loud hoorays and the trays were circulated amongst the guests so they could help themselves.

Valentina was holding a white and blue ceramic dish containing a colourful octopus salad, serving Alberto a few spoonfuls, when she raised her eyes towards the entrance and let the dish, and its contents, crash to the floor and shatter. All the others, startled by the noise and the shocked expression on Valentina's face, followed the direction of her gaze.

At the main entrance door was a tall, striking figure in a long black dress. It seemed as though a character from a 1960s movie, a Sofia Loren or Gina Lollobrigida, had just stepped out of the silver screen. The woman had a generous bust, her dress highlighting her plunging cleavage and thin waist. She had perfectly coiffed long, wavy black hair, but her face wasn't exactly beautiful. Its prominent aquiline nose and strong bone structure made it less feminine than her body. Still, a strange magnetism emanated from her. Giò could feel it from the very moment of her appearance, and it continued as she slowly moved towards the table. The clicking of her high heels filled the room, even drowning out the noise of the waves outside.

"How could you invite her?" Simone managed to whisper to Annika, and all glances moved accusingly towards her.

"I didn't!"

"Oh, but do I see my dear friends sitting here?" The woman had reached their table, her smile enigmatic. "What a surprise! How are you?"

"We were much better a minute ago," Alberto replied, his voice unusually hard.

"Margherita, what are *you* doing here?" Annika asked, charging her words.

"I needed some sea air, the winter has been so long. A pity the weather should be this terrible. But here you all are, Mummy's boy too." She looked at Erminia and Francesco before directing her cold black eyes onto Valentina. "And the poor little kitten is still so clumsy – look what a mess you've made on the floor."

Valentina remained silent, glaring at the woman. Only Alberto noticed that she was clenching her fists so hard that her knuckles had turned white as bone.

"Waiter!" Margherita waved at Giovanni, who was standing by the kitchen entrance. "Please come over here, you need to clean the floor next to this table. Some guests really should learn how to behave. Actually, I think you should *all* learn some good manners – why haven't you asked me to sit with you?"

"We're here to work," Annika replied firmly, "and you know how important it is for us to focus all the energy within the group on our writing."

"Oh come on, Annika, this is your first evening here. You seem to be doing more chattering and joking than anything, and after all, I'm no complete stranger. I was a part of this group." As she spoke, she signalled to Giovanni, who was cleaning the floor. "Would you be so kind as to lay the table for me here?" She pointed to the one empty place at the head of the table. "I want to be close to my friends, but they're all eating fish, and even the smell of it makes me sick." She unlatched her bag and looked inside. "Oh yes, my life saver is here. Please let the cook know that I'm allergic to any kind of fish. Even touching it will make me ill."

"I'm sure she knows, madam, all staff have been informed of any allergies the guests may suffer," Giovanni said. Chest swollen with pride, he cast an admiring look over the woman's body. "And I'll come back to lay the table for you after I've cleaned up here."

"You're a very efficient man," Margherita told him as she sat on the chair at the long table.

"We haven't told you that you can sit with us," Annika said.

"Ouch! Your blunt Scandinavian manner." The woman laughed. "Let's have a little reunion, even if it's just for tonight. I've got things to do myself and won't be able to spend much time with you next week. Erminia, dear, I may be wrong, but do you look older than the last time we met?"

Francesco opened his mouth as if to defend his mother, but no words came out.

"You're absolutely right," Erminia said, her mouth stretching in a grim smile. "I haven't had time to visit the plastic surgeon, as you clearly have. But at least I can smile without fearing that half my face will collapse under the strain."

"Francesco, honey," Margherita accepted the blow with lazy indifference, "shut your mouth so you don't look so much like a boiled cod. As you can see, your mummy can defend herself better than you can. But then again, this mummy can do so many things better than her baby, including writing books for him while pretending her offspring has some genius."

"You shouldn't offend people just because they're not as awful as you are," Vittoria intervened. "That's a rare talent, luckily."

"Oh, the Brontë sisters. Did I mention how much I've missed you?"

"I think I'll go to my room, I'm no longer hungry," Valentina said, standing up and leaving before anyone could stop her.

"Oh, did she leave because of me? What a shame! I do tend to have that effect on grumpy teenagers… even those teens who are at the end of their thirties."

"Did you think she would stay to be offended by your venomous tongue?" Vittoria said.

"Oh, but it was hard for me to be thrown out of the group and not even receive an invitation to join you for your second meeting."

"There was no point in inviting you," Annika said. "I had already informed you that you didn't fit in with the group and our work."

"But I had paid my fee."

"Which was refunded as soon as you were informed of my decision."

"I didn't get a full refund."

"Of course not, you took part in the first retreat."

"I'd never have wasted my money nor my time if I'd known I was going to be thrown out on the slightest pretext."

"Then if you want to be accepted in writers' groups in the future – not mine, for sure – I'd advise you to learn how to behave civilly around your companions."

"OK, I admit I said nasty things last time. I was hurt, a lost soul, but I will behave from now on and won't meddle in your retreat."

Giovanni came over to take Margherita's order, and again she was polite with him. But as soon as he left, she continued to insult the group of writers.

"My dear photographer, I wonder what you're doing here. No offence, but surely your talent lies in the realm of pictures rather than writing?"

"I'm taking a chance. It's better to be resourceful in life." Guido replied coolly, but Giò could feel a tension in him, as if he wasn't as detached as he pretended to be. "And what has brought you here?"

"Business. I tend to work too much – all the time. I can't disclose any more, but when I saw my next engagement would bring me to Maratea… well, I couldn't resist the temptation to move the meeting forward a few days to have the chance to meet up with all of you. And do I see a new face? Are you the one replacing me?"

"I think so," Giò replied.

"Giò Brando, aspiring guide scribbler?"

"And you are…?" Giò tried not to show any surprise at the woman knowing who she was.

"Margherita Durante, writer, screenwriter and PR in the tough publishing industry."

"Are you visiting Maratea for the first time?"

"Oh no, I'm not new to Maratea. I actually lived here for a while. I used to own Villa degli Incanti – I'm sure you're familiar with the place."

"Of course I know it. But it's been a B&B for years now."

"Unfortunately, I had to sell, and yes, that was many years ago…"

Margherita paused. The younger doctor at the next table had choked on his food and his loud coughing was drowning out any chance of conversation.

"Decades, I dare say." Margherita continued as if the

interruption had never happened. "It was a pity the people who took it on had nothing better in mind than converting it into a place for tourists to stay. It used to be a wonderful villa."

"It still is," Giò replied. "There's a beautiful park running all the way around it, and of course it overlooks the sea. It also has a small private beach enclosed by the rocks that cannot be reached from anywhere else."

"Yes, I know. We used to take long swims before breakfast, then sit on my beloved patio amongst the yellow summer brooms. We spent many a happy hour there…"

"We?"

"My late husband and I. But those memories, as well as the brooms' perfume, belong to a different era. I was young and happy then. Possibly the most joyful days of my life."

"So what happened?"

"Nothing much, really. All things in life must pass, and pass they did."

"So was your husband from Maratea?"

"No, he was from Rome. He owned Villa degli Incanti as a second home. At that time, Maratea was attracting all kinds of stars, from football players to famous actors and directors; from Sanremo singers to movie producers. Nothing like today's cheap hordes of tourists, eating home-made sandwiches and not even having the money to hire deckchairs and parasols, but lying on their towels."

"That's only for a couple of months a year." Giò had to defend her town. "Maratea is too far from everywhere to attract mass tourism."

Margherita ignored her words. "That's why I only come here out of season, when you can still enjoy it."

"And that's why," Annika explained to the rest of the company to switch the attention from Margherita, "I decided to start my three-month stay in Maratea now. I will leave in early July."

"Will you be staying at the Pellicano Hotel the whole time?" Vittoria asked.

"No, I'm renting a small flat at a much lower price."

As the dinner went on, the tension didn't exactly disappear, but it relaxed a bit as the guests rolled their forks in a delicious linguine allo scoglio.

Alberto whispered to Vittoria, "Should I call Valentina back?"

"Oh no!" The woman shook her head. "When she's in a bad mood, it's better to leave her alone. But I will tell her how worried you were, I'm sure she will appreciate it."

AFTER DINNER, ERMINIA ANNOUNCED SHE WAS GOING TO RETIRE TO bed. Francesco said he'd stay up a little longer, but his mother reminded him how arduous their journey had been to get to Maratea and how much he needed rest too.

"Don't worry, Mother, I won't stay that much longer."

"You know we have to start writing tomorrow morning," she insisted softly.

"Come on, Erminia." Margherita was whispering as if to Guido, who was sitting by her side, but not so softly that the others couldn't hear her. "The boy is almost 40, let him go to bed when he wants. In any case, we all know who's going to do the writing."

Erminia's face turned purple. "If a certain woman is found stabbed to death by the morning, we won't have to wonder why it happened." With that, she turned her back on the table and left.

"Mother, wait, I've changed my mind." Francesco sent a look of hatred towards Margherita. "I'm coming to bed after all."

5

EVIL IN THE AIR

When Vittoria retired a few minutes later, Giò and Annika decided to leave the restaurant too. Annika wanted to vent all her frustration to her friend, so as soon as they'd walked through the inner door leading to the hotel corridor and hall, she let fly.

"Oh Giò, I can't explain how much I hate that woman. She came here on purpose to stir things up."

Giò tried to console her. "From tomorrow, we will be OK. She said she's got other things to do."

"She was lying. I bet she's got nothing on her mind but creating trouble within my group." Annika stopped walking, as if standing still would give more emphasis to her words.

"Come on, nobody would go to all the trouble of coming down to Maratea in this awful weather just to be a party-pooper."

"You don't know her, she is that nasty. I could happily kill her."

"I guess today has been a tougher day than we expected, but we won't share our table with her tomor…" Giò's voice fell silent all of a sudden.

"What's the matter?" Annika asked.

Giò stood frozen in place, her face tilted slightly forward, her nose pointing to something ahead of them. Annika followed the direction of Giò's stare and saw Mrs Galli sitting on one of the armchairs along the part of the corridor that was used as a reading room. The lamp on the windowsill was switched off, but in the dim light they could still make out that the old woman was in an unnatural position. Her head had fallen forward onto her chest and was sagging slightly to one side; her right arm lay, palm upwards, on top of her body.

"Oh my goodness!" cried Giò, jumping towards the woman, not exactly looking forward to what she knew she had to do. Fortunately, Annika was by her side, ready to help. Only partially comforted by her friend's presence, Giò softly touched the woman's shoulder. Mrs Galli didn't stir.

Frantically, Giò started shaking her.

"Wake up! Wake up!" she cried in a frenzy.

A second later, all three of them were screaming: Giò, Annika and… Mrs Galli.

"Wha… wha… what's happening?" uttered Mrs Galli finally, pressing her hands against her heart as if the fright had hurt her physically.

"You… you… you're alive?" Giò asked, startled.

"I'm not sure for how much longer after such a fright," the woman growled, her hands not leaving her chest as she tried to deepen her breathing.

"We thought you were… err… not feeling well," Annika explained.

"And so you decided to help me by scaring me to death?"

"We didn't mean to…"

"I knew from the beginning you were trouble."

The night concierge, alarmed by the screams, came over to ask what was going on.

"My friend and I thought Mrs Galli wasn't feeling well," Giò explained.

"They woke me up so abruptly, I could have died on the spot.

ADRIANA LICIO

I've already told the hotel owner she shouldn't allow troublemakers in if she wants dignified guests to keep coming back."

"Madam, I'm sure these two women didn't alarm you on purpose."

"Really? They shook me from my sleep with a great deal of purpose. They want to get rid of me because I have already complained about their loutish conduct."

The man tried again to soothe her. "Can I bring you some water and sugar to help you recover?"

"Yes, and a double whisky will help," the woman replied. "Then you'd better accompany me to my room. Too many dangers lingering here."

"Then I will accompany you first and bring your drink from the bar soon afterwards," the man said, helping the woman to rise from the chair and winking at the other two.

"You won't be charging the drink to *my* room, will you?" Mrs Galli cried. "It's purely medicinal because of the kind of guests *you* allow on the premises."

"No, madam, the drink is on us to apologise for what has happened."

"Then you'd better make it two double whiskies. I will need a second one when I inevitably wake up in terror in the middle of the night."

"I'll be happy to do that, madam."

As the lift doors closed, the two friends caught the last of Mrs Galli's words.

"You're such a charming boy. Well mannered, and good-looking too."

Giò and Annika burst into uproarious laughter.

"How about we sit here for a while? I need to recover from both the fright and the dinner."

"How did I ever think she was dead?" Giò wondered, sinking into a comfy sofa.

"Margherita Durante has cast a dark shadow on the place,"

Annika said, her sulky voice contrasting with her expressive face. "There's something gloomy in the air, and it's got nothing to do with the weather, nor with Maratea. I'm unhappy that the men are still sitting with her. She has an arcane power over them."

"I don't think it's that arcane." Giò smiled. "But it's true – even Guido, for all his confidence, seems to be rather taken with her."

"They had a sort of relationship during our first retreat. Or maybe 'relationship' isn't the right word."

"Oh," said Giò, disappointed. "I thought he'd be stronger than that."

"Well at least he wasn't falling at her feet. Maybe he felt attracted to her, but he soon realised what she was really made of and has not been pining after her, as I've seen other men doing."

The main door opened and Vittoria dragged her sister in from the hotel terrace. They were clearly not aware of the two friends sitting on the sofa in the dim light of the corridor.

"You're drenched!" Vittoria was saying. "I thought you had gone back to our room…"

"I did, but I was too angry and restless to stay. I hate that woman and I'm going to kill her if she is still here tomorrow."

Vittoria pushed the lift button. As they waited, she whispered, "I'd kill her too if I thought I could get away with it."

As the sisters left, Annika sighed. "It's going to be hard to hold a retreat in these conditions. I feel responsible…"

"We all know it's not your fault. Do you think she went on your website and read when and where we were going to meet?"

"Isn't that what she said in the restaurant? She moved her supposed engagement to coincide with our retreat. I would have just written personal emails to all of you with the details if I'd suspected what she was up to. But for marketing new courses and classes, it's good for people to see I organise retreats, and I love putting the 'sold-out' tag on them. I confess, it's my best marketing tool."

"Of course, I understand."

Two figures came out from the restaurant, one of them upset.

"It's not the first time she's told me to my face what an awful writer I am. Frankly, I believe it's true."

"Come on, man, your readers have a very different opinion of both you and your books. I wouldn't give a damn about what that woman says…"

"My poor Simone," Annika whispered, her heart tightening in tenderness.

"Let's have a drink at the bar and forget about it," Alberto added, leading Simone in that direction. "Erminia was right – I wouldn't be surprised if Margherita ended up stabbed in the back. She's done enough of that – metaphorically, of course – to other people."

"I can't believe Guido decided to stay and chat with her," said Simone. "I could no longer bear to be near her."

"I think he's just teasing her, and she is too full of herself to realise it." Alberto smiled. "He's got good reason to take his revenge on her."

6

AFFINITIES AND BEYOND

G iò awoke early the next morning. Looking outside, she was greatly disappointed to see the weather was as bad as it had been the day before. The beach was still obscured by the waves, the sea stopping just below the wall separating it from the hotel terrace. The wind was howling through the trees next to the car park. At least the rain had stopped for the time being, which was good news as she needed a walk before breakfast.

"Hello, aren't you staying for the yoga class?" A voice stopped her as she reached the threshold of the hotel. Guido was sitting on one of the sofas in the hall, his laptop on and a number of papers spread on the table in front of him.

"Not really a yoga person, I'm afraid. I prefer a little fresh air. Are you already at work?" she asked, noticing the dark shadows under his eyes.

"I need to move fast this week to get as much done as possible."

"Frankly, I thought you were at risk of a hangover, after seeing you neck back all those Sambucas last night."

"I love them," he laughed guiltily, "but they shouldn't interfere with my work. Would you like a companion on your walk? I need a break."

"Of course."

"I will leave my laptop at reception; I think I can leave all these papers here."

They walked along the road that ran above the coastline, stopping quite a few times to admire the tumbling sea and the view of the gulf.

"That's the road you were on yesterday," said Giò, pointing to the rocky mountains above and beyond the hotel. "That's the Acquafredda rock tunnel," she pointed to a spot where the grey line of the road was eaten up by the mountain.

"That's an impressive road, a real marvel. I stopped my car quite a few times, despite the pouring rain," he replied, following her gaze. "An awesome place, thanks for inviting us here."

"Well you should thank Annika, really."

"That woman knows how to organise things."

Giò smiled. He'd just given her the perfect opening.

"No matter how good an organiser you are, there's always the chance someone may turn up and ruin all your efforts."

He nodded. "Margherita is a pain…"

"You seemed quite happy to see her last night."

"You were all running away. I didn't want to give her the satisfaction of believing we were all affected by her power."

"Her power?"

"Yes, her power to ruin our meeting, to hint at things, to dredge up ghosts of the past, as she did with Valentina, Francesco and Simone. I don't like the woman, but I want her to know she's got no power over me."

"Annika told me you enjoyed her company on the first retreat."

He laughed. "You're quite well informed, aren't you? I could see you and Annika chattering last night."

Giò flushed, but kept looking at him. "So?"

"So I did. She attracted me and I didn't turn her down. I agree, I was a little foolish. At times I can still behave like an adolescent who wants to show the world how strong and gallant he is. But in the end, it was just an innocent fling."

"Innocent?"

"I'm a free man, she's a free woman – or at least, that's what she told me. Why not?"

"Is this going to be how you behave this week too?"

He looked along the horizon, all the way to the clouded shape of Mount Bulgheria on the other side of the gulf, then slowly shook his head.

"No, I don't think so. I don't like her. It just happened last time. As I said, at times I am too eager to accept all sorts of challenges. But frankly, I don't care about her, and I've got my project to work at."

He spoke with simplicity; there was no bragging in his words. But as usual, Giò wanted to go deeper now she'd started digging.

Assuming a casual tone, she asked, "Why did you stay on with her in the restaurant after dinner?"

"We just had a couple of drinks together. As I said, I wanted to show her I'm my own master." He laughed at himself. "Then I left as I wanted an early start this morning. And in fact, you did find me up and working, didn't you?"

His humour was infectious. Giò found herself not only laughing at his ways with Margherita, but also trusting he had told her nothing but the truth.

A seagull left one of the rocks where a crowd of birds were chattering and flew low above the water level, as if challenging the waves to catch him.

"He's the only one flying!"

"He must be a free spirit."

"We've found our Jonathan," said Giò, thinking of *Jonathan Livingston Seagull*, a book that had always inspired her.

"Yes, must be him. He's doing what the others dare not," Guido murmured. Then from the horizon, his eyes turned back to Giò. "So you're going to write a travel memoir about Scotland. Why did you choose that country?"

"I lived there for five years, it's my second home. I've been hiking there, getting on trains to the middle of nowhere, met the most incredible people, shared a flat with two Scottish girls in Springburn, Glasgow. If I could live in two places, Maratea and Glasgow would be my choices."

"Glasgow is a bit on the rough side, isn't it?"

"Maybe it's not as charming as Edinburgh; you've got to dig deep to understand what a warm heart it has. But I felt welcome there from the first moment I arrived. It's a sincere city. It has had its ups and downs, but its wish to improve has always been there. There's such a special energy, an openness to foreigners I rarely found anywhere else." She stopped, almost out of breath. "Do you feel the same about Iran?"

"I wouldn't say that. It's a country I love, but I wouldn't call it my second home. I've got many favourite places around the globe, and it's my current love. But I'm afraid I'm not as faithful as you are, and this is why I want to finish this project as soon as possible so that I can jump on to the next one. But I will return to Iran; you can never have enough of its colours, its light. I'll show you a few more photos and videos, if you wish. Yesterday I didn't want to take too much time with my presentation so I only shared a small selection."

"Yes, I'd be glad to see more."

"We'll do that, then. And I hope the weather will clear up; it looks as if Maratea is an amazing place filled with treasures to discover."

They had arrived at the end of the road and Guido was pointing at a path stretching amongst the rocks, emerging only when the waves retreated back to the sea.

"Yes, there's a path connecting this beach with a much smaller one in the southern part of Acquafredda. In the next few days, if it's not been damaged by the storm, we could walk there. It leads to Villa Nitti, a beautiful villa from the 19th century that rests on the rocks above our heads. You would hardly guess it's there. But I'm afraid it's time for our breakfast, so let's return to join the others."

Guido's eyes followed the seagull, now high in the sky. Wings stretched to ride the wild winds, the bird was gliding above the sea in large circles. Guido paused to take it all in before turning back to follow Giò.

THE HOTEL WAS BUSTLING WITH EXCITEMENT WHEN THEY RETURNED. Some of the group had completed their first writing session and were enthusing about it, while others had gone to practise yoga with Annika. Chattering as they made their way along the corridor, the writers moved towards the restaurant for their well-earned breakfast.

Once inside the large restaurant, they again stopped to look from the arched windows at the view of the waves hitting the walls and flying high just under their noses.

"Thanks so much, Giò, you've brought us to an amazing place," Simone said.

Giò smiled at him, and then moved towards the other side of the room to have a look from the most exposed corner of the restaurant. Their table was already laid out, but Giò ignored it. She had stopped suddenly with a puzzled expression on her face.

"What's up?" asked Guido, following her.

Giò shook her head, smiled. "Nothing, really. Sometimes my imagination runs away with me."

She shook her head once more and looked towards the window. Her face fell. She rubbed her eyes, looked some more, and finally cried out.

"It can't be!"

"What?" Guido was now beside her and followed her gaze. "My goodness!" He kneeled down by the figure lying on the floor, touched her wrist to feel her pulse, but as he'd suspected from the body's unnatural position, he was too late.

"She's dead," he said incredulously.

Margherita was no longer going to make any trouble for the group.

7

EVERY QUESTION HAS AN ANSWER...
OR TWO

"The police?" Erminia asked, her face turning white as a few figures in black uniforms crossed the hotel terrace to enter the restaurant via the outside door. "What are the police doing here? I thought the woman had died of natural causes."

"It's the carabinieri." Giò warned her that the new arrivals wouldn't appreciate being called 'police' at all.

"It's a sudden death in a public place," Annika explained. "They have to make sure it's nothing suspicious."

They were all sitting on the sofas and armchairs around a low table in the hotel hall.

"What kind of illness could have killed her? I wonder. She seemed to be brimming with good health," Giò thought aloud.

"Do you think so?" Vittoria said, plunging on to the sofa beside Valentina. "She looked very pale to me, and... I don't know how to put it... rather... rather..."

"Rather off colour, I'd say," Erminia agreed, nodding.

"It seemed as if she was aware she wasn't well," Alberto added quietly.

Giò looked at them in surprise. To her, the woman had looked happy to be there last night, playing her part in disrupting the writers' retreat. She had never thought for a moment that Margherita might have known she had something wrong with her, as the others were hinting. But then again, they had shared a whole week away with the woman only a few months earlier, so surely they knew her better than Giò did.

As if reading her thoughts, Valentina looked up at Alberto.

"Did you really feel there was something wrong with her last night?"

"Yes, she looked like someone who was merely pretending to be well. It was just an impression that popped into my brain, but I couldn't shake the feeling."

"I agree," Erminia said. "That sums it up exactly. She was only pretending to be her usual self, but there was something wrong with her..."

A carabiniere came forward. Not too tall, he was slightly chubby with frank hazel eyes and a pleasant voice that could gain him instant empathy. He nodded to Giò. In a small town such as Maratea, most people knew each other, but in their case, they had also done a fair bit of sleuthing together in the not-so-distant past.

"Good morning, I'm Brigadiere Rossi of the Maratea Carabinieri. As you're guests of the hotel, I hope you won't mind if I ask a few questions of you."

They all nodded.

"As I understand, you're here for a writing retreat."

"We are," Annika confirmed. "I'm the organiser, and this is my group of authors."

"Are you the whole group, or is someone missing?"

"No, there are nine of us, and we're all here. Do you want the names of each of us?"

"I will need to take statements from you all individually later, but let's see what Dr Siringa, the pathologist, says first. And yes, if you have a list of names, that would help."

While Annika took out her notepad and pen and started to write the list of names, Brigadiere Rossi continued.

"For the moment, I want to ask a few generic questions. Did any of you know the woman who passed away?"

The writers looked at each other with such guilty expressions on their faces that Giò felt quite alarmed, but Paolo didn't seem to take any notice and waited patiently.

"Well," Annika stopped writing and drummed the tip of her pen against the notebook page, "we all knew her. You see, she participated in our previous retreat."

Paolo looked puzzled. "You mean she was part of your group?"

"Not any longer. She only participated in the first retreat, and was here accidentally this time."

Paolo's brows shot up to his hairline.

"Accidentally?"

"Coincidentally, I mean."

Paolo let the silence that followed stretch on until it became uncomfortable, and Annika found herself explaining that things had not worked out well at the previous writers' retreat.

"If that's so, how come you met up again here in Maratea?"

"As I said, it was just an acc... a coincidence."

The others nodded in silent approval.

"You didn't know she was coming?"

"None of us knew. It was quite a shock when she turned up."

"In the woman's bag, we found two EpiPens to counteract anaphylactic shock. Were any of you aware she suffered from some form of allergy?"

Again, all heads nodded in unison.

"During our first retreat, she told us many times." Vittoria spoke for all. "She suffered from a fish and crustacean allergy, a rather severe form, so wherever she went, she made sure that people knew. Especially people in hotels and restaurants."

"Do you have any idea if she informed the staff of the Pellicano Hotel too?"

Alberto told him how the waiter had reassured Margherita that all the staff knew about her condition. By now, Brigadiere

Rossi had taken a chair and was making notes, asking whoever was speaking to introduce themselves.

He must have realised that he can get more spontaneous answers right now than in the official statements later, Giò said to herself.

"Did you notice her tasting anything that might have contained fish or crustaceans?"

"You should ask the kitchen staff," Alberto suggested. "I take it you suspect she died of anaphylactic shock…"

The second Alberto mentioned the words 'anaphylactic shock', both Vittoria and Erminia sighed softly and, possibly unaware of their own reactions, sat back against the sofa pillows, looking far more relaxed than they had a few seconds earlier.

"That's for the pathologist to say. We're trying to understand the dynamics in the meantime. And yes, we will question the kitchen staff too, but I happen to know you were passing around trays of antipasto. Any chance the victim might have picked up something from the wrong tray?"

"Absolutely not," Annika said, her voice typically firm. "Margherita was extremely mindful of her allergy. She used to say that even the smell of fish made her sick, which was why she picked a chair at the head of the table, further away from the rest of us."

"Any chance the waiter may have inadvertently dropped a bit of the wrong food in her dish while serving?"

"No, all her dishes came covered by a plate. As for the antipasto, we were circulating the trays, not the waiter. We never passed them anywhere near her. And you can be sure she would have screamed at us if we did."

"Got it," Paolo said. "I'm very sorry for what happened to your friend. Do you know who's her next of kin?"

They all shook their heads; Margherita had never spoken of her family, if she had any, apart from a legion of former husbands. And it was all too easy to lose track of them.

"Then I hope you can help me with this. At what time did

you leave the restaurant, and did any of you notice anything strange about Mrs Margherita Durante?"

"I was the last one to leave," said Guido. "Margherita and I talked and drank a couple of Sambucas together, then I left her at around half past ten. And no, I didn't suspect anything was wrong with her..."

"Well, that's not strictly correct," Erminia interrupted him. "A number of us noticed Margherita wasn't her usual self. She seemed to be... how should I put it?"

"Like someone who's not well, but is doing her best to hide it," Vittoria came to the rescue.

"What made you think that?"

"Well, it was the small details. She looked pale and tired, maybe her voice was not as firm as usual."

"Something was wrong with her," Alberto continued, "but it's difficult to put my finger on exactly what."

"So you didn't suspect she was at risk of going into anaphylactic shock?"

"Oh no, it wasn't anything as obvious as that," Erminia answered.

"Would you all agree that there was something different about Margherita Durante last night?"

Before anyone could speak, Giò gave her opinion.

"I thought she seemed fine, but then, it was the first I'd met the woman, so I had no point of reference. But she looked well to me."

"Oh, she could be a good actress," Alberto said.

"Along with other things..." Erminia began. For once, it was Francesco who silenced her with a look, but Paolo hadn't missed her words. He interrupted his scribbling to look up at her.

"Other things like what?" he asked.

"Well, she wasn't a pleasant woman at all. I'm not saying I'm happy she died the way she did, but I'm not desperately sad either."

But Paolo didn't seem interested. He turned his gaze towards Guido.

"When you were having your chat with Mrs Durante, after all the others had left, were you still sitting at your dinner table?"

"No, the waiter had come over to clean the table and set it up for breakfast. He asked us if we wouldn't mind sitting at the next table, closer to the window – the one where we found her this morning. So we sat there for a couple of drinks."

"Why didn't you move to the bar?"

"I suggested that, but Margherita said she had a manuscript to read, and she liked the idea of sitting there with the sound of the sea. She asked the waiter if she could linger there, and he replied he'd tell the receptionist to switch off the lights later on when she was done."

"Did she complain of feeling dizzy or show any signs of distress?"

"No. When I left, she was enthusing about her unusual working environment."

"And you left at what time?"

"As I said, it must have been around 10.30."

"And did you go directly to your room?"

"No, I stopped at reception and asked for a thermos of coffee to take upstairs."

"Did you meet any other guests on the way to your room?"

Guido thought about it. "No. As I said, I only met with the receptionist, and when he came back with the coffee, I let him know that Margherita was still in the restaurant."

"What did he say?"

"That the waiter had informed him and he'd leave the lights on until Mrs Durante was done."

"Any of you others see her after 10.30?"

Before answering, Vittoria and Alberto looked at Valentina, Erminia at Francesco, Simone at Annika. Finally they all shook their heads.

"Lucky it's not murder or I'd be the suspect," Guido joked.

"If there was any negligence on the part of the restaurant staff in dealing with a known allergy," Paolo's face was grave, "it might well be considered murder."

STANDING UP FROM HIS CHAIR, BRIGADIERE ROSSI SPOKE FORMALLY to the group sitting in front of him.

"Please stay in Maratea till the end of your retreat. You need to inform the carabinieri if you are leaving the area even temporarily as we might need to speak to you. Finally, I'm afraid we need to tape the hotel restaurant off for the next few days."

"But this will totally disrupt our schedule," Annika said. "We were meant to have all our meals here to have more time for our writing."

"The owner has already contacted a nearby hotel. You'll be able to take your meals just 200 metres from here."

As the brigadiere left, the group looked at each other.

"Such a pity, I loved our restaurant," Valentina said.

"I know, dear, but at least that's the last time that woman will upset our lives," Erminia consoled her, patting her back.

Excusing herself quietly, Giò followed Paolo along the corridor.

"Paolo, wait. What's happening? Why all these questions?"

He turned towards her and spoke rather abruptly. "Giò, someone just died."

"I know, but that's not our fault. She shouldn't have been here in the first place."

"She liked to muddy the waters, didn't she?"

"I hardly knew her, but from what I heard and the little I saw, that's exactly the impression I got."

He looked at her intensely, but didn't reply.

"So what's on your mind?" she asked.

"Nothing much, really, I just find it strange she didn't even try to reach for the EpiPen in her bag, nor ask for help."

"Are you sure it was anaphylactic shock?"

"That's for the pathologist to say."

They had reached the other end of the corridor, next to the entrance to the restaurant, and Giò recognised the hotel owner talking to Maresciallo Mangiaboschi. He had his back to her, but Giò had no doubt it was him. His rugby-player's figure and deep voice were unmistakeable.

But the hotel owner, as small as she was, was not intimidated by him. "We've had guests with allergies staying before, attending weddings with 200+ guests, and nothing untoward has ever happened. All my staff have been fully trained…"

"Maybe your chef…"

"Maybe my chef nothing! She's been with me for the past 15 years and she's scrupulous about every single item of food – all ingredients, labels and possible contamination. She was informed of Mrs Durante's allergy and passed the detail on to all her staff. Ask Giovanni, the waiter; he will tell you the instructions he received to deal with Mrs Durante's food."

"But still she died."

"Maybe she had other health issues. Maybe she took a bite of food from the wrong dish. I don't know, but we did all that we had to do to ensure her safety."

"That's for the judges to decide, if it comes to it." Mangiaboschi turned and spotted Paolo. "Where were you?" he asked gruffly. "The owner has arrived and you should have been here to take down her statement."

"I was interviewing the other guests. They also knew about Mrs Durante's food allergy." As the brigadiere moved forward, Giò followed in his footsteps, desperate to hide herself.

"Who's that behind you?"

Paolo moved sideways and Giò emerged, her mouth already emitting a sigh.

"The Brando woman? What's she doing here?"

Oh, anyone but Maresciallo Mangiaboschi, thought Giò. Saying their relationship had never been an easy one was an understatement.

"As I told you, some of the hotel's guests are holding a writers' retreat," Paolo replied.

"I thought they were serious people..."

"How dare you!" Giò cried.

"How dare *you* stick your nose in carabinieri business all the time?" Then turning his gaze towards Paolo, Mangiaboschi asked, "Have you questioned her?"

"Just finished."

"Do we have good reason to hold her?"

"No, not really." As used as he was to his superior's brusque manner, Paolo was embarrassed by how rude he could be, not just with criminals or suspects, but with anyone who didn't conform to his exacting standards – standards, as far as the brigadiere was concerned, that only the rich or the powerful met.

"Then let her go, but keep an eye on her and don't allow her to leave Maratea until we've solved the case. Now let's look at the kitchen – the forensic team is already at work."

Mangiaboschi followed the hotel owner into the kitchen. Paolo had just enough time to whisper, "Go back to the others, I'll speak to you later," to Giò before his boss's voice demanded that he'd better join him – now!

8

VOLEUR DE ROSES

A gnese felt deflated as she looked at the long line of rejected lipsticks lying on the makeup shelf. How many were there? About twenty? They were all shades of coral, but apparently not one of them met the expectations of Romina.

Sometimes it happened that a customer had something in mind that Agnese simply didn't stock, but why was it that every time Romina came into her shop, it was always – and her mind stressed the word *always* – with a request that took well over an hour of her time, only to be fruitless? In the past five years, had Romina bought a single thing from her shop? Nope.

Romina had just left and Agnese was still ruminating when a little man, wearing square spectacles almost as big as his face and a long raincoat that made his chubby body look even shorter, entered her shop.

"Hello," he whispered sheepishly.

"Hello, is there any way I can help you today?"

"Indeed, that's what I hope," he said, looking around with the pitiful expression of one who wouldn't normally dare to enter such a feminine environment.

"Yes?" said Agnese encouragingly. The man didn't seem about to add any more words to his request.

"I don't know exactly how to put it…"

Agnese tilted her head, wondering what was coming.

"The thing is that our wedding anniversary is coming up and I still have no idea what to give to my wife."

Agnese sighed with relief. If that was all he needed, she had plenty of ideas. She showed the man the nicest of her necklaces, her set of travel perfumes in beautifully decorated little bottles, the silkiest of her scarves, some gift boxes filled with makeup items that would make any woman's heart skip a beat in excitement. But each time, the man shook his head sadly, unconvinced.

Is he going to be the second customer to leave my shop empty-handed and disappointed this morning? thought Agnese as she showed the man a set of luxury items for the bath and body care. But unlike Romina, who looked victorious every time she left, as if she took pleasure in showing Agnese how useless her shop was, the man wore an expression of quiet despair.

Finally, shaking his head one last time, he got ready to leave.

"I'm so very sorry to have taken up this much of your time, but I guess I'm on an impossible quest."

The palpable sadness emanating from the man made Agnese's heart contract with sympathy.

"I'm sure you will find something, there are so many shops around for you to try," she encouraged him.

"I don't think so. I've been everywhere, but there simply doesn't seem to be anything that's good enough."

"Good enough for what?"

"Good enough to keep my wife, I'm losing her."

"Oh my goodness, is she sick?"

"Oh no, not at all. She's simply bored, tired of me…"

"But that's wonderful!" cried Agnese in relief. The man looked at her in amazement. "I mean, if she's not sick, there are plenty of things you can do about it, believe me."

"On Tuesday, we celebrate our 24th anniversary. I will buy her something at the last minute, maybe some flowers, but I already know how disappointed she will be. I've been searching hard for ideas, but none have come to mind. She tells me I'm such a boring, unambitious man, but I love Maratea, our home, our garden, our kids phoning us in the evening or coming over during the holidays. But this is no longer enough for her, and I know it's all my fault. I don't know what else to do to make her happy..."

The man was shocked at the words that had flowed unchecked out of his mouth. He had always kept his family affairs to himself, but he had been bottling up too much recently: all the sighs; all the contemptuous expressions on his beloved wife's face; all the powerlessness he was feeling as he realised she was slipping away from him.

"I'm sorry, I shouldn't have burdened you with my troubles..."

"Oh no, not at all," Agnese reassured him. Whenever she was faced with a problem, she felt relieved. It was so hard to deal with the unknown, but finally she had recognised Angelica's husband, she hadn't seen him for so long. Even better, now she knew how to help him.

"You go and sit there," she directed him to the ebony table in the alcove and went to close her shop door, putting up the 'Back Soon' sign. She then sat in front of him and started her perfume session. The man followed all her instructions blindly, an anguished expression on his face.

When Agnese finally turned the perfume table face up, she cried enthusiastically, "Voleur de Roses! Your preference for patchouli and roses has led you this far. There's a bold man inside you."

The man looked after her in dismay as she went to fetch a bottle of perfume from one of her cabinets.

"Hold out your wrist," and she sprayed him generously with the musty, velvety fragrance. The man breathed in the scent, and then smiled at her.

"This is a beautiful fragrance. But do you mean it's for me, not for my wife?"

"Indeed it is. Voleur de Roses is a French name, meaning 'thief of roses'. I believe it represents those men who wouldn't hesitate to steal a bunch of roses from a secluded garden to gift their woman with the rarest of flowers."

The man in his oversized raincoat looked at her incredulously.

"But stealing is not a good thing, Mrs Fiorillo."

"Nope, it's not a good thing, but sometimes women need something out of the ordinary, something once in a lifetime. There comes a moment in our life when we need to dare to do dangerous things, walk the unbeaten path. Keep this scent on all night long and let the fragrance inspire you."

The man paid for his fragrance. Trying to assume a dignified air, he stumbled over the belt of his raincoat just before he reached the door.

Let us hope for the best, said Agnese to herself as the man finally managed to recover his equilibrium and leave the shop.

9

TOO HAPPY AT DINNER

Once the brigadiere had left, the writers' group had a light breakfast at the Pellicano's bar, a simple cornetto and cappuccino. Later, Annika invited them to return to their rooms in order to get some writing done before an early lunch at the hotel nearby, encouraging them to do their best despite all the disruption.

Giò had just reached her room when she realised she had left her notebook somewhere. She'd had it in her bag during the walk with Guido, then had pulled it out to write something in the breakfast room, and left it… on the breakfast table when she made her grisly discovery. Surely the carabinieri would not object to her retrieving it? After all, it wasn't a piece of food, nor had it been there the evening before. No, it had definitely played no part in the crime – if crime it was – so she could at least ask the carabinieri if she could have it back.

When the lift doors opened on the ground floor, there was no one at the reception desk, nor in the hotel hall. Giò went towards the restaurant. The door had been cordoned off, but there was nobody around to ask if she could enter. Maybe she'd find someone inside.

With her typical impetuousness, she reached for the door

handle beyond the tape, but the door was locked. She gave it a couple of useless shakes.

How stupid of me, all my notes are in there! Goodness knows when I'll see them again.

Her fingers were still holding on to the handle when she felt it turning. Somebody was coming out of the room.

Before she had the time to think, she'd hidden behind a thick curtain, probably used to isolate the relaxation areas from the rest of the hall. She wasn't in a hurry to encounter Mangiaboschi again, let alone ask him if she could fetch her notes.

But it wasn't Mangiaboschi who emerged. The door opened to reveal two men, one holding the tape up to allow them both to pass underneath it. She recognised Dr Siringa, and he was speaking to Dr Gimondi, the MD she had been introduced to the previous evening. Dr Siringa was inviting his companion to sit at the table just in front of Giò. From her hiding place, she was able to see Dr Siringa's face, but the other man sat with his back to her.

Dr Siringa pulled out his forms and wrote some notes, thinking out loud.

"We'll see if the autopsy finds any fish traces in her stomach, but it might be too small a quantity to detect."

"Maybe you'll have better luck from the analysis of the ingredients in the kitchen."

Dr Siringa nodded. "I wouldn't be surprised if that's the case – some stock cube, sauce or salad dressing. Something that may look like an innocuous ingredient, but still contains traces of fish. We'll also need her medical records."

"To find out if she has suffered from anaphylactic shock recently?"

"Yes, and how severe any previous attacks were," Dr Siringa said. "But I'd also like to know if she suffered from any other medical condition."

"You're thinking her death might not be due to anaphylactic shock after all?"

"It's something I can't rule out, especially as no one witnessed it."

"Did no one notice anything wrong with her during dinner?" Dr Gimondi said.

Dr Siringa shook his head gravely. "Brigadiere Rossi mentioned something about the guests thinking she was under the weather, but they didn't think it was related to her allergy. And the fact the woman didn't even try to reach for her EpiPen makes me wonder if her death wasn't due to something more sudden, such as a cardiac arrest. I guess we need to wait for the post-mortem results."

"What about the time of death?" the MD asked.

"From the body's condition, I'd say between 11 and 12pm, maybe slightly earlier. That would fit with what the waiter said: that the writers' group finished dinner around 10pm."

"And most allergic reactions occur within an hour," Dr Gimondi completed his friend's thoughts.

"I imagine she was taken suddenly and violently ill, giving her no time to react or call for help."

"Maybe she dozed off. She had been drinking, so maybe she was tired after the trip. Trying to work on a manuscript at that time of day may be more conducive to sleep than efficiency."

"That would explain quite a few things. Perhaps she fell asleep, and when she woke up, she was in the middle of a crisis, her throat already blocked, her body in hypoperfusion and her heart close to collapse."

"Also, with the noise coming from the rough seas and the storm, there's a chance that anyone at reception wouldn't have been able to hear her distress, even if she had managed to scream."

"The only other strange detail is the broken glass that had contained red wine," Dr Siringa said. "If she had been drinking and was taken ill all of a sudden, we're back to the heart attack hypothesis. She let the glass go and fell on top of it. But if it was anaphylactic shock, she certainly wouldn't have been holding a glass of wine."

"Maybe the glass was on the table, and in the frenzy of the attack, she knocked it over."

"That's a reasonable assumption, at least until we have the full post-mortem results, with a report from the victim's MD and the forensic observations from both the kitchen and the place of death."

"That will give you a full picture of the case and rule out – or not – anaphylactic shock."

"Exactly." Dr Siringa sighed, putting away his notes. "But whatever the case, it's such a pity. She was a beautiful woman."

The other man was nodding when Doctor Siringa called out.

"Excuse me, madam, where do you think you're going?"

Giò recognised the voice that replied immediately. It was Mrs Galli.

"I'm going to sit and watch the fish in the aquarium."

"The aquarium?"

"Yes, it soothes my nerves and inspires my imagination."

"I see. But the restaurant has been cordoned off by the carabinieri, only authorised people can go inside. Both this and the outside doors have been locked."

Mrs Galli had moved away from the door to the restaurant and Giò saw her stand beside the table where the two men were sitting. "That's a pity," she said, "as I get a great deal of satisfaction from watching what goes on inside the aquarium. It allows my thoughts to wander, which is when I get the best ideas and clear my mind."

"Are you one of the writers here for the retreat?" Dr Siringa asked, his voice more polite than curious.

"Oh no, I work for *real* publishing houses, great names in the industry. Nothing to do with those self-publishing charlatans."

"I see," said Dr Siringa, although he looked as though he wasn't sure he really understood what the woman meant.

"And you're an MD?" Mrs Galli asked, looking down at the younger man.

"Yes, I'm in Maratea visiting my friend, Dr Siringa, and as we had dinner here yesterday, I decided to accompany him when he was called out on duty this morning."

"I won't disturb you any more now – I see the carabinieri are coming back – but I might need some medical advice while I'm here. Can I have your card?"

The MD pulled out his card somewhat reluctantly and handed it to the woman, who smiled at him.

"You will hear from me soon. Bye-bye for now."

As she disappeared, Giò heard Dr Siringa teasing his friend. "You've made quite an impression on her."

The other man just shook his head.

By 8PM, THE HOTEL HALL WAS FILLED WITH THE WRITERS. AT FIRST they were shy and reserved, but before long they were chattering and joking. If it hadn't been for Strazio, the carabiniere who was still patrolling the place, no one would have suspected that Death had passed by so recently.

"That's all of us," said Annika, counting them. "I'd say it's time to go to the Veliero Hotel for our dinner."

"Such a pity," sighed Giò. "I loved our restaurant by the sea."

Valentina nodded; she felt just the same.

"At least we should get fresh, tasty food," Francesco tried to cheer them up. "I've read good reviews of the Veliero on TripAdvisor."

They all moved outside. The wind had calmed down, but the air was still damp and the intense smell of the sea was everywhere.

"How about tomorrow's weather?" asked Vittoria.

"Still a bit cloudy, but little or no rain, and from Monday the sun should be shining," Francesco replied, smiling at her.

"Finally!" said Vittoria, sliding her arm through his. He flushed with pleasure, glancing shyly at his disapproving mother.

"Yes, we've all come to Maratea to enjoy the sunny side of the Mediterranean," Annika commented.

"Giò has not been a good host in this respect," Guido said in mock disapproval. Giò protested, but the others all laughed at her.

"Come on, old grump," said Guido, imitating Vittoria and linking arms with her. "Let's go."

Giò tried to hide the gulp as her throat tightened. Guido felt her stiffening.

"Are you OK?"

"It's just the cold air," she replied, grateful for the chilly weather giving her the perfect cover for her discomfort.

They had taken their seats in the restaurant and given their order. The waiter offered them white pizza with garlic, olive oil and oregano to accompany some home-made local cheese as they were waiting for the main dishes to arrive. Alberto approved of the Aglianico Red that was served.

"It will warm us up," he said, taking a careful sip, "despite the cold weather."

"So, while we wait for our food to come, would you mind if we did a quick round-up of how everyone's writing day went? I hope the interviews with the carabinieri weren't too much of a disruption. Or the... other thing."

For the first time since Giò had met Annika, it seemed like she was stumbling over her words.

"Really," she went on, "I didn't know whether to encourage you to carry on with your projects or not. Maybe today we should have abstained from writing."

"Why?" said Erminia icily. "We're all professionals, we know life gets in the way, but we still have to keep to our deadlines. As in any other job."

"What else could we have done?" said Guido. "We were

ADRIANA LICIO

stuck in the hotel with nowhere to go. For my part, I got on with my project and had a most satisfactory day. The words kept flowing."

"Not too many words down for me," Alberto said. "But I'm always slow when I start a new project. Besides, I have worked on my outline and I hope that might stimulate more productivity in the next few days."

"Our hotel," said Vittoria, leaning her elbows on the table and cupping her face between her fists, "and the whole setting is so very romantic – the storm outside, the cosy interior. Need I say more? My romance has been given a huge head start today."

Valentina shook her head. "Not good news from me, I'm afraid. I found the whole sequence of events a bit too much. I could neither write nor think about my story. At times, reality is so harsh, there's no need to write fiction."

"Sequence of events?" asked Erminia, wringing her puffy hands. "There was just one event and that was Margherita having the temerity to die in the hotel we'd chosen for our retreat."

"No, there *was* a sequence." Valentina's eyes were half closed as if she was seeing it in her head. "The storm, the pouring rain, the howling wind, the raging sea. Then Margherita appeared when she was the last person we wanted to see. And all the things she said – she was rather harsh with us. Then we found her dead. No, I couldn't write with all those thoughts, all those wrongs…"

Vittoria took her sister's hands and held them tight.

Annika nodded. "You are right, Valentina, it's been a tough day. We've had loads to cope with. I'm glad you shared your feelings with us."

She waited for Valentina to add more if she felt like it, but the woman just shrugged her shoulders and kept quiet.

At that moment, Mrs Galli made her way into the Veliero Hotel's restaurant. The waiter invited her to sit in the corner, but the woman asked for another table – one closer to the writers.

68

"She wants to be *closer* to us? Maybe she feels lonely," murmured Giò to Annika.

"Do you think we should ask her to join us?" Annika asked.

"We've just got rid of Margherita, now you want to unleash a new source of unpleasantness on us?" Vittoria said dryly.

Guido burst into his trademark loud laughter, then lowered his voice and added softly, "We can't say you don't speak your mind, Vittoria. But yes, Annika, let her join us. It will add to the fun."

To everyone's surprise, Mrs Galli accepted Annika's invitation. As the woman sat down at their table, a fat black beetle happened to pass close to her feet. Mrs Galli got up instantly and placed the leg of her chair on the poor insect, then pressed down with all her might. Nobody particularly liked beetles, but the woman's unexpected meanness left them all feeling somewhat dismayed.

"No point in allowing useless beasts to live," she said dryly.

"Does that apply to humans as well?" asked Guido in his usual laid-back style.

"There are some humans that don't deserve to be called such."

"You're joking!" Guido cried, banging his forehead with his right hand.

"If you read the Bible, you'd know God himself had no pity on some creatures: '*I will remove wild beasts from the land*'. Some people don't even deserve to be called creatures."

"While I'd agree with you that some people act appallingly," said Alberto, "I'd be careful drawing a line between worthy and unworthy people. Every time human beings have declared themselves superior to other human beings, that's when atrocities have started..."

"Are you sure you're not quoting from Nietzsche?" Simone asked Mrs Galli.

"No, definitely the Bible. Leviticus."

My goodness, I thought she was a grumpy old woman, but in

reality, she's a monster, thought Giò. Annika's eyes met hers, conveying that she felt the same.

"'One thing I said,' said God, 'and a thousand different things you heard,'" Alberto replied with a wry smile. "Or rather, you misunderstood."

Heads all around the table nodded in agreement.

"Enough," said Mrs Galli. "And you, young man, shouldn't you be passing the wine around?" She held her glass out so that Guido could fill it.

"To our health," Alberto said, raising his glass and inviting all his companions to do the same. Mrs Galli drank her whole glassful in a single long gulp.

"You mentioned working with publishing houses, are you an editor?" Simone asked her, hoping to switch the conversation on to a less contentious topic.

Mrs Galli cast a long look all around the table, and then shook her head. "I'm not an editor, I'm a writer. A ghost writer."

"That's interesting," said Vittoria. "Did you ever write under your own name?"

"I'm not looking for fortune and fame," the woman replied bitterly. "I love writing for writing's sake."

"They would have to pay me loads," joked Guido, "to spend painful hours writing something in someone else's name."

"Money will never reward me for what I put out. But as I said, I don't believe in writing for money."

"Well, we try our best to put the two things together," Annika said. "We love writing too, but if, at the end of the day, it doesn't pay the bills, then we'll have to do something else for a living. And that in turn leaves us with very little time for writing."

"Self-publishing isn't writing at all. It's just a form of marketing to steal money out of people's pockets."

"I beg your pardon, but we put our hearts and souls into our books. If they didn't resonate with our audiences, no one would buy them. They might be fooled into buying our first book, but they'd never stick with us. But our readers choose us, love what we've written and keep asking for more…"

"Then they're not cultured readers, they'd just buy anything with a nice cover."

Giò had had enough. "Well I wouldn't call people who read a book when they don't know who really wrote it very smart. Personally, I think ghost writing is far more misleading than being an indie author who has to work their way up from a complete unknown, conquering one reader at a time using only their writing skills."

The writers' group all clapped their hands.

"You understand nothing!" Mrs Galli said angrily. "You've no idea which authors I write for."

"Authors?" Vittoria said. "If they're not writing, you can hardly call them authors. And you call what *we* do misleading?"

"Well, I understand that celebrities often require a ghost writer," Erminia said. "They don't have the skills nor the time to write their stories. What I don't understand is why they don't state openly that they haven't written their own books and let the readers know it's a joint enterprise. The ghost writer could then have his or her share of the plaudits."

"That's exactly what my clients don't want: to share the limelight, the accolades, the applause. And the book wouldn't sell as well without their famous name on the cover."

"And you call your readers cultured?" cried Vittoria.

The two women were still glaring at each other when the waiter arrived to distribute the dishes.

"Do you think the carabinieri will allow us back into our restaurant this week?" Simone asked, again trying to change the subject on to something safe. He disliked conflict of any kind.

"Why wouldn't they?" asked Mrs Galli.

"I guess it all depends on what the forensic scientists find," said Alberto. "Was Margherita's death due to negligence on the part of the restaurant staff? Or was it a fatal mistake, a trace of fish in a dish you wouldn't expect to find it in?"

"I don't think the restaurant staff are at fault for what happened to the silly woman," Vittoria said.

"Not knowingly, for sure," Alberto continued. "But still, they were the ones preparing her food."

A satisfied grin appeared on Mrs Galli's face. "So that's what you believe, is it." It was a statement rather than a question.

Ignoring her, Erminia asked Alberto, "Do you mean the restaurant may be shut down for good?"

"No, nothing that serious. If neither the forensics nor the health and hygiene institute find anything that could represent a danger to the general public, they will reopen the restaurant shortly. Then the legal process will decide who's at fault. There'll be no harm to the Hotel Pellicano if the owner and her staff are found to be blameless."

"That's a relief," said Annika. "I like it here, but our restaurant is super. I love the view from there – I can't get enough of it."

Mrs Galli, after downing a few more glasses of wine, which she seemed to enjoy much more than the food, left before dessert was served. As she departed, she bent down and whispered something into Guido's ear.

His face flushed, he replied in all seriousness, "I'll give it some thought, thank you."

The rest of the company stared at him. As the cantankerous woman hobbled out of sight on her walking stick, they bombarded him with questions.

"My goodness," he admitted finally, pushing his chair away from the table and raising his hands in a gesture of surrender, "I'm not particularly proud of this conquest. Mrs Galli just gave me her room number. Am I getting that old?"

They all laughed.

"I'm afraid you aren't the only one on her radar," Annika said. "I've seen her making advances on the receptionist."

"Don't be jealous!" Simone smiled at Guido.

"And there's Dr Gimondi too," added Giò. "I saw her asking

him for his card this morning, pretending it was in case she needed to consult him about some medical condition. At the time I took it at face value – I thought she was really sick."

Guido banged his hand on the table with a loud "Ah!" and laughed in the infectious way that other folk couldn't resist, not knowing if they were laughing at whatever had amused him or as a reaction to Guido's response.

"Are you hitting the Sambuca tonight?" Alberto asked him.

"No, I'll stick with a double espresso. I need to get some more work done."

"Tonight?" Vittoria asked. "Hasn't it been a tiring enough day?"

"I'm no early bird; I work better during the night."

The spoons tinged against the thin porcelain espresso cups, their sound almost drowned out by the group's lively chatter and laughter.

"Oh, I'm ever so sleepy." Annika yawned languidly. "What do you say to calling it a night? It's early for a Saturday, I know, but I suggest we have a writing sprint early tomorrow morning, and then go visit the centre of Maratea and stay there for lunch."

"Yahoo!" cried Guido, while all the others clapped their hands in approval.

"Lovely idea," said Vittoria, glad to see her sister finally smiling.

～

"Giò, will you keep me company? I fancy a last cigarette before bed," said Guido as they rose from the table.

"A last one? I thought you were going to be writing – and smoking – all through the night?"

"I'm trying to cut down. Bad habits, you know?"

She stared at him. "Are you kidding me?"

"No, I mean it, I'm serious," he said. "One cigarette after

lunch, one after dinner, a third for emergencies. But I try to resist that third one."

They went out into the darkness of the night, crossed the road leading from the Hotel Veliero and leaned over the balustrade that gave onto the ocean. The sea was gradually calming down, the waters retreating to allow the beach to emerge again. They could just make out the gravelly grey strip appearing from underneath the white foam of the waves as they walked along the pavement, like they had done that morning. When they'd left the hotel's lights behind, they could distinguish the million stars in the sky, the Milky Way wrapped up in its opalescent cloud.

It was only on the way back that Guido broke the silence.

"A penny for your thoughts."

"Just some silly idea of mine," said Giò, startled. "I was thinking at dinner that it's weird – despite the fact Margherita died suddenly only last night, everyone seemed more relieved than anything. Our mood tonight was so much better than it was at dinner yesterday."

He shrugged, took a last puff of his cigarette and put it out in an outdoor ashtray.

"Frankly, my dear," he said, quoting one of the most famous lines in cinematic history, "I don't give a damn."

10

LIMONCELLO TALES

"And what's that?" Francesco asked, pointing at the colourful shutters of La Farmacia dei Sani.

Giò grinned. "Just what it says," she said. "A pharmacy not for the sick, but for healthy people who consider food and wine their best medicine."

"It doesn't look like one of those awful health food stores," said Simone, looking at a long row of prosciutto and salami hanging from one of the wooden beams.

"Not at all," laughed Giò. "It's more of a delicatessen. Here you'll find all sorts of local delicacies, from herbs, spices and chillis, to pasta sauces, cheeses and salami. I'm glad it's open on a Sunday morning."

The group of writers filled their bags with all sorts of goodies. The pleasant shopkeeper, her sweet smile softening her square face, helped each of them, explaining every single item they pointed at and sharing a plethora of recipes for each ingredient. Alberto bought a few bottles of the Aglianico Red he'd enjoyed so much the previous evening, supplied to La Farmacia dei Sani by the small local producers. He'd had some on his shopping list for a long while and beamed with happiness at the unexpected opportunity to tick that item off.

"Giò, where are you taking your guests for lunch?" the shopkeeper asked.

"We're just having an aperitivo at Leonardo's, but we'll be back in Maratea for a proper dinner one evening this week."

"If you want to have a walk around town, you can leave all your bags here. We're open till half past one."

"That's an excellent idea, I've been buying things as if there's no tomorrow," laughed Vittoria.

"Then, Mum, we can buy some more, too," Francesco said, picking up a bottle of Limoncello.

A few minutes later, they were walking briskly up the paved alleys taking them to the upper part of the village. Stone houses, ancient wooden doors, terracotta pots with the first flowers of the season enchanted them, and every now and then a small side alley opened on to a view of the sea, the gulf embraced by the mountains.

Simone walked next to Annika, who was panting slightly from the climb.

"You made a splendid choice to spend the next few months here, it's a gorgeous place."

Annika laughed. "I'm no longer so sure. I'm supposed to lose weight, but I keep finding all sorts of food here that's far too tempting."

"I don't think you should lose any weight," Simone said, looking at her with admiring eyes.

"I love you for saying that." Annika laughed again and Simone's cheeks turned bright red.

"Giò, what are you doing here?" An elderly woman with a slim figure, rebellious white hair and deep grey eyes suddenly appeared beside the group from a steep alley.

"Hello, Gran, have you just been to Mass?"

The woman nodded. At Giò's greeting, all her companions could easily make out the strong family resemblance between the two women.

"I did, but there's not much going on, really."

Giò introduced Granny to the whole company and Guido invited her to join them for the aperitivo.

"At my age, I'd better stay away from certain foods," Granny said.

"Don't believe her!" admonished Giò. "She eats all sorts of food, as long as she's cooked it."

"Well, that makes all the difference because I can pick and choose every single ingredient. It's so important... but why don't you come over for a cup of coffee after lunch?"

"There are nine of us," laughed Annika.

"Then I'll just have to use the Moka pot three times. Well, I do have a larger one, too, but as I never use it, I'm not sure the coffee would be too good from it..."

"OK, we'll come." Giò stopped Granny before the old lady could bore her companions with the entire history of all the Brando family Moka pots that had appeared and disappeared over the years. "But for now, we'd better go, before Don Anastasio leaves the church and demands to know why we weren't at Mass."

"On the contrary, you're safe. It's Rosario who closes the church, but he will hang around for a while yet. Don Anastasio was in an awful mood – there were less than 40 people this morning for Mass."

"Who's Don Anastasio?" asked Erminia.

"The local priest," Giò answered coolly, "who cannot accept that the clergy no longer has complete power over the lives of the congregation."

As they parted company with Rosa Brando, Valentina said to Giò, "It was very sweet of your granny to invite us for coffee."

"Sweet? Oh no, there's nothing sweet about her. She must have heard about Margherita's death and wants to know more."

Startled, Valentina shook her head. "Oh no, more talk about that awful woman."

"THESE ARE MY BISCUITS WITH LAVENDER AND RAISINS," SAID Granny, pointing to the different silver trays, "these are rosemary and lemon, and these are my puffs with vanilla custard."

"Did you bake them all yourself?" Erminia asked.

Granny nodded modestly. Giò laughed at her.

"And are you the granny who helped Giò prepare the bocconotti on Friday?" Guido asked mischievously.

"Oh yes, I am," Gran answered nonchalantly. "Not that she needed my help, mind you. She's such a passionate cook, she can defrost almost any kind of food. And you should see the wonders she can perform with a microwave."

Giò flushed as all her companions roared with laughter at her.

"Do you all want coffee, or would you like to try my Limoncello?"

"Both, please," said Guido eagerly.

"Guido's right, it's unfair to make us choose, Gran."

"Don't you need to go back to work this afternoon?"

They all nodded, and Erminia added, "We thought an aperitivo would just be a light meal, but it ended up being more than a full lunch, which has made me feel a little sleepy. But yes, we're supposed to go back to work once we've returned to the hotel."

"Then I'll serve you the Limoncello first, and the coffee later."

"We're in your trusty hands." Guido winked at Granny, who without hesitation winked back at him before disappearing into the kitchen. She came back with a painted ceramic tray on which stood ten icy thimbles and a frozen bottle containing a pale yellow liquid. Silently filling nine of the thimbles, she only gave herself a small drop.

"This is my Sunday treat, I love the smell of it."

And then they were all breathing in the pungent and refreshing aroma of lemon.

"It's the Mediterranean through and through," said Alberto.

"It's creamy," said Annika, tightening her lips to enjoy the taste a little longer.

"This is my version with a little condensed milk, a special treat."

"Excellent."

"I thought I'd better treat you well, after all you went through yesterday."

Oh, here we go. Giò shook her head, looking at her granny gravely. The old lady pretended not to see her granddaughter's expression and continued leveraging her fragile appearance and innocent, sympathetic expression.

"Ah, that hideous woman," said Francesco, banging his thimble glass back on the table more loudly than he had meant to. Valentina sighed. The lighthearted expression that had been on her face all morning disappeared in seconds.

"Not really a great loss, for us or the rest of the world," Simone said bluntly, for once seeming to forget about his shyness. Vittoria and Erminia nodded in agreement, while Granny's eyebrows rose as she flinched in surprise.

"You must be thinking badly of us," Annika explained, "but, you see, that wicked woman, Margherita Durante, was part of our group a few months back, and she managed to alienate every one of us."

"I didn't know you knew her, I thought you just happened to be in the same hotel."

"No, we knew her, and since I had asked her to leave our writing group, I suspect she came here on purpose to stir things up."

"That'd not only be very mean of her," said Granny incredulously, "but also such a waste of time and money. I mean, isn't she supposed to be a famous author with a rather busy schedule?"

"You're right. In fact, she told us she had some business to conduct in Maratea, and apparently she brought it forward to coincide with our retreat. But the most wicked part of it is that we had no idea she would be coming at all."

"And what kind of business did she have in Maratea?"

Annika shook her head, as did all the others one by one.

"We have no idea, we weren't that curious about it. Maybe you spoke to her some more, Guido?"

"No," he replied after some consideration. "She told me about her social life, all the presentations she was going to host during a long Italian tour, but she never mentioned her engagements in Maratea."

"And the people she was supposed to meet, didn't they come to the hotel or contact the carabinieri?"

"I don't think they ever came to the hotel," Giò replied. "Not sure if they got in touch with the carabinieri, though."

"Yes, maybe they called in at the carabinieri station directly," Gran said as if thinking aloud, "though I would have expected them to show up at the hotel at least to enquire what had happened."

"Maybe they didn't want to intrude," Alberto said.

"That'd be strange," Gran replied, shaking her head. "In Maratea, we love to intrude."

Alberto looked at her, half amused, half in amazement.

"Don't think badly of us, but nothing ever happens in a small town, and so if something unusual does happen, we tend to be rather..."

"Nosy, just like my granny!" Giò interrupted.

"I hope you will excuse my granddaughter," said Granny. "She's lived in London so long, she's lost touch with the reality of a small town, where people look after each other and need to be alert to changes going on in the community, to bad things happening. They must be on their guard against any evil approaching."

"Or you might simply call all this hypobole 'gossip'!"

Granny waved her hand in front of her nose as if to whisk away a little mosquito, and then went on, asking all of the questions the carabinieri had already asked, but in such a delicate, intriguing way that Giò's companions felt compelled to reply, sharing rich details they hadn't disclosed to Brigadiere Rossi. She asked about Margherita's food allergy, if she had been concerned about her food on their previous meeting, if she used to carry an EpiPen with her.

"Actually two," said Annika. "During our last retreat, she made sure at least some of us were familiar with where she kept them and how to inject her in case of an emergency."

"And when you left her, she showed no signs of distress?"

They all shook their heads.

"Actually, she looked remarkably well," Simone added instinctively.

"No, she wasn't that well," Vittoria corrected him.

Erminia explained to Granny that the hideous woman had not looked her usual self from the very moment she had entered the restaurant, but they'd had no reason to believe it was due to her allergy.

"There was no shortness of breath, or evidence that she would later go into anaphylactic shock. But to be sure, her health wasn't as good as it had been last time we met."

"And who was the last one to see her alive?" Granny went on, churning out question after question like a machine throwing out tennis balls on a training court.

"I guess it was me," said Guido. "I was the only one who stayed on for a longer chat with Margherita."

"I see, and she showed no sign of dizziness, confusion, or difficulty breathing?"

"Certainly not, or I wouldn't have left her alone."

"That's important, it puts the whole thing in a different perspective. Do you remember what time you parted?"

Guido's face held a funny expression, as if he was enjoying being quizzed. Or was he just pretending? He was a little hard to read. Behind his agreable nature, behind his sense of humour, was there a hidden part to this man that he had not yet revealed?

"Of course I do, it was around 10.30 when I left her, and she was alive and kicking then."

"And she stayed at the table in the restaurant?"

"Yes, she had her manuscript on the table and said she was going to work on it."

"The pathologist," Erminia explained, "said that she could have died any time between 11pm and midnight."

"Which most likely means around 11.30," Giò intervened. "They can be so accurate nowadays."

"And did you see if she had her bag with her?" Granny carried on.

Guido shook his head. "I'm afraid I took no notice at all."

"Because we have a girl here in Maratea who suffers from a nut allergy, but she's fanatical about always having her bag with her EpiPens inside to hand. Also she's very alert to any warning signs of an attack coming."

"I saw her bag," said Giò. "It was on a chair next to where she was sitting. I guess she didn't have time to reach for it."

"And the man at the hotel reception, did he not hear anything?"

"Nothing at all," Giò answered.

"With the sea and the storm raging outside," said Guido, "I doubt he would have heard anything from the restaurant."

Gran nodded in agreement, offering more Limoncello to Guido and Alberto while the others gently refused before continuing.

"And the lights in the restaurant stayed on all night?"

"Granny, stop sleuthing! The carabinieri have already asked all these questions. The waiter had told the receptionist that Margherita would be working in the restaurant, so he had to leave the lights on until she went back to her room and told him she had finished."

"Which I guess she never did, so the lights stayed on all through the night."

"No," Alberto intervened, "I heard the police asking the night

Peril at the Pellicano Hotel

receptionist that very thing. He admitted that he'd been catching up on TV on his laptop, and then he must have dozed off for a while, but at 3am, he went to the restaurant to check if Margherita needed anything. Seeing no one there, he assumed she had gone back to her room while he was asleep. It was then that he switched off the lights."

"So he didn't see anything?"

"Nope," Giò almost growled as she could see her friends' faces getting more and more concerned at Granny's flood of questions. "Margherita's body was on the other side of the table, perfectly hidden unless you were on that side of the room. I didn't see her the next morning until I went to look out of the window on that side."

"How convenient!" The words, although softly spoken, exploded into the room.

"What do you mean?" Annika finally asked.

"Nothing, really," babbled Granny. "It's just strange that a woman, aware of her severe allergy and knowing what to do if she should feel an attack coming, didn't even try to reach for her bag. I would have expected to find her in full view, having either made a last attempt to alert the receptionist, or grasped her bag and pulled its contents out to find her EpiPen."

Three things struck Giò simultaneously. One was the troubled expression on Alberto's face. He wasn't gazing at Granny; his stare was on Valentina, who looked pale and kept her fists tightly clenched on her lap. Secondly, Giò had been so distracted by all that had happened, she hadn't realised that the woman with the wry smile she had met on Friday, at least before Margherita made her appearance, had completely vanished. Valentina was a worried woman now. And the third thing was... Gran's words had jogged a memory, but Giò wasn't able to grasp it – something she had seen on Saturday morning when she made her grisly discovery. Her brain had registered it, but not her conscious mind. The more she tried to grasp the memory, the more it eluded her.

Let it go and it will come back, Giò reminded herself.

Annika looked at her watch and exclaimed, "Golly gosh, it's 3.30! The hotel shuttle driver will wonder where we've got to."

"Is the driver waiting for you?" Gran asked.

"Yes, we said we'd rejoin him at half past three in Piazza Buraglia."

"Well, you'll be there in five minutes, and down south no one notices when you're a little late."

Annika smiled, relieved. "I love this relaxed place. I feel like I'm the master of my own time, instead of continuously rushing after it." She stooped to kiss Granny's cheek, and the old woman took the chance to whisper in her ear.

"He's a nice man and you'll be the perfect match for him. He just needs a bit of confidence and security."

Annika gasped, then blushed, which was not the way she'd generally act. As soon as she recovered, she whispered back in the old woman's ear.

"Giò's right, you really are something."

The old woman twinkled, but her piercing eyes were on Valentina. The woman nervously said thank you for the coffee and the biscuits, but it didn't require Granny's powers of observation to see she was relieved to go.

By the time Granny was saying farewell to Giò and Guido, the others were already standing on the little cobbled alleyway outside.

"It was a pleasure to get to know Giò's grandmother," said Guido, kissing the old woman. "And I loved that Limoncello of yours."

"Someone said you're a good photographer. Next time, I hope we'll have a chance to talk more casually, but today it was important I warned you."

"Warned us?" Guido and Giò asked together.

"Yes. Did you not hear how many times the words 'hideous' and 'wicked' came out while we were chatting? There's something evil going on in that hotel, just be aware."

"I'm so sorry," said Giò to Guido as soon as Granny had closed the door behind them. "She's got such a powerful imagination, I never know how to stop her. Maybe it was the things she saw during the war, maybe..."

"Shhh." He smiled softly at her.

"What?"

"You don't have to justify what your granny says."

"Maybe you have a point."

Giò's relief turned to surprise a second later.

"Especially as she struck a chord. I don't think she's wrong. I've felt the evil myself."

11

JUST ANOTHER SUNDAY

During the night, strange visions of castle ruins above a deserted plain, the smells of campfires and spices, populated Rolando's dreams. When he woke up, he went straight to his small office in the attic of the apartment, browsed through some of his magazines and searched for the ad. Yes, it was the exact place he had seen in his dream. Strange, he hadn't even been aware he'd read the text, but something must have stuck in his memory. Anyway, there was a mobile phone number to call. He didn't hesitate a second, even if it was Sunday, even if it was not yet 8am.

A cheerful voice answered at the other end of the line. Yes, it was possible to join at such short notice, the group wasn't full yet. As for the visas, they could be obtained from the airport on arrival, as long as they both had valid passports that weren't due to expire within the next six months. Rolando was grateful that Angelica had prepared in advance to visit her sister in the States and their passports were well in date. They had never travelled outside Europe before.

Rolando then made his specific request. The woman took some time before answering. It could be done, but could he call back at 10.30 to give her time to check it out? Of course, he could call back, even if it did leave Angelica rather surprised that they wouldn't be going to Mass together as he – the predictable and unadventurous Rolando – had other things to do.

AT LUNCHTIME, ROLANDO PICKED ANGELICA UP FROM MASS AND they drove to his favourite restaurant on the harbour. Angelica yawned as they sat at their usual table, greeting the people around them and ignoring her husband. All the families in the restaurant were the same ones she'd seen there every weekend for the past 20 years, the same people who had been beside her at Mass, and were now gossiping about all that had happened in the past week. And of course, nothing had happened, except for that strange death at the Pellicano Hotel. But was a death from anaphylactic shock really enough salt to add flavour to their insipid lives?

After the initial greetings, Angelica didn't even attempt to make small talk with the people at the neighbouring tables, let alone with her husband. She was so angry with him, with the complacent, satisfied expression on his face. How could he be so content with this miserable life? How could he not see how hard it was on her, how frustrated and unhappy she was?

The waitress appeared beside them. "Spaghetti and vongole for Mr Ariosto and orecchiette for you, madam, as usual?"

"No, I'd like some linguine allo scoglio today," Angelica said vehemently, feeling rebellious. Even the waitress knew their every move. How humiliating.

"I'll take the same as my wife."

Rolando smiled gently. Then the waitress came back with a silver tray, a red rose on top of a white envelope. Now, this was utterly unusual.

"For me?" Angelica asked. Surely there was a mistake.

The waitress nodded. Angelica picked up the rose and the white envelope, holding both incredulously.

"Won't you open it?" Rolando asked.

"But our anniversary isn't until Tuesday," she said.

"I know, but I had to prepare something."

She opened the envelope to find two tickets for... Tehran? Wasn't that in Iran?

"We leave tomorrow, so we have the afternoon to pack."

A journey, tomorrow? And why Iran? What was there to see there? Why not Paris or London? Could women even travel to Iran? Would she have to wear a burka or at least a headscarf?

She was dumbfounded – had her husband gone mad? Then she noticed the address on the details beneath the flight tickets: the Alamut valley. Hey, that was the name of her perfume. How could she have forgotten that it was a real place, and that it was in Iran? Had Rolando seen her new perfume? Surely not, he never looked in her bathroom, let alone her cabinet. So was it one of those strange coincidences that hit our lives every now and then? Was she going to experience a *One Thousand and One Nights* dream?

He gently caressed her hand. "I thought it would be thrilling to spend our anniversary in a completely different place this year."

She looked at him uncertainly, wondering for the first time if she really knew her husband as well as she'd always thought she did.

12

THE DANGEROUS CHARM OF TALENT

It was 30 minutes before dinner when Guido sent her a text.

"Do you want to come over? I've got something to show you."

Giò felt a bit too delighted by the offer.

Come on, old spinster, you can't get this excited. It's probably a ruse – the old story of the predatory man inviting the unsuspecting woman to look at his 'butterfly collection'. But even as the thought was passing through her mind, she was trying to tame her rebellious short hair and had brushed a touch of bronzer onto her face and natural gloss on her lips – gestures that would have delighted her sister, Agnese, who was always complaining that Giò should take more care of herself and her appearance.

She knocked on his door. Inside, the room was chaotic, with a couple of cameras recharging on the floor and a number of papers spread out across his desk.

No clothes left lying around, though, it's just his creative stuff.

She pointed to a large-screen laptop standing on a chair.

"We need to sit on the bed, I'm afraid," he said, indicating more papers that were taking up the only armchair available.

"You don't believe in travelling light, do you?"

"I'm not travelling at the moment. This is a break – a working break – and I need to get things done. When I travel, I travel light

– well, sort of light, if you ignore the laptop and photo equipment."

She finally accepted his invitation to sit beside him. He moved the laptop to perch it on top of a couple of books on the desk.

"Perfect height," he said as a video started.

The video played for fewer than five minutes, and was about Iran. Mostly shot from a drone, it showed mosques, cities, mountains and deserts. Music following images, and images following music, but there was little dialogue. People buzzed around the bazaar, then a close up showed steaming tea slopping from a silver pot into small, shiny crystal glasses. From that scene, the sound moved on to the gurgling of water and they were under a waterfall in a luscious forest. The camera was moving upstream close to the water's surface, as if it was hopping from stone to stone, until it reached the top of a rocky mountain, the sky beyond filled with fluffy clouds.

The video was an immersive sequence of time-lapse effects and continuous jumps from small detail to glorious landscapes, from slow motion to speeded-up videos, from people to plants, from animals to objects. Giò found herself totally lost in what she was seeing.

When the video stopped, she could only cry, "Gorgeous!"

They sat silently for a while. Then he threw his head back, his curly red hair bouncing as he let out one of his loud bursts of laughter.

"Is that all?"

His laugh was so infectious, Giò found herself smiling, feeling a little stupid.

"Yes, that's all. It is really gorgeous. I can't add more on top of that, except I'd love to see it again, maybe more than once."

He pressed play again, but this time he turned down the volume and commented on the images as they went by. He didn't describe what he'd been filming, just mentioned the tricks he'd used to shoot the film the way he had, sharing a few anecdotes, some technical stuff Giò didn't understand, some challenges due to the wind and turbulence in manoeuvring the drone exactly the way he had wanted.

When it was over, Giò asked him earnestly, "Why do you bother writing at all, if you can create something this good with film?"

"You're right, photography and video are my natural media, but in order to survive, I must be a jack of all trades. The video you saw has been commissioned by an Iranian travel agency; the country is opening up to tourism and they needed to create imagery to sell it as a destination. From the whole video, I will have to create shorter videos to use on social media..."

"My question is still the same – why do you waste your time writing a book?"

"Once I've completed the project, the flow of money from it stops. If I write a book, I have money, even if it's only a little, coming in all through the year. And I can pitch it to the Iranian tourist board or cultural institutes around the globe. If they ask me for 100 copies, I'm a happier traveller as I get a little money in my pockets to buy more equipment."

Giò nodded, finally understanding his point of view. She appreciated how much effort he put into something he didn't like too much in order to live life the way he wanted.

"So, did you really like it?" he asked.

"I wish I could write as well as you shoot."

He laughed again. Was it to mask his pleasure at her words?

"I do have a proposal," he said.

"And what's that?"

"Tomorrow, I see the weather will have improved no end, so I'd love to do some shooting from the statue of Christ the Redeemer. I want to be there at first light..."

"I thought you were meant to be getting on with your writing."

"That's what I intend to do straight after dinner."

"And you mentioned you're not a morning person."

"Except when it comes to photography. Unfortunately, you can only get that lovely, soft early morning light... early in the morning. But I will remember that you're likely to use anything I say against me."

His hazel eyes went from joking to soft and caressing – too soft and caressing for poor Giò, who flushed and tried hard to hide the fact that her heart was drumming in her chest. All of a sudden she stood up, looked at her watch and spoke as coolly as she could manage.

"I think it's time to go for dinner."

Guido looked around, grabbed his jacket from the back of one of the chairs and held the door open so that Giò could walk out first.

"So will you be joining me tomorrow morning?"

"I'd love that. It's one of my favourite spots – you can see for miles from up there – and I'm curious to see how you work and... mostly... what you will see..."

She stumbled over her last few words. She had meant to say that maybe the way Guido saw the world was different from other people, that she was sure he could see beyond the obvious, connecting images in unexpected ways as with the Iran video, but for once, words were failing Giò miserably.

He nodded as if he understood all the same.

In the corridor, they met Erminia and Francesco, and Giò was rather pleased to see them. She needed a little time to process what was happening between herself and Guido; she had felt too close to a man she barely knew. But maybe she didn't want to think about it at all. She moved in front of Guido and bombarded poor Francesco with an avalanche of questions on his work, her voice once more determined and confident.

13

ON THE ROOFS OF THE WORLD

I t was still dark when Guido's car began the steep climb that led from Maratea to the statue of Christ the Redeemer, tall viaducts spanning the voids as the serpentine road wound its way around a series of sharp hairpin bends.

"I'm glad that it's still dark, it looks as if the road might be quite scary in broad daylight."

"Don't you worry, there'll be plenty of opportunities for sightseeing on the way back," laughed Giò.

"Not for the faint of heart," Guido said.

"We're almost there," said Giò, directing him towards the best place to park. "This early in the day, we can drive almost up to the Basilica of San Biagio, so there's no need to leave the car this far down, especially since you'll need all your equipment."

"OK, Boss."

They parked where Giò had shown him. As soon as they were out of the car, the chilly air enveloped them.

"My goodness," Guido said, shivering.

"I told you to wear something warm." Giò laughed again, pulling a woollen scarf over her mouth.

"I wasn't expecting it to be this cold," he said through chattering teeth. "Let's hurry, I'll warm up while walking."

"You're not taking any of your cameras?"

"I need to study the place first, see what it's like, and then decide how I'm going to do the shoot."

"OK."

They glanced briefly at the small Basilica of San Biagio, but soon carried on along a tiny path leading to the white statue of Christ, standing 22 metres high.

"Wow, it looks like a passage up to the sky," said Guido, admiring the path, his mind already seeing how his cameras would capture it all. Darkness was beginning to give way to a deep blue light, and behind them a whitish halo was marking the horizon below purple-tinted rays. One of them touched the white statue at the end of the path, and Guido cried out in surprise.

"But He's looking at us! I thought He'd be watching over the sea."

Giò nodded. The statue of Christ was indeed looking inland, watching over the Basilica. She'd never known why He had His back to the sea, but found it fascinating nonetheless.

"And what are those ruins?" asked Guido, pointing to the remnants of fortified walls below them to their left.

"We can have a walk there later. It's called Castello; it's what's left of old Maratea before people moved to the lower part of town."

Christ's face was emerging from the darkness.

"He looks like one of us, an ordinary young man."

"Now stop looking around and just concentrate on the statue," said Giò as they walked on briskly to ward off the cold. When they reached its base, Guido looked up as far as the eye could see to take in the sheer size of the statue. Giò placed her hands over his eyes.

"Now let me guide you. Don't open your eyes till I tell you so."

"Won't I trip over the cobbles?"

"Trust me," she said, carefully guiding him over the rough

terrain beyond the statue. It was a game her father used to play with her.

"And now you can open your eyes," she cried, pulling her hands away.

The peaks of the rocks where they stood were suspended over the valley below, opening up to the sea in front of them. Along the coastline, parts of the mountains were highlighted by the first rays of the sun, the shadows adding to the depth of the scenery. The sea was a dark blue, except towards the northern part of the gulf which was embraced by the shining cone of Mount Bulgheria and already bathed in sunlight.

Giò let him take in the vista in his own time before gently pulling his shoulders to turn him around. Chains of mountain ridges invited his eyes to caress an edgy green carpet, plumes of lazy clouds suspended here and there.

"YAAAAAWP!" he cried with all the breath he had in his lungs, and then in unison they yelled, "I sound my barbaric yawp over the roofs of the world." They laughed, looking into each other's eyes until Giò felt she couldn't hold that look for a second longer. Luckily he chose that moment to start exploring, moving around the base of the statue, reading lovers' names carved on the toe emerging from the white tunic before marching down to the parapet of the belvedere to look below to Maratea Harbour. He calculated the speed at which the light was advancing, pushing back the veil of darkness.

"This is exactly the light I want," he cried, catching hold of her right hand. A second later, they were both rushing down the path, happy as playful children. Pushed by the wind, they let out a final cry, stopping, breathless, at the Basilica.

"That wasn't disrespectful," he said, looking towards the simple little church. "Just our cry of joyful thanks." And before Giò could think, before she could take refuge in some silly remark, blurting out words for words' sake, he pulled her tight against him and kissed her with a tenderness she would not have suspected this man – so energetic, so wilful, so full of life – could possess.

"And this is my thanks to you," he whispered, gently pushing her away. Then he winked at her. "Now to get to work."

As he moved towards the car, Giò stood there, an unusually dreamy smile painted on her face. For once, she was unable to think. Had her heart collapsed, or was it beating so furiously she didn't recognise it as such?

In a few minutes, he had returned with some bags and a rucksack strapped over his shoulders, a thermos in his hands.

"I asked the receptionist for something warm to bring with us."

"Not alcohol at this time of day?"

He laughed. "Sorry, I didn't think of alcohol. It's just some hot fruit tea with honey."

"I didn't mean I *wanted* some alcohol. On the contrary."

But he was still smiling, and she understood he was teasing her. She shook her head. Where had all her defences gone?

Fortunately, Guido was now concentrating on his work. He said something about using the path up to Christ's statue as a launch pad and, once he had placed the camera on the drone, it started to lift from the ground with a buzz, moving along the path and pointing just above the statue. They followed it as he guided the drone all around the head of the statue to capture the bay below from all perspectives.

"Now to the castle." He showed her the display, grinned when he was happy, shook his head when disappointed. Then he'd call the drone back and repeat the process until he had exactly the sequence he wanted. From what he was saying, Giò realised he had already visualised the finished film in his mind.

"I thought you'd gather your material and edit it later, depending on what emerged from your shoot…"

"That's one way to work, but usually I envisage things in my head, and I want to make sure I get the right sequences on the camera. It's so annoying if I don't shoot the things I want."

He flew the drone around the church, and from there on to the mountains inland, flying it towards the ridges perpendicularly, as if he meant to crash against them, to capture the rising sun. He checked around once more, took some shots of the serpentine road, the Castello ruins, and finally packed the drone back into the rucksack with a satisfied grin. He then opened the thermos, offering her the first cup.

"It's still hot, so delicious," she said, feeling the liquid warming up her mouth, her throat and, most pleasantly, her chest and stomach.

"I love the feeling of being in the mountains, but I wasn't expecting to experience it here in a Mediterranean town. Giò Brando, you live in paradise."

Giò nodded.

"Have I got a right to disrupt your life?" he said, taking her hands in his.

Giò again felt that words were failing her, as they did every time this man spoke to her seriously. She could laugh at his jokes, speak to him about dreams, ambitions, difficulties, but now he was looking at her as if he could see into her life with the same clarity as his drone had filmed the landscape. He'd understood from the start; she hadn't been so fast. She hadn't even realised until now how attracted she'd been to him from the first moment she'd met him.

"Good morning." A young priest was standing in front of the little church, wearing sandals despite the chill of the morning. He showed them the key in his hand. "You can come inside if you want," he told them as he opened the metal gate protecting the inner door.

Giò went over to him and, from the inviting open portico, beckoned Guido forward. The sanctuary was small and intimate, and Giò let Guido look around in his own time. She then took him to stand in front of one of the columns and showed him a fresco in vibrant reds.

"It's the Madonna of the Pomegranate," she said, gesturing

towards the Virgin holding the Holy Child in her hands. "I know it's far from perfect, but I love its bold colours when the rest of the church is so simple and low-profile."

Guido nodded, and she signalled to him to follow her below the arches on the left. There was nothing to see there, but she waved a hand towards the empty space.

"There used to be a beautiful crib here with terracotta statues, on display all year round. It was this large," and she held out her arms in front of the columns. "It was animated, with a mill splashing water, a man pulling out freshly baked bread from the oven, a blacksmith beating and forging iron in the fire." And Giò went on, describing the crib as if it was there. "And I never knew why they removed it. When we were young, my siblings and I would beg Dad to bring us up here just to see the crib."

He smiled at her while quietly shooting the interior of the church. Giò lighted a candle below the Madonna and, despite no longer being a regular churchgoer, asked her silently, "*Please, help me clear my mind before I make a decision.*"

"I'd say it's time to go back to Maratea," she said aloud when Guido had replaced the lens cap on his camera, "and eat a large breakfast to warm ourselves up."

"I'm starving," Guido agreed, pulling the heavy rucksack on to his shoulder.

14

THE QAZVIN BAZAAR

Angelica glanced at the cute red-brick café with high arched vaults on Imam Khomeini Street. They were in Qazvin, a town three hours north of Tehran.

"Time for a break?" Rolando said as if reading her thoughts.

"Indeed," replied Angelica, smiling with gratitude. They had arrived in Tehran at 5am, only to get straight in a taxi to Qazvin. There, they had rested for a couple of hours in their hotel, then curiosity had got the better of them and they had gone out to discover the city.

The waiter crossed over to them and handed them a couple of menus. They both ordered tea, then Angelica wanted to get closer to the glass counter to make her selection from the goodies on display there. She'd already learned that the Iranians could cook delicious bread and tempting sweets of all sorts.

With her finger, she pointed what she wanted out to the waiter. She was not confident speaking English, and so far had let Rolando do most of the talking. When the waiter returned to their table, he was holding a number of small porcelain dishes in various colours, carrying food of all shapes and sizes. Rolando looked at her in amazement.

"Did I order too much food?" She chuckled. "I feel so curious, I want to try everything."

"It seems Iran has stimulated your appetite."

"And my curiosity too. I'm not sure Qazvin is the best city to be... I was expecting a traditional city centre full of ancient monuments, but here the little gems are scattered between rather mundane places."

Her thoughts went to the Tehran gateway, its splendid mosaics and tilework displayed in the middle of... a traffic island; the neglected Jameh Mosque; the ruined facade of the now closed Grand Hotel, which she had insisted on going to see because of its atmosphere of long-gone glory days.

It had been different at the Aminiha Hosseiniyeh, the luxurious mansion of a rich Qazvin merchant. There the central hall had left her speechless, with its decorated sash windows and incredible vaults. Painted masterpieces, mirrors, stuccos, wooden panels, the intricate designs of the ancient rugs on the floor, the decorated windows hit by the sunlight... that's where it had struck her that she really was in a place far away from home. But once they'd left the house, they were back in the streets of anonymous low buildings, large and ugly shop signs. Only the people made a difference – they were curious, shy and kind. She had only to approach them and they would take the trouble to help her find her way. Even if they couldn't speak a single word in the same language, they would try hard to understand what they could do for her.

In any case, Qazvin was only a short stop. The next day, they would wake up early and head for the Alborz mountains and Alamut, the legendary Assassins' Castle, sleeping in a lodge nearby.

How strange, she thought, stirring her amber tea, *that Rolando should choose this very place.* Now that she was depending on him for guidance – he'd got directions and selected the driver who had taken them in the early hours of the morning from Tehran airport to Qazvin – all the bitterness she had felt against him had at least lessened, if not disappeared. It was so easy to be happy now she was out of her daily environment.

"I wonder if we will manage to eat anything tonight at the hotel," Rolando said when every last morsel had disappeared from their dishes.

"I don't know how good their food will be, but I'm glad we stopped here for lunch. I loved it all."

Rolando nodded, paid the bill and asked her if she felt like visiting the Sa'd Al-Saltaneh, the Great Bazaar just behind the café.

"Of course, I'm looking forward to that."

As they entered the imposing building, she felt once again that the country was surprising her. She had envisioned an overcrowded market with sellers shouting to grab her attention, yet here they were in huge, empty vaulted corridors – red bricks, beautiful mosaic patterns, tall arched wooden doors leading to elegant modern boutiques, all immersed in an eerie silence. There were hardly any visitors around.

Rolando stopped at a carpet shop; he loved to see how the designs were created and the skills with which the artisan worked. He had found a seller who spoke decent English, and the man was more than happy to show him the workshop in the courtyard out the back.

Angelica, who had no great interest in the noble art of carpet making, had spotted a shop selling antique jewellery and trinkets.

"I'll wait for you there." She pointed to the shop opposite and left, curious to see what was on display. The bell rang as she opened the door, but nobody came to say hello. A fair-haired man with grey eyes, probably another European, was waiting at the counter. He gave her a distracted look, and then went on examining some items in front of him.

Angelica was too enchanted by the silver jewellery on display to take any more notice of him. A woman she hadn't noticed before left the shop and the bell rang again. Five minutes later, the Iranian seller was finally back, followed by a man who could have been a boxer, so large were his shoulders, so flattened his nose. His hard eyes glared icily at Angelica, then he headed towards the fair-haired man.

"It's OK, that's my wife," Angelica heard the fair-haired man say as the small Iranian disappeared into the back of the shop.

"So, did you like the jewels?" the boxer said. He spoke English with a strange accent – was he Russian?

"Indeed," the other replied, still checking the contents of the box on the counter.

"You show me your stuff then."

The fair-haired man handed him a leather bag. It was so big, it took both hands to lift it. The boxer opened it and took something shiny out, looking at it carefully.

"Deal closed," he said and went out the back towards the courtyard. Through the window, Angelica saw him gesturing to the Iranian seller, as if to tell him he could return to the shop now. The Iranian came in and tried to speak to the fair-haired man, who ignored him.

"Karen?" he said, walking in Angelica's direction. Angelica shrank back into the corner. As the man moved towards her, she hid behind one of the brick pillars, wondering how she was going to explain why she was there when the man discovered she wasn't actually who he'd thought she was.

Just then, the shop door opened again.

"Liam?" a woman called.

The man turned round. "There you are! I thought you were browsing the jewellery here. I was wondering why you didn't reply."

"Done?" she asked.

"Done and closed." He smiled, turning back and dropping something in the Iranian man's hands. The Iranian didn't say a word, just nodded.

The couple, who Angelica still assumed were European, left and she made her presence known to the seller. The man gulped in surprise, but she smiled reassuringly as she headed for the door to return to her husband. Rolando was still chatting with the carpet seller, and so enthusiastic was he that it was some time before she was able to tell him what she had seen.

"Smuggling, most likely," he commented.

"Yes, and the European man thought I was the one who had left the shop when the bell rang, when in fact, it was his wife."

"Lucky he didn't realise his mistake," he teased.

"What an adventure!" she said. "I felt as if I were a child again, up to mischief and hiding from the adults."

"And now, my great adventurer, shall we go back to our hotel? A hot shower, dinner and an early night?"

"Yes, I'm looking forward to some sleep."

They passed the Chehel Sotun Palace they had seen that morning, its light architecture, porches and garden with its early spring leaves even more beautiful and romantic in the sunset hour. From there, it wasn't too far to the reassuring entrance of their hotel. As they walked back, Rolando put his arm around her shoulders, and she felt like she had done when they were young and in love with life and each other.

15

A LOST MANUSCRIPT

That afternoon, Giò worked hard on her travel memoir, going through the diaries and photos of her various trips in Scotland. Reading her notes, she found that describing the people she had met – friends, friends of friends, other walkers, chance meetings in a B&B or hostel lounge – was a perfect way to introduce readers to the country's lesser-known attractions.

She jotted down a chapter dedicated to Rannoch Moor, a place in the middle of nowhere. Around Loch Ossian, the only human beings you'd encounter for miles were other wanderers. There was no road to get there, and even the train would only stop at the tiny platform – you could hardly call it a station – if a passenger asked to be dropped there.

She reread what she had written, and for once felt happy with it. For sure, it needed some revision and tidying up, but it was all there: her sense of marvel; her sudden fear at the total isolation on a harsh winter's day, the wind howling over Loch Ossian. How gradually that scary place had become more familiar as she passed time there and heard the stories of the few hardy people she met. By the next morning, a hint of sun was peeping from behind the clouds, and the loneliness had turned to an absolute sense of freedom. She had felt more liberated than she had ever done before or since... until this very morning at the statue of Christ the Redeemer.

She parked the thought in the back of her mind and returned to her piece of writing.

If only I could write like that every day, she thought, looking at her watch. A quarter to six – almost time to meet Guido in the hall. He'd promised to show her how he'd processed the videos they had shot earlier.

All day, Giò had done her best not to think of what had happened that morning. She had repeated to herself over and over again that it had just been the euphoria of the moment – that amazing view; the cold air; the sense of freedom that had overcome them. Maybe the kiss meant nothing. It had been too sudden, too unexpected. She hardly knew this guy, after all. True, he was... well, he was a tad attractive. True, he was living a life she had always dreamed of. True, he could be a fascinating man, with so much to tell. Heaving a deep sigh, she remembered being spellbound as he'd shared his impressions of Iran with the group.

Giò Brando, she addressed herself seriously, *please don't pretend to be a romantic soul. You always end up in trouble when you start down this route. It was just the stunning beauty of the landscape at dawn, the amazing light. He hasn't spoken a word about it since; I'm sure he's as embarrassed as you are and doesn't know how to handle it.*

She looked again at her watch, put a touch of gloss on her lips.

What if I don't turn up? I can text him, say I'm too busy writing and want to carry on while the inspiration lasts.

She looked at her phone: five to six. The short text she started to type seemed to take longer to put together than the ten pages she'd written about Scotland. She deleted it, started all over again, deleted, and finally threw her phone in her bag.

Why should I run away? I'm not afraid of him.

∼

GUIDO WAS ALREADY SITTING IN THE HOTEL LOUNGE, A CUP OF coffee beside him and his laptop on.

"Hello," she said, more sheepishly than she would have liked.

"Hi." He invited her to sit beside him with a winning smile. "We did some good work."

He had already edited the first part of the video. Offering her one of the earplugs he was using, he spoke about the music he had selected.

"The beat slows down here, which is a perfect way to open the film up to the landscape behind Christ the Redeemer's statue."

He cut past chunks of video quickly, his fingers flying on the keyboard.

"This is our short sequence in time-lapse," he said, showing her the gulf and how the light of the dawn overcame the darkness. Giò was fascinated. "But the best part comes next."

The drone had shot a close-up of the San Biagio church and Guido had already edited, in his dynamic style, the flight sequence to incorporate what he had shot with the hand-held camera inside the church. From the quick flight over the church, they were inside all of a sudden; from light to darkness. And from the darkness, they took a quick tour round the church's interior, its altar and arches, then darkness again. From that darkness, a woman's shape materialised. Picking up a candle, she lit it and set it amongst the others flickering in front of a pretty Madonna. Then the woman turned towards the camera and smiled; close up on her face, the flickering candles reflecting in her green eyes.

"I love that smile," Guido said, hugging Giò's shoulders and kissing her cheek.

"Is it really me?" Overwhelmed by emotions on too many levels, Giò hardly recognised the figure in black who was standing in front of them, asking something.

"Giò, may I talk to you, please?"

Guido looked in surprise from Paolo, the brigadiere, to Giò.

"Can you please come with me?" Paolo asked Giò again, his expression sombre. "It won't take long."

"Sure," she stuttered finally, standing up.

Paolo didn't speak a word as he strolled down the corridor, giving Giò time to recover.

"So what's going on?"

"Maybe you should tell me?" was the dry reply.

"Tell you what?"

He shook his head. "Leave it."

Was he angry? She couldn't remember ever having seen Paolo look so serious, and she had known him well for a few months now. Sleuthing when the crime is murder is enough to create a strong connection between anyone. There's nothing like surviving danger to bond people together.

Having said that, there wasn't much camaraderie between the two of them just now.

Paolo stopped in front of the restaurant. Strazio, the carabiniere who had been left to oversee things at the hotel, opened the door for them, greeting Giò shyly. Paolo sat down at one of the tables and invited her to do the same.

"So, what's going on?" she repeated, more alarmed by his silence than anything else.

"I have the first, if unofficial, results from the post-mortem and the forensic team."

"And?"

"And the post-mortem didn't find any particles of suspected allergens in Margherita's stomach and gastric juices, which confirms the food analysis: none of the food used in the preparation of her dishes was contaminated."

"You mean she died of natural causes?" she said, unable to make the connection between his sombre expression and what looked like good news at face value.

"Maybe," he said.

Another long, unnerving pause.

"Aren't you happy? I mean, the hotel, the owner and the chef will be cleared after all."

"Yes."

"But you're not convinced, are you?"

"Your group didn't have a good relationship with the woman, did they?"

"They all loathed her," Giò spat, immediately regretting the harshness of her tone.

"I suspected that," Paolo replied. "Even though your friends were not so open about their feelings when I questioned them, with the exception of Mrs Spilimbergo, I still got the sense that there was something unpleasant in the air."

"Margherita Durante wasn't exactly a lovely soul, from what I've gathered," Giò admitted. "So what are you thinking?"

"Frankly, Giò... maybe it's just a cop's hunch, but Mrs Durante comes all the way down to Maratea. By chance, she stumbles on her former writers' group, all of whom seemed to hate her, and then she dies of an allergic reaction without even trying to open her bag and get her EpiPen out."

"Maybe she fell asleep and didn't realise the crisis was coming."

"Dr Siringa mentioned that possibility."

"And from what you've just told me, maybe it wasn't an allergic reaction at all."

"Something like a heart attack is a possibility we cannot rule out. But we spoke to Mrs Durante's doctor; she'd had her yearly check-ups a couple of months ago. No problems with her heart, nor anything that might explain her sudden death. As for her allergy, the attacks she'd had were severe – I mean life threatening."

"So we circle back to anaphylactic shock?" Giò enquired.

"Yes, anaphylactic shock and no evidence of her having eaten fish or crustaceans."

"Well, what if the kitchen staff stirred Margherita's food with a contaminated spoon? That might be difficult to prove."

"Then we will never know. Everything in the kitchen had been thoroughly cleaned before the restaurant closed for the night."

It was easy to tell something was bothering him. Giò pondered his words, then looked him in the eyes.

"And you came over here just to share your doubts with me?"

"Is that so strange?"

"Indeed it is. You usually go to great lengths to keep me out of your investigations."

He smiled for the first time since they had met that day. "You're right. Let's just say this time I have no choice. Mangiaboschi is far too happy that there's no proof against the hotel – you know, bad publicity for tourism, the usual pressures from superiors and politicians not to shed a bad light on the area as a whole, and all that stuff. This woman had no close family members who will demand to know what happened. I can already see the results of the inquest: sudden death from natural causes and peace for everybody."

"So you called me in," Giò said with a proud smile. But his reaction wasn't what she had expected. A shadow obscured his face.

"The thing is, I didn't realise how involved you were with the group…"

"I'm not *that* involved!" she snapped, realising that by 'group', Paolo meant a certain person.

He raised his hands. "I would have said a kiss was a dead giveaway to a certain amount of involvement."

For a moment, Giò wondered if Paolo had been present at Christ the Redeemer's statue, then she realised he was referring to the much more innocent kiss she and Guido had shared in the hotel lounge not long ago. This fired her courage.

"That was a reaction to a successful bit of work we'd done together."

"If that's how you celebrate a bit of work, I don't want to be present when you accomplish something major!" Sarcasm wasn't generally a trait of Paolo's personality, but Giò was angry to see it raise its head now.

"Are you checking out my personal life?"

"It would seem you're getting far too close to the very person who last spoke to the dead woman, so it's pointless to ask for your help."

"The last person who spoke to Margherita? Are you really thinking that Guido had something to do with her death? How silly!"

"How do you know?"

"How do I know what?"

"That it's silly? That the guy had nothing to do with her death? How well do you know him, and for how long?"

"Is that a carabiniere's question or a personal one?" Giò growled. Why was it that every time something good happened in her life, people had to question it and stir up trouble?

"It's an official question," Paolo replied after a short, uncertain pause that did not escape Giò.

"Unless I've got a short memory, you're the one who arrested Andrea Aiello, only to find out a few days later he was as innocent as a lamb," she snapped, reminding him of a previous case where she had been... well, sort of involved with one of the suspects.

"Look here, Giò, as you said, I always try to keep you away from danger. You cannot deny that."

"Yes, you're always complaining I'm too nosy."

"I spoke to your fellow authors, but only got generic answers. They are not telling the whole truth, and I wondered if you, as an insider, could discover more. Maybe one of them knows the real reason why Margherita came all the way from Rome to Maratea. Was she planning to meet someone? I thought you might be unbiased as you'd only just met them, but then I see one of them hugging and kissing you..."

"That was just a friendly kiss!" Giò protested, even as her

thoughts went back to the *not-just-a-friendly* kiss of that morning. She felt a frisson of excitement run down her spine, causing goosebumps to appear on her arms and neck.

"Yes, brotherly love, whatever, but I'm inclined to think you're not as impartial as I'd hoped."

"Let us not argue, Paolo." Giò was more intrigued than angry now. "It was only yesterday that Granny asked me exactly the same question: was Margherita here to meet someone, and the fact is she did have a business meeting in Maratea. So, has anybody come forward to let the carabinieri know they were meant to meet with her?"

"No, no one has said they were expecting her. I wonder if the news of her death made them reluctant to come forward."

"Hmm," Giò said. "As Granny said, that'd be a strange way for a Maratea local to behave."

"I'll check on that, then. But what I want you to do…"

"Yes?" Giò interrupted eagerly.

"Is some digging within your group. Encourage them to speak about Margherita and see what they say about their relationship with her. I still find it weird she decided to come when you were here, even if she was to meet with someone in Maratea. Could her appointment actually have been with one of the group?"

Giò nodded, but in her heart of hearts she didn't find it all that strange that Margherita had simply turned up to annoy the writers who had snubbed her. Then all of a sudden, a memory came back to her – the memory she had been trying and failing to grasp since the previous day.

"The manuscript!"

"What manuscript?" Paolo asked.

"Was there a manuscript at the crime scene?"

"A printed one, you mean?"

"I think so," Giò said.

"No, nothing of the sort. Whose manuscript was it?"

"I assume Margherita's. When we were at Granny's, there

were three things that struck me." She told Paolo about Valentina and how her demeanour had changed during her stay, about Alberto's concerned face. "And I had the feeling that there was a third thing that had passed unnoticed under my nose. I couldn't figure it out, until now. Guido had said that when he left Margherita in the restaurant, she had a manuscript on the table in front of her. But when I found Margherita the next morning, I'm sure there was no manuscript anywhere near her, and you just confirmed that."

"So a manuscript has disappeared from a writers' retreat," Paolo thought aloud. "What's the meaning of that? I wonder. I've asked Strazio to look at all the files Margherita had been working on recently. We'll see if there's anything interesting there."

When Paolo left, his demeanour was definitely less friendly than usual, and he exited using the outer door of the restaurant instead of the inner one. Was that so he didn't have to pass where Guido had been sitting? Or was that just her imagination?

Before they joined the others for dinner, Giò asked Guido about the absent manuscript. He insisted it had been there when he left, on the table in front of Margherita.

"Quite a substantial pile of paper it was too, it's strange it should have disappeared."

But when Giò mentioned that the carabinieri were investigating the possibility that Margherita might have had an appointment with one of the writers in the retreat group, Guido didn't burst into his trademark contagious laughter, nor did he deny the possibility. Was he intrigued by the hypothesis or concerned that the carabinieri were still investigating Margherita's death?

16

WAS IT BLACKMAIL?

After dinner, Giò asked Annika if they could have a short talk before going to sleep.

"Is it something confidential?" Annika asked.

"Let's say rather delicate."

"Then we'd better go to my room." Annika winked at her. "I get the impression the hotel hall is the worst place to try and keep things private."

As they entered her room, Annika added, "Now let me guess, does this have something to do with a certain red-haired man?"

Giò looked at her, pretending not to understand.

"Come on, Giò, it stands out a mile. Are you and Guido falling for each other?"

Giò gasped and went crimson. Just as many people had done before her, she had thought she and Guido were being perfectly discreet about their budding feelings for each other.

"Who told you that?" Giò blabbered.

"Come on, Giò, it's obvious. You're always sitting next to one another, always chatting and sharing private jokes, and when you're not close, you keep looking at each other. And today when you came back from your trip to the statue of Christ the Redeemer, you looked like a different woman."

"Oh my goodness, I never thought it'd be that obvious!"

"I'm so happy for you. You're two kindred spirits, two free souls that dream of travelling the world. And I'm sure you could mitigate that certain hardness of his."

"Hardness?"

"Maybe that's not the right word. But I've known Guido for quite a long while. I don't know if it's ambition or just perfectionism, but I've found there comes a point, especially when he needs to conclude a project, where he becomes as stubborn as a mule. He's completely blinkered, and it seems he would do anything to achieve his objectives."

"You mean he's a man without scruples?" Giò asked her in surprise.

"I'm not saying he'd do anything illegal, but yes, he can get carried away and be quite unpleasant. I mean, in a way that's good – he's an achiever, but at times… He should know when to put the brakes on in life, when to stop no matter what. And I believe you might just teach him there are other things in life than results."

"I'm not sure I understand, but yes, I do get a feeling he launches himself headlong into everything he starts, if that's what you mean."

Annika laughed and shook her head. "Please, I don't want to preach. Now you look so worried; it wasn't a warning. I believe these things just happen spontaneously, you'll naturally complement each other. At times I feel you should be more confident in your own skills and he might be a good boost for you to believe in yourself."

"I've got plenty of confidence," lied Giò shamelessly.

"Sure!"

"You're wicked! Now tell me about you and Simone – I think *you* complement each other. That poor guy really does need a confidence boost and you're the right woman for the job."

Annika turned towards the small fridge in her room, took out a bottle of prosecco and filled two tulip glasses on her desk.

"Friends can never hide anything from each other," she chuckled, raising her glass. "You're right – salute!"

They clinked their glasses in a toast, laughing and teasing each other for a while.

"But you know the funniest thing of all?" Giò asked.

"Funnier than what we've just confessed?"

"Indeed it is – I came to speak to you about something completely different. Nothing to do with my messy love life."

Annika didn't try to hide her surprise. "I thought you had come to confess your feelings to your Scandinavian friend. So, what's the matter?"

"The carabinieri, and my granny, wonder if Margherita had some business to discuss with someone in our group, other than her business in Maratea."

Annika looked alarmed by what Giò had just said.

"Could it be true? But they all seemed surprised and definitely not pleased to see her. To me, her arrival came as a real shock. She had given me such a hard time on the previous retreat."

"And you don't think she kept in touch with any of them afterwards?"

"If she did, none of them has ever mentioned it. Did you ask Guido? After all, he spoke to her more than the rest of us on the night of her death. They were the only ones who seemed to have anything to discuss."

"I asked him briefly, but maybe I need to dig deeper with him. And what about you? Did you notice anything strange going on?"

"After Margherita arrived, everything seemed strange. But that feeling didn't last long as the next day, she was dead. Do you have anything specific in mind?"

"No, I just wondered if you'd noticed anything unusual, even if it doesn't seem to be related to Margherita's death."

Annika shook her head. "I wouldn't say so. It's just a retreat, not too dissimilar to all the others I've run. Mind you, each one has its idiosyncrasies, but there's a set pattern to them, if you see what I mean."

"I think so: some personal matters, some love interests, some creative crises, some creative genius, a new determination and loads of good resolutions. Does that sound like a typical retreat?"

Annika nodded.

"I see." Giò looked at her empty glass. "As tempted as I am to share a second prosecco with you, I'd say it's time for bed now."

"Yes, especially as I've got a rather intense writing sprint planned for tomorrow." Annika rose up from the bed where they'd been sitting and accompanied Giò to the door, then stopped abruptly. "Oh, there was something. I'm not sure if it's of any interest to you, but Vittoria mentioned something about Mrs Galli."

"Huh?"

"You remember the day Margherita died, we invited her to join our table. Vittoria said something like, 'Oh, the thrill of having a blackmailer amongst us'."

"I didn't hear that."

"She whispered it in my ear. We couldn't speak further with her sitting at our table, so I resolved to ask her for an explanation later, but then I totally forgot about it."

"That might be worth following up," murmured Giò, leaving her friend's room to go back to her own. But instead of turning right, she headed left, stopping in front of the sisters' room.

There was a considerable amount of noise coming from inside, despite the lateness of the hour. It sounded as if two people were arguing, hissing at each other in a vain attempt to keep their voices low. Giò was wondering whether to get closer to the door to eavesdrop when a turn of the knob made her jump. A second later, a woman exited and bumped straight into her.

"I'm sorry!" Vittoria cried in surprise.

"Ouch," said Giò, massaging the point at which her nose had

been hit by Vittoria's head. The door slammed behind Vittoria and she peered more closely at Giò.

"Did I hurt you awfully?" she asked.

"I think I'll survive."

"What were you doing out here?" asked Vittoria, then her gaze travelled across the corridor to where Guido's room was. Clearly imagining Giò had just left him to return to her own room, she added, "Oh, I see."

Giò flushed a bit, but thought better than to put her right.

"And you, where are *you* going?"

"My sister's driving me mad," Vittoria said with a sigh. Giò looked at her quizzically. "How about a drink at the bar?" Vittoria added. "It might do me good to talk to someone."

Giò wondered if alcoholism wasn't opening its doors to her, but wasn't Vittoria the very person she wanted to speak to? Some things require sacrifices, so she followed Vittoria down the stairs. The bar was actually closed, but the night concierge was kind enough to serve them a couple of gin and tonics in the hall.

"So, what happened? You look worried."

"Valentina is a dear, but at times she's just too sensitive, almost like a child. Since this thing happened here – Margherita's death, I mean – she's been so… disconcerted. We paid a lot for this retreat, but she isn't really into it. What I mean is we joined the writers' group because *she* was so enthusiastic about it. She's always looked up to Annika as a role model, so when she found out about this group led by Annika, she insisted we had to join…"

"And was she as eager to come on this second retreat?"

"Yes! She hadn't liked Margherita at all, but we were all happy we'd got rid of her… possibly that's the wrong expression to use in the present circumstances." As usual, Vittoria was doing both the questioning and the answering, making Giò's job easy. "What I mean is we felt relieved she was no longer part of the group. And then when Valentina saw her walk through the door, it came as a huge shock to her, but hers was a childish reaction. Life is never easy – the very thing you dread the most has a tendency to turn up. It's a pattern that repeats again and again throughout life; you can't hide away from it."

"But why did she in particular dread meeting Margherita so much? I mean, I know how unpleasant Margherita was, I saw it for myself, but she seemed harmless."

This time, Vittoria didn't seem too keen to answer the question. "You see, our mother died when we were children, and I became a surrogate mother for my younger sister."

"I know what you mean," said Giò. "It's exactly the same with my sister and me, though we were adults when we lost both our parents in a car accident." She shook her head to dispel any melancholy thoughts. "But yes, from that moment onwards, Agnese became a mother to me to a certain extent, besides being my sister. At times, we argue about it, but overall I'm grateful for what she does for me. And though I've never acknowledged it to her, I love to know she's there."

"You younger siblings never giving us any credit." Vittoria grinned, grasping Giò's hand as if to thank her.

"We're not always that aware of our own feelings." Then Giò remembered her original quest. "And what do you think of Mrs Galli? I think she's an odd character."

"She *is* odd. There's something I don't like about her. The evening we arrived, during dinner, just before they started to serve food, I left the restaurant to fetch the photos of the previous retreat from our room upstairs for Annika. On the way back, I caught Mrs Galli talking to someone in the hall. They were sitting in a dark corner, and I couldn't see the other person, but I heard Mrs Galli say, 'You don't want me to spread that around, do you? Then you'd better do as I say.' There was something so hard in that voice that the words struck me, even though I was in a hurry. Since then, I've wondered what it was about."

"And what do you think?"

"I don't know. She sounded menacing, evil." Vittoria paused as if looking for the right words. "I think it was blackmail."

Giò was startled at the frank admission. "And who do you think she was talking to?"

"I wouldn't be able to say."

"A woman? A man?"

"I couldn't make out the other figure, but from the way the voice sounded, I'd say another woman. And the likelihood is that a woman would only be that threatening and merciless towards another woman."

"But there was only our group at the hotel at that moment," Giò whispered, "apart from Dr Siringa and Dr Gimondi sitting at the other table, and they never left the restaurant until they'd finished their dinner."

"That's what we thought at the time – that no one else was there. But a few minutes later, Margherita made her appearance."

"Do you think it might have been her?"

"I couldn't say for sure, but when I returned to the restaurant, no one from our table was missing."

17

A CONFIDENTIAL INFORMATION CLAUSE

The aroma of orange flower water and pastry baking filled the air in her kitchen as Granny religiously watched the golden pastiera in the oven with one eye and the timer on the marble kitchen top with the other. As the alarm rang, she opened the oven slightly, tested the cake with a long toothpick and sniffed.

I'd say from the smell the pastiera is ready. It was her own mother who had taught her to tell whether the cooking was perfect by scent alone. Nonetheless, closing the oven quickly, she passed her fingers along the toothpick. There were a few traces of ricotta, but none of the dough. The pastiera was ready.

She switched off the oven, opened it slightly again and waited for the vapours to clear, the temperature to drop and the cake to settle. Only when five minutes had passed by did she take out the cake and put it on a rack so it could cool down.

Looking at the lattice pie crust she had patiently woven, Gran nodded in approval. It had lived up to her expectations.

She looked at the clock: 10.30am, the best time of day to go to Maria Lucia, the hairdresser. The shop was closed on Mondays, as are most hairdressers in Italy, so on Tuesdays it would fill up with customers with a backlog of gossip from the weekend. Most women would do their cooking and chores at home early in the morning, so by now the shop would be crowded – something Granny tended to avoid, except on special occasions. And this was a special occasion, she decided as she buttoned up her bright yellow duffle coat.

∾

"Good morning, Mrs Brando," Maria Lucia said, her chirpy voice hardly audible over the hubbub and chatter coming from the sofa in the salon. Five women were sitting there, happy to have to wait while Maria Lucia and her young assistant Clelia did their job.

"Weren't you happy with your haircut last time?" Maria Lucia added.

Granny liked to go to the hairdresser four times a year, once each season, and she had only been there the previous week.

"I was delighted, but we might have Emmegra down here for Easter and I want to be ready." Emmegra, her posh granddaughter-in-law who lived in Rome, was as stylish and refined as she was empty-headed, but she was useful at times like this.

"Then we will have to do something special," Maria Lucia said, scrutinising Gran's profile as if seeing her for the first time. Emmegra had once gone to the salon and complained about how classic and old-fashioned the hairdresser's style was, and Maria Lucia was not someone who'd forget, nor forgive.

Granny, as respectful as a schoolchild, took her seat on the sofa to wait for her turn.

"Have you heard," the blonde woman sitting next to her asked, "about this woman dying at the Pellicano Hotel?"

"Of course." Trying not to show her pride, she added in a whisper, "My granddaughter is staying there."

"So I was right!" The blonde looked at the other women with

her best I-told-you-so nod, then turned her attention back to Gran. "You must know all the details, then."

And Gran was only too happy to launch into a description of what had happened, taking the attention from Mrs Pecoriello who'd just sat down on the hairdresser's chair. With her head inclined backwards as Clelia shampooed her, Mrs Pecoriello could only listen, but as soon as she got back to a sitting position and noticed Granny had no more to say, she spoke up triumphantly.

"What you don't know is why this woman came to Maratea."

"Indeed, that's what I've been wondering."

"I heard," said the brunette sitting on the other side of Gran, her voice sheepish, "that she already knew the writing retreat organiser, that Swedish woman. She came on purpose to create trouble."

"And God in his righteousness decided to punish her for having such a wicked heart." Another of the gossips had her own peculiar views on religion.

"If God were to punish every wicked heart in this world," Maria Lucia said, "there would be very few of us left... if any!"

The hairdresser switched off her hairdryer and Mrs Pecoriello could finally speak again.

"The thing is that Mrs Durante was meant to meet my husband on Sunday."

Silence. A long, long silence.

All five women on the sofa looked up at her, acknowledging the power of first-hand information. Mrs Pecoriello enjoyed the sight of the open mouths, and only when they started breathing again did she decide it was time to tell them the rest.

"That woman is – was – well connected in the publishing industry. And my Mimì is going to write a book – you know we've had quite an adventurous life. He moved to Venezuela when he was a young boy and there he made his fortune, starting as a dishwasher in a restaurant."

The women looked at each other in dismay. They had heard

the story of Mimì Pecoriello at least a million times, how he'd progressed from dishwasher to owning a huge chain of restaurants in Venezuela before deciding to retire to Maratea for no better reason than to show his fellow citizens, who had always taken him for stupid, how disgustingly rich he had become.

Maria Lucia sighed, switched on her hairdryer again and was as violent as she could reasonably be with the hot air and brush strokes in a desperate attempt to speed up the woman's tale. She switched off the hairdryer only when the story was over and Granny could finally fire her questions.

"So you're saying that Mimì not only knew Margherita Durante, he had actually invited her here?"

"Well, he didn't know her in person, but a friend of a friend told him she was the right person to speak to. Mimì was to send our driver to pick her up from the hotel at lunchtime – her and someone else who'd help by creating a book trailer, or something to that effect, but then we heard what had happened."

"You mean your husband didn't meet Mrs Durante at all in the end?"

"No, not at all," and they could all see how desolate she was. She would have been the star of the gossips if only that stupid woman had had the good sense to die *after* the meeting with Mimì.

"And you said your husband has written his autobiography?"

"I'm not sure he's finished, but Mimì has good business sense. I think he wanted to make sure he already had a publisher to support him with marketing and all those things I don't understand, and that woman was an expert in the field."

"They must have spoken to each other, though," Granny insisted.

"Of course they did, many times before she came to Maratea. And when she arrived, they agreed that the driver would pick them up at 1pm on Sunday, and I had everything organised for lunch."

"Did you say 'them' – was there someone else coming?"

"Yes, the man making the trailer."

"You don't know his name?"

"I'm not sure Mimì mentioned him, but I guess he'd be staying at the hotel too."

More gossip followed about whether the hotel chef was at fault for Margherita's death, but even this group of harridans could find no fault with her.

"We don't ever really know what we're eating," said the shy brunette sadly.

Mrs Pecoriello's hair was finished. She paid Maria Lucia and said farewell, put on her elegant blue jacket and left, only to return in fewer than two minutes.

"Ladies, I forgot to say something. Please understand that Mimì doesn't want to make the book public yet; it's a secret. So everything we discussed in here is strictly confidential."

They all nodded solemnly and Mrs Pecoriello left with a lighter heart. But as she walked away, two sisters came in, and within 30 seconds they had been updated on the fact that Mrs Margherita Durante had come to Maratea to meet Mr Pecoriello. By the time Granny left, half the women of Maratea knew of Mr Pecoriello's plans to write an autobiography, but to be fair to Maria Lucia and her clients, they never forgot to add that the news was strictly confidential.

ONCE BACK HOME, GRAN LOOKED AT HER HAIR, HORRIFIED. HER white bangs, normally framing her face nicely, had been pulled back into a crest pointing upwards. She tried to comb it down again, but there was no doubt that Maria Lucia could comb hair for lasting effect. Far from being traditional, the hairdresser had gone all out for modernity.

Sighing, Gran gave up. In any case, she had something more important to do. She picked up her phone and called Giò.

"I know how busy you are, but we need to act fast before the rumours reach the carabinieri, then the man won't speak to us at all."

"Are you sure I'm the person you wanted to call? It's Giò here, not one of your gossipy friends. I've no idea what you're talking about."

"Mr Pecoriello – we need to speak to him as soon as we can."

"Why would I need to speak to a man I didn't even know existed until two minutes ago?"

Gran sighed heavily. *How slow this young generation is.*

"Because he was meant to have lunch with that Margherita woman on Sunday to talk about his book. And I have reason to believe someone else from the hotel, very likely that Guido of yours, was invited too."

"I think... I'm on my way..."

GIÒ WAS TOO FLABBERGASTED TO ASK ANY MORE QUESTIONS. HER heart was pounding violently as she ended the phone call. From experience, she knew Granny was hardly ever wrong when gossip was involved.

"What's up?" asked Annika, who was sitting beside her in the hall, waiting for the others so they could all go to Il Veliero for lunch together.

"Something weird. I can't tell you more until I know more, but I'm not coming for lunch."

"You look as pale as you did when you lived in Scotland."

"I promise I'll tell you later. Let me go before the others come down."

She marched towards the main door of the hotel just as Guido came down the stairs.

"Hello," he said, all smiles.

She muttered a greeting, but avoided looking him in the eyes.

"What's wrong?"

"I'll tell you later, I need to go now. Bye."

Guido, looking confused, turned around to see Annika with an equally puzzled expression on her face.

"What happened?" he asked her.

"Her grandma invited her for lunch."

"But she looked so shocked, I hope it's not bad news."

"Hmm, I hope so too."

18

THE MEXICAN VILLA

"Aargh!" Giò cried when Granny opened the door to let her in.

"What's the matter?" Granny asked in alarm.

"Whatever happened to your hair?"

Granny shrugged. "Maria Lucia vs Emmegra."

"Eh? Are you feeling quite well today, Granny?" Giò asked, hoping that everything the old lady had said on the phone was as exaggerated as the punky crest standing up on her head.

"But I said no to having my hair dyed fuchsia."

"Oh my goodness."

Granny tried again to comb the crest flat against her head, but only succeeded in making it stick out all over the place like thorns on a rose stem.

"Leave your hair, you're only making it worse. What were you telling me about Margherita Durante earlier on?"

Granny told her all she had learned at the hairdresser's. Giò wasn't too bothered that Margherita had been due to meet Mr Pecoriello, but she objected to the notion that Guido might be involved.

"We've discussed Margherita's death at length and he's never mentioned having an appointment with her in Maratea."

"Well, you're grown up enough to know the truth: people lie all the time."

"Why would he lie to me, though?"

"Maybe he didn't. Filomena Pecoriello never mentioned his name, but she did say that someone in your group was putting together a book trailer, so I naturally assumed it was him."

Giò thought it over. "I'd assume the same, I'm afraid. I'm going to have to confront him."

"How about finding out a little more before you roast him alive?"

"How?"

"I phoned Filomena, told her she had been a little naive in sharing her husband's business in a hairdresser's salon, that by this evening the whole village would know about his book. She was terrified, the poor dear. Mr Pecoriello would do anything for her, but when it comes to business, he can be single minded."

"What have her marital problems got to do with me?" said Giò, pretending an indifference she didn't feel.

"I suggested that if you and I were to visit him, we could pretend that the news of their lunchtime meeting had already spread around the hotel before Margherita passed away. He will appreciate having a chance to talk to you so that he knows what to expect from the carabinieri. They will be the last to know, of course, but in the end they will hear about the meeting and might not appreciate the fact that the man didn't come forward."

"I'm not sure the carabinieri will appreciate us being informants either."

"We won't be informants," Granny said firmly. "Mr Pecoriello would have found out sooner or later that everyone already knew about his planned meeting with Margherita, we're just using time to our advantage. After he's spoken to the carabinieri, he won't be willing to speak to us, but as things are now, he and Filomena are waiting for us to join them for coffee."

VILLA CHIARA WAS ALSO CALLED THE MEXICAN VILLA, FOR NO reason other than the fact that Mr Pecoriello had made his fortune in Venezuela, and Maratea people had little idea of the geography of South and Central America. It was situated on the outskirts of the village and could only be reached by a serious hike, or by car.

Giò drove through the tiny rural streets of Maratea, realising how unfamiliar she was with some of the peripheral parts of the town. The satnav directed her up a street that climbed steeply, passing through such a narrow space that she could only hope nobody would be driving down. Most of the view was hidden between unkempt walls made from chipped stone, beyond which she could spot treetops revealing the presence of gardens. They finally found number 224 and, stopping in front of an imposing iron gate, Giò announced her presence into the intercom.

When the gate opened, both Granny and she were stunned. Although the world outside had been scruffy and rough, inside was a beautiful green park, three terraces dealing with the sloping terrain. The lush grass, a real luxury in the southern part of the country, was cut very short; beautiful palms were stretching their large leaves towards the mountains behind them; centenarian olive trees with their convoluted shapes were scattered among white rocks in large terracotta jars and vases.

Giò's car climbed some more. On the second level was a beautiful swimming pool overlooking the gulf and the pier. One more climb and they were in front of a huge villa dating from the early 20th century, all turrets and gables and stucco decorations covering its facade. A portico overlooked the swimming pool below and the majestic view beyond.

It was rare that Giò, not to mention Granny, stayed speechless for long, but that's exactly what they did now. It took a few minutes before Giò could suggest a shy, "Shall we go?"

Filomena Pecoriello, her short, sturdy body spilling out of a yellow and black dress, came over to welcome them. If she was concerned about how indiscreet she'd been, she didn't show it. The woman invited them to sit in one of the rooms behind the portico, passing through some thick blue curtains held open by a white ribbon adorned with shells.

Elegant sofas and a crystal table were arranged so as to make the best of the view outside. A small gas stove warmed up the room as the weather was still cool from the recent storms. A housemaid appeared, enquiring what they'd like to drink, and Mrs Pecoriello asked her to call the master of the house as well.

Mimì Pecoriello was a short man, even shorter than his wife, with a square face that was more shrewd than handsome.

"Good afternoon, Filomena told me you were coming. How are you?"

"We're fine," Granny said, wishing he was one of her former students. She could still command instant respect from those she had once taught.

"We were admiring this place, Mr Pecoriello, it's simply beautiful."

The man nodded in approval, inviting the Brando grandmother and granddaughter to call him by his first name.

"I'm sure my wife will be only too pleased to show you around. We had a much bigger property back in Venezuela – which is a beautiful country – but we missed our Maratea, despite the government over here seeming determined to prey on all our hard-earned money. So we had to downsize quite a bit, didn't we, dear?"

And Filomena Pecoriello nodded, her dreamy eyes surely still seeing all the luxuries she had left behind. Giò and Granny glanced at each other; they could hardly imagine anything richer than where they were just now, but a luxury lifestyle wasn't their area of expertise.

The housemaid returned carrying a heavy silver tray on which a pretty old-fashioned Moka pot sat and poured the hot liquid into thin porcelain cups with a red and golden design. As she disappeared, Mimì drank his coffee in a single gulp.

Watching Giò, his piercing black eyes partially hidden by his bushy eyebrows, he then asked her a question.

"So you knew Mrs Margherita Durante?"

"Not exactly, but she was staying at the same hotel where I am attending a writers' retreat, and she had once been part of the same group."

"Did you have much chance to speak to her?"

"She had dinner with us the evening before the accident occurred."

"I see." He looked as though he was pondering on her words, maybe deciding how much to reveal.

"I heard that she was due to meet you on Sunday."

Filomena's lips twitched nervously, but Mimì missed it as he was absorbed in his two guests. He was evidently used to making decisions quickly as he replied without hesitation.

"Indeed, my driver was going to pick her up from the hotel. We were meant to have lunch together, until I heard what had happened. A terrible thing, poor woman. I'm not sure they have allergies in Venezuela; I think it's something that only plagues civilised countries."

Giò thought that it was more a case of being knowledgeable about one's own immune system's reactions than anything else, but she kept the thought to herself. It was other information she was looking for.

"And may I ask you how you knew her? If it's not an impertinent question, I mean."

Granny nodded in approval. With this kind of man, you had to take a polite approach. A confrontational one would yield no results.

"It's no big secret," he said. "You see, I have lived what can only be considered an extraordinary life. I've taken risks since I was a young man, and I believe life rewards the brave. Act like a rabbit and you'll stay a rabbit. At my age, many successful people feel the urge to share all that we've learned, maybe inspiring other young minds. Although the more I see of youngsters – and

I'm afraid that includes my own nephews and nieces – the more I think they are just a mass of spineless spoiled brats."

Filomena had kept very silent up until now. Realising that her husband was about to tell the story she had let out of the bag earlier, she relaxed, knowing she could no longer be held responsible. Looking relieved, she was anxious to have her say.

"My husband won't acknowledge that the times have changed, that the new generations have a different drive…"

"Their only drive is buying things," he frowned, "from video games to clothes, all sorts of useless stuff. But they have no will to become someone, create their own business, earn their own money. Anyway, I know I'm old fashioned, but I've long held this romantic notion of writing my autobiography. A mutual friend advised me to get in touch with Mrs Durante, and she told me she could come over this weekend."

"You mean you hadn't met her before?" Giò asked.

"No, it was going to be our first meeting, but we'd spoken over the phone a few times."

"And I understand she was going to put you in touch with a publishing house to get you a deal."

"Yes, my friend said she's quite influential and has plenty of contacts. More useful than an agent as she covers all kinds of extra services too."

Giò looked at him questioningly. *What was the man referring to?* Again there was a short pause as he looked straight into her eyes.

"I'm an excellent businessman, but writing is a different story."

"Margherita was to provide you with a ghost writer?"

"She was going to be the ghost writer. I'd be no good at that, but she told me she'd study articles, have a researcher with her, a video maker. They'd interview me, present me with an outline and work with me to review the text if things weren't correct."

"So on Sunday, you weren't only expecting Mrs Durante?"

Granny asked as Giò had been struck dumb the moment she'd heard the words 'video maker'.

"No, it was to be three of them: Mrs Durante, the video maker and the researcher."

"You don't remember their names?"

"Not really, but I may have them in emails."

"Was one of them Guido Gagliardi?" Giò ventured.

"Yes, that's right. He was the video maker."

Giò felt her heart tighten. He hadn't been honest with her, not mentioning a thing about having business to conduct in partnership with Margherita. And he'd had the temerity to kiss her! She felt so angry, she wanted to get up and run away from this lovely house, go to confront him there and then. Why had he lied to her? Why had he wanted to get close to her in the first place?

She remembered the way he'd described his affair with Margherita. Had it really been in the past? Well it was certainly in the past now the woman was dead, but how about Giò? Was she meant to be just another trophy in this man's collection?

A kick on the leg, and not a gentle one, called her back to the present. The Pecoriellos were looking at her, and she realised she didn't have a clue where the discussion had gone.

Granny repeated the question that Mimì had just asked of her. "Do you want to tell Mimì your other friends' names? Maybe he can identify the researcher?"

Giò did as she was asked on autopilot, but Mimì shook his head, not recognising any of the names.

"I'm sure it was a woman, and she wasn't young from what I understood."

"Not Mrs Galli?" asked Giò with little conviction.

"Exactly, Augusta Galli! So you know her too?"

"Not really, but she's a guest at the hotel, and after the accident we got to know each other a bit more."

The man simply nodded.

"Do you plan to go ahead with the researcher and the video maker?" Granny asked.

"I doubt it. I was interested in the full package Mrs Durante was offering me, but now I will have to look for a publisher who wants to take on the project. It will be the publisher who will supply the ghost writer and researcher, and decide whether we need a video maker or not. I'm less clued up about these things than Margherita was."

"So you're not going to meet either of them?"

"I can't see the point of meeting them as there will be little chance we'll work together. Retired though I am, I still have limited time."

"My husband is just too good at finding things to do, though he did promise me that once we were back in Maratea, we'd relax a little, travel more and visit our children."

"Men need a purpose in life," he said, bending to kiss his wife gently. "Actually, I hope you will excuse me, but I have to go now. It's been a pleasure meeting you, and please come back any time to visit my wife."

He shook hands with them in his strong, energetic fashion and left.

"Men are so different to women," said Granny. "Never take their work away from them, they need that kind of stimulus."

"That's so true," Filomena Pecoriello said. "Shall we have a walk in the garden? Although I'm afraid this year, springtime is proving elusive and we don't have many flowers in bloom as yet."

Giò was grateful to Granny for doing all the talking as she followed the two older women silently. While Granny exclaimed in delight over some rare plants, Giò couldn't help thinking about that stupid kiss at the statue of Christ the Redeemer, the intimate chats, the enthusiasm with which they had worked on the video. Damn! She had trusted him.

As Giò tuned back into the conversation, Filomena was inviting them in.

"We'd love to," Giò heard herself saying, "but I'm afraid I can't. I left my group at the hotel and we're supposed to stick together. I hope you don't mind."

As they moved towards the car, Filomena invited them to come over whenever they felt like it, adding, "It feels a bit lonely here every now and then. I do have a couple of good friends from my youth, but they're often busy with their grandchildren as their families live nearby…"

"You should join the Pink Slippers Society," Gran suggested. "I'm sure you'd love the President, Ornella Capello. The Capellos, of course, are one of the noble families here in Maratea."

"Are you a member yourself?"

"Not really, I'm more into bookish things, but they do lots for the community and I'm sure you'd find yourself well received. I could come back for a visit with Ornella if you wish?"

"I'd love that."

When they got back into the car, Giò remained silent despite Granny's remarks about the villa and the garden and the view.

"And how about Mimì?" she said. "Didn't you find it strange he never asked any question about Margherita's death?"

Giò flinched, her mind foggy as if she were waking up from a dream. "Maybe he's just not as nosy as we are."

"He's a shrewd businessman, I'm sure he must be curious about it. I find it weird he didn't ask you anything about what happened during the dinner, or afterwards. Giò, are you listening to me?"

"Of course I am, but I don't have an answer."

"Remember, men lie for all sorts of reasons. It's not necessarily because he wanted to mislead you. And he seems to be a nice guy."

"Who?" Giò cried, now fully awake with all her senses alert.

"That Guido guy."

"I wasn't thinking about him!"

"Not much," replied Granny smugly.

19

THE VALLEY OF THE ASSASSINS

By 8am on the Tuesday, Rolando and Angelica had already enjoyed their generous breakfast at the hotel, checked out and were waiting in the foyer for their travel companions. Soon a taxi would take them to the Alamut Valley, also known as the Valley of the Assassins.

A couple about the same age as them stopped at the reception desk and the concierge pointed to Angelica and Rolando. The two came forward to meet them.

"Nice to meet you, I'm Karen." A puffy-faced woman with brown hair and a pleasant smile stretched out her hand.

"And I'm Liam," said her companion, a tall man with blond hair and sparkling grey eyes.

"How do you do?" replied Rolando in a friendly tone. "This is my wife, Angelica."

It took a little while for Angelica to offer her hand as she was recovering from her surprise. Liam was the man she'd seen in the bazaar, conducting some shady deal with the boxer.

"My wife has not yet got over the long journey," Rolando added.

"I'm sorry, it was a *very* long journey," Angelica muttered.

"Tell me about it!" Karen nodded. "We come to Iran a

number of times a year, but every time it requires a few days to get over the flight."

Liam looked at Angelica as if evaluating her before inviting them all outside.

"I think our car has arrived."

Had he recognised her from the bazaar? Was it just a coincidence that they should meet again?

The driver, Sajad, had a pleasant round face, thick beard and even thicker eyebrows. He welcomed them, put their luggage in the back of the car and asked if they suffered from car sickness.

"Is that a warning?" Angelica asked, smiling.

"No, Sajad is right to ask," Liam explained. "The journey is long, and as we get closer to the Alborz Mountains, the road will get rather rough."

"If you need, we can stop at the pharmacy before leaving," Sajad said. But all the passengers shook their heads. No, they would be fine.

"So you mentioned you're often here in Iran," Rolando said to Karen once they were in the car. "How come?"

"Partly for pleasure, partly for business," Karen answered. "We have an antiques shop in Birmingham and we love to look for hidden treasures from North Africa and the Middle East. Iran is possibly our favourite country."

"Though *possibly* the most difficult to deal with from a business point of view," Liam added. "So *possibly* our worst supply market."

"But we finished the business side of our travels yesterday, and from today we're officially tourists."

"Unless we spot a good opportunity," Liam added.

"The random deals are often the best," Karen agreed.

The two went on, chatting amiably about the country's hospitality and its rich beauty. They were very knowledgeable about Iranian traditions and customs, attractions and food. But as friendly as Liam was being, Angelica felt rather ill at ease with him, and she was sure he was sizing her up. Why, though? Surely, as far as he knew, she had left the shop before the mysterious transaction had taken place, so why would he be suspicious of her? Had her surprise at seeing him given her away? But why would he care if, as the couple had been implying, their business dealings in Iran were all above board? She must be overthinking things; perhaps he was just surprised to meet her again too.

The road got more and more narrow and started to climb. Occasionally, trucks and cars overtook them, even though there was only just enough space. A few centimetres' error and they could have ended up in the deep ditch on the side of the road. But Sajad kept his cool, slowing down to let the cars pass while managing to explain what they were seeing.

Then the mountains that had been tempting Angelica from a distance since she and Rolando had landed in Tehran were right in front of her, breathtaking in their imposing glory. The overcast sky had partially cleared, apart from some long streaks of low cloud. The rays of sunlight hitting the pinkish-brown rocks made the valleys come alive as if in Technicolor, the vegetation consisting of low bushes and a few scattered groups of hardy trees that could resist the wind.

Sajad had to stop the car quite a few times so his passengers could take in the view, and he seemed to know the best places for the most dramatic sights. Many of the rest areas were near small cafés that served a strong, aromatic tea. The first sip was bitter and unusual, but then Angelica discovered it was delicious, as was everything she'd consumed in Iran, and the pungent scent cleared her thoughts.

She felt both intimidated and captivated by the landscape, so natural and yet so powerful. With the snowy tops of the mountains so close, she felt as if she could reach out and touch them, her heart thumping with awe and excitement. She looked at Rolando, who was gazing out of the café window, fascinated. For the last 20 minutes or so, he had been silent, refusing to get involved in small talk with their travel companions.

Should she tell him about Liam? No, not now. Later maybe, in their lodge.

Once another cup of hot tea had disappeared, they returned to their car. As the road rose higher and higher, chains of mountains revealed themselves from behind crests. Amazing. She had thought of Iran as a desert, always hot and sunny. It was a good job Rolando had warned her to pack warm clothes.

"Gâzor Khân welcomes you," Sajad said. They were finally beneath the Alamut Castle. "I suggest we have a quick look round first."

A pity about the scaffolding, which had been placed around the ruins after an earthquake and never removed, but what a view! No wonder the assassins had decided to build their fort there – they could dominate the whole valley around them, see what was going on, and at the same time defend themselves easily. The place must have been impregnable.

Angelica searched for the bare walls behind the scaffolding, wanting to touch the stones full of history. Sajad led them on to a path from which they could see the fort and the rocky valley behind. A streak of sun lit up the rocks and the pastures, a silver stream of water at their feet, the snow-tipped peaks of the Alborz Mountains. They stood enchanted, despite the cool wind blowing against their faces.

"Is that our car coming?" said Karen.

"Yes," Sajad confirmed. "My colleague Hossein will take you back."

"You're not staying overnight?" asked Angelica.

"It's too cold and we're not as hardy as you are. I need the solid wall of a building around me. We're off, my friends, but we'll see you tomorrow. Enjoy your stay here."

Angelica watched as the couple walked over to the car.

"I think it's time to set up our lodge," Sajad said as Hossein drove away.

"*Set up* our lodge?" cried Angelica. "Do you mean we're

sleeping in a *tent*?" She had been dreaming of a hot shower in some romantic but comfortable accommodation.

"We'll have a fire and food under the stars," Sajad replied. "I'll wait for you on the plain below so you can enjoy the sunset."

As the man left, Angelica glared at Rolando.

"Are you kidding? Are we really sleeping in a tent?"

"It's just for tonight."

"Why didn't we go back with Karen and Liam to a decent hotel?"

"I thought it'd be a nice experience, and you didn't contradict me when I mentioned camping at Alamut."

"You didn't mention camping, you called it a lodge. I thought it'd be a nice deluxe place, not a tent. I need a hot shower, a warm bed."

He didn't reply, just looked at the sunset and the amazing pinkish colours in both the sky and the mountains. Apart from a few baaaas from a group of goats following a shepherd home, they were surrounded by complete silence.

They were alone.

THE NIGHT WAS BEYOND STARRY. ANGELICA HAD NEVER SEEN THE like of it: a feast of lights, the Milky Way looking so close, thick as a spoonful of clotted cream, she believed she could touch it with her hands.

Sajad offered them a delicious stew of beef with split peas and aubergines.

"I've never tasted beef like this," said Angelica, who had decided to make the best of a bad job – a decision she'd found unexpectedly easy.

"It's my wife who does all the cooking," replied Sajad. "I've only warmed up what she prepared."

The crispy Barbari flatbread with sesame seeds was so tasty,

Angelica could have eaten it on its own, and the hot, aromatic tea accompanied the meal perfectly.

I can't believe I'm sitting by a crackling fire in the middle of nowhere, Angelica thought.

Rolando was asking questions about the history of the place, and Sajad was only too happy to share tales from Alamut and its surrounding area, occasionally throwing dry wood into the fire from the pile he'd collected. Angelica looked at her husband: the boring man, the steady employee who now looked so at ease in this wild place, conversing in stumbling English with Sajad. And all of a sudden, she felt happier than she had been for years. She slid her hand into Rolando's, and he kissed her on the head.

"Honey, you look a little tired. Perhaps you should go to bed now."

"I think I'll do just that, but don't stay up all night yourself. That goes for you too, Sajad."

The two men smiled and resumed their conversation, their chat interspersed with long stretches of comfortable silence. In the tent, Angelica found a sleeping bag, a thin mattress. Would she sleep a wink? After the first few minutes, though, her body started to warm up, thanks to the hot-water bottle Sajad had given her. It certainly helped, and before long, her thoughts were drifting.

But just before sleep overcame her, a pair of hands covered her mouth and she was dragged out of the tent, unable to make a sound. To add terror to terror, Angelica saw no trace of Rolando and Sajad near the fire as she was dragged away. What had happened to them? Who was kidnapping her and what did they intend to do to her?

She tried to kick out, move her arms, but they were pinned too tightly. As they reached a four by four, she felt handcuffs snap on to her wrists before she was thrown in the back. A strip of sticking plaster covered her mouth.

"I'll take it off," said one of the kidnappers, "but if you scream, it'll go straight back."

She shook her head and pleaded with her eyes, letting him know she promised to stay silent. Maybe having her mouth free would afford her more chance to escape later.

"Good."

He tore the plaster away. She did her best not to cry out. It hurt.

By the inner lights of the car, she recognised who one of her kidnappers was: the man with the mean eyes she had seen speaking to Liam at the bazaar. The boxer. He laughed mirthlessly at her attempt to open the door with her cuffed hands.

"It's locked, so you'd better behave. If you do, nothing bad will happen to you. We want to keep you as healthy as possible – you see, you're precious to us."

"What do you want from me?"

"The gold your husband was meant to give us."

"My husband what?"

"You're starting to talk too much for my tastes." The boxer with the mean eyes turned towards her and sprayed something around her mouth and nose – something sweet almost to the point of rottenness...

20

AN HONEST CONFESSION

G iò had just parked her car when Guido spotted her from the hotel terrace. Smoking a cigarette, he approached her.

"Hello, Giò, is everything OK? You looked rather worried when you left."

"I'm not worried any more, just furious. I simply hate liars of any kind," she replied, slamming the car door.

"And who has been stupid enough to lie to you?" he asked with the soft smile and slightly ironic wink she had become so fond of.

"A certain video maker, engaged by Margherita for a project when he'd told me he'd intended to have nothing more to do with her. I've just come from Mimì Pecoriello's house."

"Ouch! Yes, that was very stupid of me," he said, still speaking softly, but he didn't seem too worried. He put out his half-smoked cigarette in an ashtray on one of the tables on the terrace, and then said, "Let's have a walk, I want to explain."

"It's a bit late for that…"

"Come on, Giò," and he invited her to follow him, descending the little staircase leading from the terrace to the beach. The sea had retreated after the storm, so the gangway between the rocks was again usable. They reached Anginarra Beach without difficulty.

"You let me believe you no longer had anything to do with Margherita." Giò spoke as soon as they had passed beneath the windows of the restaurant and she was sure they were alone.

"Which was true. By that time she was dead, so I couldn't have anything to do with her."

Giò stamped her foot and looked at him with furious eyes.

"As I said, it was stupid of me, and I shouldn't have done it. But you didn't like it when I talked about my past relationship with Margherita, so if I'd added that I'd come to Maratea to conduct business with her, you would have told me to bugger off."

"Which is exactly what I'm going to do now."

"Giò, things happened so quickly. If I were going to work with Margherita, if she were still alive, then I would have told you all. But as things are, it would just have created friction between you and me, and we have so little time to get to know each other. I didn't lie to you... I simply didn't tell you the whole truth."

"Unfortunately, to me there's no difference between telling a lie and not telling the whole truth."

Guido sighed, thought things over, then spoke in a contrite tone of voice.

"You're absolutely right. It was so stupid of me, but I swear I didn't ever think along the lines of *Giò's never to know the truth*. Just believe me when I say I'm sorry."

"The thing is, I'm not sure I can trust you, now."

"Giò, it was just a job. We were to meet with this Pecoriello guy, who Margherita said might have some work for me, and you know every little helps."

"Did she contact you before you came to Maratea?"

"Yes, a couple of months ago."

"And was that the first time she'd got in touch with you after your other writers' retreat?"

"No, she phoned me a couple of times soon afterwards. I made it clear that what had happened between us was over. It took a while for that to get through to her, but then she came back with this deal involving a man who needed a team to put his book together."

"Are you sure you told her things were over? Or did you tiptoe around that as you seem to do with uncomfortable truths?"

"You're welcome to check all our emails as soon as we get back to the hotel," he said seriously.

"I might just do that."

"Suits me. It's my fault you're doubting me."

"Mr Pecoriello mentioned that Mrs Galli was also due to meet him on Sunday."

He looked genuinely surprised. "I didn't know that. Margherita never mentioned it when we spoke after dinner."

"So what did you talk about?"

"We spoke about the customer, Mr Pecoriello, and what Margherita was expecting me to do."

"Were you going to do some shooting when you met on the Sunday?"

"Not at all, that would come later. But since I was here, I could show him my work and outline what he could expect from me, hand him my proposal."

"It was very nice of Margherita to suggest your name."

"I didn't lead her on, Giò, if that's what you're hinting at. That's not me. I told her our affair was over and this was just a business meeting. She told me he could pay good money, and work is work. I had no reason to refuse this job, especially as I'd be here in Maratea anyway."

"But why didn't she tell you about Mrs Galli?"

"I've no idea." He thought it over, then added, "You know what? The woman told us plainly she's a ghost writer, and I can hardly imagine Margherita putting in all the hard work that takes: interviewing the man, working with him draft by draft. I don't think that suited her personality at all – a ghost writer is someone who avoids the limelight, but Margherita had to be the centre of attention all the time."

"So what are you suggesting?"

"That Margherita was intending to introduce Mrs Galli as the researcher, but in truth, she'd be the dedicated ghost writer. Maybe they had some form of private agreement."

It was Giò's turn to think things over. He might be right. From the way Annika had described Margherita, Giò could hardly imagine her, with her glamorous lifestyle – attending social events of all kinds, meeting people – finding the time for the complicated work of a ghost writer.

"And was it Margherita who told you not to mention the meeting to us?"

"Yes, she asked me to maintain the highest confidentiality for the project. After all, she hadn't signed the deal yet. That's one of the reasons I never mentioned anything to you – it wasn't my secret to tell. And I didn't think it was relevant to our relationship, so yes, I glossed over it. Will you forgive me?"

Giò suddenly felt better, the heavy weight lifting from her heart. She could cope with harsh reality, with bad things happening in life, but lying was an altogether different thing. Still, she needed time to think over whether she could trust this man or not. No impulsive decisions, no silly feelings running away with her.

His eyes met hers, his hand gently moving her chin upwards.

"I won't lie to you, I promise."

Giò felt goosebumps cover her skin, all good intentions abandoning her. Those hazel eyes searched her soul as if he could read her mind and his touch was having a strange chemical reaction on her, something she had no control over. She closed her eyes, shivering with pleasure.

But disappointingly, his lips never met hers.

"And I won't kiss you either." He was still looking at her

intently, so very close. "No, not until I've told you one more thing…"

It was at that moment they were interrupted by people shouting to them from the gangway. Vittoria and Erminia were calling their names, telling them to return to the hotel right away.

~

"WE'RE SO SORRY," VITTORIA SAID TEASINGLY.

"Yes, we hope we didn't interrupt anything." Erminia chuckled wickedly. "Anything important, I mean."

"That's exactly what you did do, and at the worst possible moment," Guido replied. Giò blushed beyond crimson, but possibly in the orange light of the sunset, the other didn't notice.

"Not our fault," Erminia said. "It was Annika who sent us looking for you, after she'd tried knocking at the doors of your rooms. And your mobiles don't seem to be connected either."

Giò stuttered something about there being no signal on the northern beach.

"It's almost 7pm," Vittoria reminded them. "It's time for our group meeting to sum up the day."

The other writers were all in the small seminar room, sitting in a circle. Annika sent a look towards Giò, as if asking what was going on. Giò nodded and smiled to reassure her friend that everything was fine, but she felt as if she was still in a dream. So much so that Giò started when it came to her turn to speak at the meeting; she'd barely heard what the others had said. She stammered a summary of what she had done before she had gone out to meet Granny and the Pecoriellos. Luckily, she had managed to squeeze in a few hours of concentrated work in the morning. And yes, she was quite happy with the direction her project was taking. Writing a travel memoir was so much more personal and creative than writing a travel guide. Not as straightforward, though.

Valentina followed her, but once again, Giò found herself unable to concentrate on what her companions were saying. She glanced at Guido, who seemed to be much more present than she was. He was listening, encouraging and speaking words of advice when he felt he could help someone. As for Giò, she was just waiting for the painful meeting to be over. What more did he have to tell her? Had she fallen for this guy in a few days without even realising what was going on? Had she already passed the point of no return?

She remembered the beginning of her very short relationship with Andy, a charming architect she had met in September, soon after her return to Maratea. But back then, she had fought against her feelings. She had felt her interest, realised what was going on... Or had she? Maybe love is meant to take you by surprise, no matter what.

How could Annika be so cruel as to keep them here for so long? And what was Francesco saying? It was his turn now and he was explaining the rather convoluted path his mind had gone down today, using a million words to say he hadn't even managed to write 500. Then Erminia intervened, saying that it wasn't the quantity but the quality that mattered, although she herself had had a productive day with 8,000 words down. And a gazillion words followed to describe her creative process.

Giò's eyes, despite her best efforts, fell again on Guido, who winked at her. Erminia's verbal stream was a monologue; she didn't seek any feedback from the others. She simply wanted them to admire her ability to write and produce work constantly, to feel she was a role model. She seemed indifferent to how hard it must be for her son to live up to such a monster of productivity, despite her attempts to appear encouraging and understanding.

Annika summed up all they had said, dispensed advice on what could work better for each writer, asked what their expectations were for the next day, and finally called the meeting to a close.

"Let's go to Il Veliero. It's time for dinner."

"No chance they'll open our restaurant again?" Alberto asked.

"The carabinieri said that tomorrow, they will remove the tape. I'm not sure about lunch, as it will take some time for the chef to sort out her kitchen and do all the shopping, but tomorrow evening we should have dinner at the Pellicano Hotel."

"Yahoo!" Simone said. "We love it here, and it'd be a pity not to use the restaurant now we know the kitchen staff weren't at fault."

"I agree," said Alberto. "And the wine list here is excellent."

On their way out, the writers met Mrs Galli holding a paper bag in her hands.

"Are you joining us for dinner?" Alberto asked her politely.

"No, got some work to do. I'm taking my dinner to my room. I need to go on writing; can't waste my time with yoga classes, meetings, long lunches and even longer dinners, drinks and cafés. I have a schedule to respect."

"I feel so miserable whenever I speak to that woman," Francesco said as Mrs Galli hobbled away.

Vittoria took his arm. "Please don't. Not all that glitters is gold."

"Besides," Guido said, "as far as we know, she might be writing the screenplay for a sleazy porno movie," and they all burst into raucous laughter.

21

MORE REVELATIONS

The dinner dragged as much for Giò as the meeting had, but finally it was over and Guido was standing beside her.

"Would you come to my room? I'd like to show you a couple of things."

As she followed him in, he turned on his laptop and opened his email.

"I want you to read all my correspondence with Margherita."

Giò was uncertain for a second. Had she been so unforgiving that he felt he had to prove he'd been speaking the truth?

"Please, go ahead, I'm begging you."

He had entered Margherita's name and a number of emails had appeared in date order. Giò could see that it had been Margherita who'd contacted him, that much was true. The woman had also alluded to how much she was looking forward to meeting him again, and he had replied, leaving no room for ambiguity, that to him it would only be a business meeting. He had been very clear on the fact that any personal relationship between them was well and truly over, and he had no wish to resurrect it.

From the replies, Giò could see that Margherita had been rather resentful to start with, but then it appeared she'd accepted things when she'd invited him to join her to meet the entrepreneur who wanted her to write his autobiography. In the following emails, they simply discussed the details of their meeting and what Guido had to prepare to show to the entrepreneur. He had done other book trailers, short documentaries and author introductions, and she mentioned a couple of these that it'd be worth taking along.

Giò put the laptop back on the desk. She was sitting on the only free chair.

"Earlier, you mentioned that you wanted to tell me something else?"

"Yes, Giò." He ran both his hands through his curly hair, and for the first time since they'd met, he gave her the impression he was at a loss for words. "I'm not too sure how to go about this one. You see, I wasn't expecting... to meet you."

Giò tensed, feeling her body go rigid. She didn't like the sound of where this was going.

"If it helps," she said icily, "I hate it when people try to sweeten the pill."

"What I want to say," he sat on the bed in front of her chair, "is... well, you've seen how hard I've been working on my book. I want it to be finished, or mostly finished, by the end of this retreat, because next week, I'm flying to Istanbul. And from there, I will travel the Silk Road."

Giò was somewhat relieved. As far away as he was going, it wasn't the secret love affair with another woman she had been dreading he'd been about to confess. It was just a journey; he'd be back.

"Sounds exciting."

"The thing is, I plan to explore all the locations, passing through Samarkand, Kyrgyzstan, the northernmost part of China, then its east coast, finally ending up in Jakarta."

Giò was startled by the list of places, her brain becoming a version of Google Maps, the Silk Road a long, long line reaching from country to country.

"How long will it take?"

"About a year."

"Did you say a year?" Giò cried.

He nodded.

"And you haven't said anything to me about this until now?"

"I really wanted to, but at the same time, I felt that if I did tell you, things between us would stop there and then. I thought it was better to let things happen and see where we were heading." He took her hands in his. "I wasn't expecting to feel this way about you – you took me by surprise."

She snatched her hands away. "And is this trip definitely going to happen?"

"It is, but I'd love it if you were to join me and spend some time with me..."

"Why are you going?"

"It's something I've had planned for years. I have been looking for sponsors, and a few brands have commissioned videos and will be supporting me financially."

"That means you can't change a thing – postpone your departure; shorten the trip?"

He shook his head. "It's one of those once-in-a-lifetime things, Giò. I know you love travelling and I thought you'd understand. And you could join me from time to time and we could see what happens. Hey, come here."

He tried to pull her close, but Giò pushed him away.

"I need time to think, I'd better go now," Giò said, turning her back on him and leaving the room, shutting the door violently behind her.

In the corridor, Giò stumbled into Annika, who read her agitation and confusion.

"Oh, Giò, did he tell you?"

"You knew he was leaving?"

"I knew. He asked me if he should let you know, and I told him to tell you at the right moment. To let things follow their natural course, not to force them. After all, you can always join him – you love the travelling lifestyle, and I can just see the two of you wandering the world together..."

"We hardly know each other!"

"I didn't tell you to marry him, just spend time together and see if you're made for each other."

"But Maratea's my home."

"Maybe you're not meant to have a fixed abode. And Maratea will always provide a safe nest any time you need to return."

"I'm not sure I have itchy feet any more. At the moment, the ground's just settling under them."

"Life never goes as planned."

"That's easy for you to say. With Simone, you'll settle in either Ystad or Tuscany and run your business from there, then travel and hold seminars all over the place."

"Has the nomadic bug left you, Giò?"

"I don't know. I need fresh air."

"I'll accompany you."

"No, please, I need to think alone."

Leaving her friend, she went out into the starry night, the moon suspended over the sea. It was a quiet night, with just a gentle, cool breeze rippling the water. The only wild storm now was inside her.

Why did you have to come into my life, you stupid man? Couldn't you have just stayed away? If you want to go to Asia, fine, go, but forget about me.

She descended on to the beach and walked briskly until she was close to the waves. There she looked for pebbles and started to throw them into the sea as far as she could, listening to the plop as they dropped into the water. So great was the turmoil of her emotions, she put all her energy into the exercise and had worked up a sweat in no time.

"What the heck?" she cried. "Were you really expecting me to follow you, just like that?" She snapped her fingers furiously. "Forget it, Prince Charming."

She had just resumed her walk when she saw the lights of a car in the parking space overlooking the beach. Was someone else about? Had they heard what she'd been yelling?

"Can't I be left in peace in this stupid country?" she hollered, her temper getting the better of her. "There aren't even 400 souls living in Acquafredda, so why is there always one in the wrong place at the wrong time?"

A figure waved at her from the balustrade.

"Is that you, Giò?"

"Paolo? What on earth are you doing here?" she cried. Although she felt angrier than ever, she still approached him. He switched off the car lights and came down to join her.

"I was doing my night watch and saw someone on the beach. At this time of night, I wanted to make sure everything was OK."

"How long have you been here?"

"Oh, I heard everything you said, if that's what you mean."

"Do you know how much I hate you right now?" she said, too angry to be embarrassed.

"At least I'm in good company."

She had to laugh, despite herself. "It wasn't really gentlemanly not to reveal your presence."

"I had my headlights pointed onto the beach. I thought that was more than enough to let you know I was here, but you were really on a roll. So, who's upset you? Is it that Guido guy?"

"Yes, him!"

"Has he cheated on you?"

"Not sure. He certainly has a habit of not telling the whole truth, of leaving things unsaid."

They sat down on a boat that had been pulled up the beach almost to the level of the road to keep it safe from the stormy sea. It had been turned upside down to protect it from the rain and it offered a convenient, if not exactly comfy seat.

"Love is so complicated. I wish it could be fair and simple; instead, it takes all sorts of tortuous routes, and no matter what you do or don't do, it's going to hurt you."

"I agree with every single word," Paolo said.

"But this time, I won't fall into the trap. I'll steer clear of it. As far as Giò Brando's concerned, that love story is over – assuming it ever started."

They sat silently for a while. Paolo's presence, as always, had a soothing effect on Giò, and before long, her thoughts started to wander along another path.

"By now, even the carabinieri must know about Mimì Pecoriello and Margherita."

"So you know about that, too." Paolo sighed. "It seems to me we – the carabinieri – are always the last to know everything."

"That's exactly what Granny said."

"Even the elderly make jokes at our expense. There's no longer any respect for the authorities."

Giò chuckled.

"It's good to see you laughing."

"Indeed, you're good medicine. But did you know Granny and I were at the Pecoriellos' house this afternoon?"

And she told him all that had passed. He listened to her, as he always did, not only with great patience, but also with interest to hear her point of view.

"Did Mr Pecoriello mention Margherita's fee?" he asked her when she had finished.

"He said she was on the expensive side, but he seemed rather pleased with it."

"It was 80,000 euros."

"Are you kidding me?"

"Not at all."

"I didn't think a ghost writer earned that much."

"Most of them wouldn't, but if you land a project for someone famous, where the book will potentially make serious money, then the contracts tend to be on the generous side. After all, we're discussing the sale of intellectual property rights. A ghost writer signs away all her IP..."

"I didn't know you had such a deep understanding of the publishing world."

"I didn't," he confessed, "until I did some research this evening and asked the advice of a small independent publishing house in Naples. It's run by a guy from Maratea – we were friends at high school, and he was willing to explain a few things to me over the phone."

"Eighty grand," Giò repeated incredulously. "It's a lot of money."

"Exactly."

"I take it you still suspect there's something fishy about Margherita's death?"

"Interesting choice of words, given her allergy. Yes, more than ever. One minute, she's fit and healthy, about to close an important and very lucrative deal; the next, she's dead. And we don't know why. The post-mortem was inconclusive – maybe there was a minute trace of fish in what she ate at dinner, but would anaphylactic shock have hit her so quickly that she had no time to call for help? Nor even reach for her EpiPen? And all the food used for the preparation of her meal was cleared by forensics."

"Is it possible that someone dropped something in Margherita's food?"

Paolo nodded.

"But," she continued, "it might also have been an honest mistake. Maybe the chef used the wrong spoon."

"Maybe."

"Let's assume Margherita was killed on purpose," Giò said. "Why?"

"I've no idea. Was anyone else aiming to win the contract from Mimì Pecoriello?"

"Not that I know of. Mr Pecoriello mentioned that Margherita had been recommended to him as an authority in her field, so I don't think anyone else would have stood a chance of going up against her. But I can see where your suspicions are heading."

"So?"

"So, as I told you, Mrs Galli was supposed to go to the meeting with Margherita, posing as the researcher. But as Guido said, it's unlikely that a glamorous woman like Margherita would do all the hard work herself. If she did, the whole thing would have been out of character."

"You think she wouldn't ghost write for that amount of money?"

"No, she'd rather hand the task to Mrs Galli, a dedicated ghost writer, paying her, I suspect, only a tiny fraction of what she – Margherita – would receive."

"You might be right. How about Gagliardi? Was he aware of how much money she stood to make?"

"In the emails, Margherita just mentioned that Mr Pecoriello was a good payer."

"What emails?"

"The emails Margherita wrote to Guido."

"How do you know what she wrote to him?"

"He wanted me to read her emails," Giò said shortly. She wasn't going to explain everything to Paolo.

"Maybe one of them thought they'd cut themselves a larger slice if Margherita was out of the way?"

"No," Giò answered stubbornly. "As I said, Mr Pecoriello doesn't even want to meet them. His interest was in working with Margherita, her services and her contacts with publishers. No Margherita, no contract for Guido or Mrs Galli."

"Or maybe that's what Mr Pecoriello wants us to think now we've found out about his liaison with Margherita."

"Maybe."

"And one more thing – if Guido Gagliardi is going away for a year, why was he so keen on getting a contract now?"

"That's not an issue. His trailer work would come last in the project, and I wouldn't be surprised if the book took a year or so to write, then that much time again for publication. He'd have a nice contract waiting for when he came back."

An ugly thought crossed Giò's mind: *Along with a stupid woman.*

"Are you OK?"

"Of course." Desperate to find anything to camouflage her despair, she threw in the first thought that came to her mind. "The blackmail!"

"What blackmail?"

"Vittoria said she heard Mrs Galli blackmailing someone the night of Margherita's death. I thought it must have been Margherita, as all the other hotel guests were in the restaurant."

"Hmm," Paolo muttered. "Maybe Mrs Galli had found out how much money was involved."

"And she threatened to tell Mr Pecoriello that she, not Margherita, was going to be the ghost writer. She really thought she could get the contract, and… my goodness, she had a reason to kill her."

"Blackmailers never kill their prey. And you said Pecoriello wouldn't be interested in a contract without Margherita."

"Only because he didn't know who the real ghost writer was."

"I'm not convinced. You said Margherita's value also lay in her contacts with publishers. I can hardly imagine Mrs Galli having the same kind of influential relationships. I believe she was simply trying to get more money out of Margherita."

"And then there's the lost manuscript. Guido says it was there on the night of the murder, but it had disappeared by the next morning. And Mrs Galli was trying to get into the restaurant that morning, I saw her. Dr Siringa had to send her away."

"But if she had already taken the document, why go back?"

"Maybe to return it."

"We would have noticed, and it was risky."

"Maybe, but she seems a little bizarre in the way she acts. Maybe she didn't appreciate the consequence of her actions."

"So how did she manage to kill Margherita when she wasn't sitting anywhere near her during dinner?"

"You're right. But there's something fishy," Giò smiled, "about her role in this story."

"I think I may have to speak to both Mrs Galli and Mr Gagliardi tomorrow. But how about calling it a night? It's almost 2am."

"My goodness!" said Giò, standing up. "I need to get up early tomorrow, I've got work to do. I want to finish the outline of my travel memoir – did I tell you that I'm working on my own project?"

"No, you didn't, but you look far more enthusiastic about it than you do about the guides you generally write. Tell me more as I walk you back to the hotel. I'll fetch the car later."

Giò was still speaking animatedly about her new book as they reached the terrace of the Pellicano Hotel.

"Paolo, I feel so much better." She didn't know exactly how to thank him, and so she hugged him briefly, feeling a little embarrassed.

"Now, be a good girl and get some sleep," he said, taking her by the shoulders and turning her towards the hotel door.

"Goodnight," she said, walking across the terrace deep in thought – so deep she didn't notice the shutters of one of the upstairs window quietly closing. By the time she got her key from reception, her mind had returned to Guido.

He's going away for a whole year. According to Annika, he hadn't meant to mislead her, he had just been waiting for the best moment to tell her. Well, obviously there hadn't been a 'best moment' at all. There couldn't be a best moment for such a painful confession.

He was leaving. No doubt about that. He'd never give up on his project, she knew that much about him, and he probably couldn't either. There were contracts to be respected, agreements, sponsorships. No, it had to be her choice. She could visit him in a month or so, spend time together. And travel was always the ultimate test for budding romances. Either they'd get along, or they wouldn't.

~

IT WAS 4AM AND SHE WAS STILL LYING AWAKE IN HER BED, HER EYES wide open, adrenaline pumping ideas into her brain. Now it was Guido, then it was the murder case. Murder? No, safer to say suspicious death. Maybe she and Paolo had just been overthinking things.

She jumped out of her bed, moving in nervous circles. She felt like she was close to solving the mystery, but there was something... something she'd heard that she absolutely had to remember.

Restlessly, Giò opened her balcony doors and went outside, the chilly air making her shiver. Looking over the balconies on either side of her, she saw light coming from one of the rooms. It had to be Guido's – he was the only one in the group who preferred to work in the hours of darkness.

Then the light went out. Had he decided it was finally time to sleep? She went back into the room and was just about to give sleep another try when she heard a light noise from the corridor. Was it someone closing a door?

She switched off the lights in her room and quietly opened her own door a tiny bit, just enough to see torchlight – most likely from a mobile phone – moving along the corridor towards the stairs. She couldn't fail to recognise the familiar physique and gait: it had to be Guido.

Did he suffer from insomnia too? It was none of her business anyway, so she pushed her door closed. And then it came to her mind.

Vittoria had mentioned Mrs Galli blackmailing Margherita. And Paolo had said no blackmailer would kill their prey. But what if Mrs Galli had known how much money Margherita was expecting to earn from the Pecoriello project? What if the discussion that Vittoria had thought was blackmail had in reality been a simple threat? What if Mrs Galli had seen the chance to get her hands on more money? From the way she dressed and hobbled around, it was clear she wasn't exactly swimming in cash. And hadn't she killed a beetle in the restaurant, just to let the writers' group know she didn't value certain people's lives any more than the insect's? Maybe she wasn't really a religious fanatic. What if she had only pretended to be asleep on the sofa when Giò and Annika had found her? Had she really returned to her room before the murder took place? What if she had instead gone back to the restaurant after Guido and the waiter had left?

Giò wrote a text to Paolo, urging him to interview the woman early the next morning. Mrs Galli needed to explain why she had used threatening words with Margherita. And Paolo could confirm whether she had tried to get in touch with Mr Pecoriello.

22

A HARD AWAKENING

Dr Gimondi was shaking his head at Brigadiere Paolo Rossi.

"I should have told the hotel to call the emergency services, but I didn't realise it was this bad."

"Could you tell me exactly what happened?" Paolo said, inviting him to sit down on the sofa in front of him.

"Mrs Galli phoned me yesterday at around 6pm and asked me to come visit her this morning as she didn't feel too well."

"How come she called you? Did you know her?"

"When I picked up the call, it took me a while to realise whom I was speaking to. Then I remembered – when I was here with Dr Siringa on Saturday, Mrs Galli asked to have my card, saying she might need the services of a doctor during her stay here."

"Did she tell you what was wrong with her?"

"Not on Saturday, but yesterday on the phone she mentioned she suffered from type 2 diabetes and a few heart troubles. I asked her to explain any symptoms she was experiencing and if she had tested her glucose level."

"And what did she say?"

"She said she was keeping her sugars under control, but that in the last few days she'd maybe had too much alcohol and was feeling a little dizzy. But she didn't specify any more alarming symptoms."

"Didn't you offer to come out there and then?"

"As a matter of fact, I did, but she said that early this morning would be fine. I advised her to alert the hotel staff should she start to feel worse, explaining that in the case of an emergency, it would take me 30 minutes to get here as I live in Capitello. I reminded her that Dr Siringa lives in Acquafredda, but she said she didn't want someone used to dealing with corpses to attend to her."

"And you didn't think of calling an ambulance yourself?"

"I admit I didn't take her too seriously. You see, on the phone she sounded rather more chatty than you'd expect from someone who's not feeling well. I thought I'd be safe to leave things until this morning."

"When did you arrive?"

"Must have been around 7.30, but the receptionist might be more precise. I asked him to let Mrs Galli know I was here, but she didn't answer her room phone. I tried her on her mobile, but again no answer. It was only then that I thought something might be seriously wrong. I asked the concierge to accompany me. We knocked on the door, and when there was no answer, we entered the room with the hotel master key and we found her in her bed. I believe she had passed away no more than three to four hours earlier."

"And what did you do then?"

"Simply called my colleague Dr Siringa and asked the receptionist to get in touch with you."

At that moment, Dr Siringa came back down the stairs and sat beside Dr Gimondi.

"Dilated pupils, pyjamas soaked with sweat, used syringe beside her… it looks like an insulin overdose."

Dr Gimondi nodded. "And the half empty bottle of whisky?"

"Only made things worse."

"Did she inject the insulin herself?" Paolo asked.

"Forensics say there's no sign of anyone else having been in the room," Dr Siringa answered slowly. "The door was locked, according to the receptionist, when they tried it earlier. No signs of burglary. The balcony door was closed too."

"And I guess it's difficult to establish whether it was a deliberate suicide attempt or a mistake?"

"Correct. The lack of a note leads us to suspect it wasn't suicide. Also the whisky might have confused her so she thought she hadn't injected herself yet when in fact she had."

"Would twice her regular dose kill her?"

"It's not a simple case of maths, it depends on many variables – her heart condition, how much alcohol she'd had, when she had taken her previous dose of insulin, what kind of dinner she had had…"

"I see. Nothing to add on top of that?"

"Yes, there are a few cases when people become addicted to insulin. They like the way it makes them feel."

"Like a drug?"

"Exactly. Mind you, it's not common. But then, it's not common for a female diabetic over 60 to drink too much. I'll let you know how much alcohol is found in her body."

Gimondi was looking admiringly at his older colleague.

"Time of death?" Paolo continued.

"I'd place her death at around 4am, no more than thirty minutes either side," said Dr Siringa.

As the two doctors discussed the state of the corpse when Dr Gimondi had arrived, Paolo listened in, his expression concerned.

"Do you think it's suspicious?" Dr Siringa asked him.

"Yep," Paolo replied bluntly.

"I know," Dr Siringa said, as if reading the thoughts behind Paolo's words, "two sudden deaths at the Pellicano Hotel, one after the other, is a bit too much of a coincidence. I'll tell you more after the post-mortem."

And with that, Paolo knew it was useless even trying to get any more out of the doctor right now, but his mind was working furiously. His cop's hunch was hammering his brain with a single message:

"*Foul play.*"

He left the two men and returned to Mrs Augusta Galli's bedroom. The forensic team is still at work, taking nothing for granted, but they only confirmed that the door had not been forced and there were no signs of anyone else having been in the room.

Strazio and another young carabiniere joined him.

"We need her mobile," Paolo said. "I want to know all the recent phone calls she'd made. Have a look at her laptop and send me all the files she'd created or modified in the last month."

"I'll see to that," the young carabiniere replied.

Giò WAS STILL FAST ASLEEP WHEN HER PHONE STARTED RINGING repeatedly. Opening one bleary eye, she looked at the handset: 7.30. She'd happily have slept for a few more minutes, but the call was from Annika and she couldn't ignore her.

"Hello?"

"Hello, Giò, please come downstairs as soon as you can. The carabinieri are here again."

"The carabinieri? What's happened now?"

"Mrs Galli. I'm afraid she passed away in the night."

That was enough to get Giò out of bed, showered and dressed in double quick time.

When she got out of the lift, the first thing she saw was the hotel chef, shouting in the face of Maresciallo Mangiaboschi.

"You've kept my kitchen closed for days, accused me of food contamination, and now another woman has died in this hotel. You've got to admit this time, it can't have had anything to do with our food. So, what have you found out? Why did she die?

ADRIANA LICIO

I'm sure the same thing caused both deaths, because nobody's ever dared to die here before!"

Mangiaboschi didn't seem as large or bold as usual. His whole body seemed to shrink as her rage made the chef look bigger than she really was.

"And now, what should I do?" the woman continued. "I was supposed to reopen my restaurant today. I've been to Sapri market, bought fresh food as everything in the kitchen will be old and rotten by now. Are you about to tell me you're closing my kitchen again?"

She jabbed a finger against his breast and the maresciallo shrank back as if it was a sharp knife.

"Please, go ahead and do all you were meant to do. There's no reason to close..."

"You'd better not, not now that I've done all the shopping. Didn't your parents teach you not to waste food?"

Now the accusing finger was moving as fast as a fencing foil just below the maresciallo's nose.

"No need to waste any food, the kitchen will be open today," he stuttered.

"And you'd better keep your eyes open and do something useful before anyone else thinks it's OK to die in this hotel. What times we live in! And we pay you a large salary to do what? Close our kitchen and let other people die?"

She picked up one of the boxes full of fresh vegetables from the floor beside her and stalked into the restaurant, shutting the door loudly behind her.

"What a woman!" the maresciallo said. Turning round, he spotted Giò, who had just decided she'd be better off in the bar with the rest of the writers than trying to speak to Paolo. She greeted him sheepishly.

"This place is cursed," he growled, turning his back on her and heading towards the opposite end of the corridor and Brigadiere Rossi.

166

~

"The hotel owner has arrived. Do you want to question her?" Paolo asked.

Mangiaboschi nodded, but as she hadn't been there the previous night, there was little the owner could add. She did, however, let the two carabinieri know that she was also mad at them for doing nothing to prevent another person passing away in her hotel. Would she have to shut down the Pellicano after it had been in her family for over 50 years?

The only question the maresciallo managed to squeeze in was to ask whether she trusted all of her staff. He was soon to regret his audacity.

"They've all been with me for decades, and I'd trust them with my life. You've already tried to accuse my chef and were proved wrong..."

Oh no, not the chef again. Mangiaboschi had fallen into the trap of being too curious. In future, he would leave the torture of interviews to his brigadiere.

As the woman left in a fury, Mangiaboschi turned to Paolo.

"She's right," the maresciallo whispered. "We'd better interview all the guests again. After all, both victims were in the writing business. We need to understand if Mrs Galli was upset enough to attempt suicide, or if she injected too much insulin by mistake."

"Or maybe it wasn't self-inflicted at all."

Mangiaboschi looked at Paolo as if he was insane.

"Always ready with the conspiracy theories, aren't you? I'll tell you what, Rossi, if you don't learn to solve problems instead of creating new ones all the time, you won't have a long or easy career in the force."

"Guido Gagliardi was the last person to see Margherita alive," Paolo insisted. "Then last night, he said he went back to his room around midnight and saw a waiter walking along the corridor upstairs. I asked the concierge, but he said no waiter was in the hotel at that time. He was the only member of staff present, and he never went up to the first floor."

The maresciallo was finally listening. After all, if he arrested a killer, especially if they were a stranger to the area, it wouldn't do his career any harm. His superiors would commend him, as would the Regione Basilicata politicians, so he began to take an interest.

"Gagliardi, you say? And he was the only other person in the writing circle who was involved in Margherita Durante's project, connecting him to Augusta Galli as well."

"Correct," Rossi replied.

"I still believe you tend to overthink issues, as if we don't have enough on our plate, but in this instance, I'm inclined to agree with you. Investigate, but be quick about it. We will talk again later when we have Siringa's post-mortem."

Paolo frowned, wondering how he was going to break the news to Giò that another of her beaus was the carabinieri's number-one suspect. She could be such a stubborn woman – after all, he was only trying to do his job, and she had been totally wrong to suspect Augusta Galli. Had she been sidetracked by her feelings, her sympathies, for Gagliardi?

"So, will you interrogate him again?" the maresciallo asked impatiently.

Paolo nodded. "Him, and the rest of his group. Will you be present for the interviews?"

"No, I've got work to do at the station," Mangiaboschi said dismissively.

I wonder what that might be? Paolo knew full well it was a slack time at the carabinieri station with nothing to do except for paperwork – there was always paperwork, but it didn't require a maresciallo to do it. So what else was so urgent for Mangiaboschi? Barking at his subordinates?

As his superior officer left, Paolo walked to the front desk and asked the concierge if he could be allocated a private room. Then he entered the hotel bar, where all the writers were sitting, called for Guido Gagliardi, and told all the others to stay where they were as he would need to speak to them again. Giò looked at him quizzically, but he just turned and left the room with Guido.

As Francesco left the room, Paolo scratched his head and spoke to Strazio, who had been beside him throughout all the interviews.

"There's something weird going on. If they're innocent, why are they all so nervous? Not one of them seems to be telling the truth."

"And that Valentina was possibly the most nervous of them all."

"Exactly. I was hoping the others would help us stack the evidence against Guido Gagliardi, but the more we dig, the more it seems they might all be involved."

"You know that movie – what's it called? The one where there's a murder on a train, they suspect an outsider, but then they discover it was all the other passengers?"

"Strazio, that's *Murder on the Orient Express*, of course. But that's fiction. We're in Maratea, and not on a train, but in a hotel."

Strazio blushed, but in his heart of hearts, he wished he was investigating on that famous train.

"Have you managed to contact the night concierge?"

"Yes, he should be here any moment. But we've not heard from Giovanna Brando yet."

"If the concierge is here, I'd like to speak to him first. Giò will be in the bar, trying to glean information from the suspects. Better leave her to last."

A couple of minutes later, Strazio returned, followed by the night concierge who, after his first round of questioning, had gone back home to get some sleep.

"Sorry to disturb you again, but we need to go through the details of…"

"You asked me everything first thing this morning," the man grumbled, none too happy at having been called in again.

"Yes, but we need to circle back to the first death. Would you remember what happened on that night? Did you see Mr Gagliardi return to his room?"

"In fact, I did, as he asked me for a thermos of hot coffee to take upstairs to his room."

"And after that, you didn't see anybody else wandering around the hotel?"

The man thought for a while before answering.

"No, that's not correct. Soon after Mr Gagliardi had left, I saw Ms Valentina Valsecchi going upstairs."

"Had she been in the restaurant?"

"I'm not sure. She'd certainly been somewhere – maybe in the foyer on one of the sofas, maybe in the restaurant. I can't say for sure."

"And how long had she been there?"

"The first time, you mean?"

Strazio and Paolo looked at him in horror.

"How many times did she come downstairs?" the brigadiere asked him finally.

"Twice that I know of. Mind you, I never spotted her coming down, but I saw her going back up in the lifts. The first time was at about 10.30. The second time, it was the middle of the night. Around 2am, I believe."

"And what did she do?" Paolo launched an angry look at Strazio. This was all news to him.

"I'm not sure as again, I didn't see her come downstairs. I had binged quite a few episodes of…" he flushed, "…*Storm of Love* on TV."

"So you don't know how long she was downstairs the second time?"

"No, I don't know. The programme has an intriguing storyline."

"Didn't it look suspicious to you that she had come back downstairs?"

"Nope, she might have forgotten something. In fact, it looked like she had a wad of papers when she went back over to the lifts. Maybe she had come down to fetch it."

"A wad of papers? About what size?" Paolo wondered if they'd finally got a lead.

"Like an A4 bundle of paper for a printer, but of course, there's no printer here that I know of."

"Why didn't you tell us any of this when we interviewed you after Mrs Durante passed away?"

"Your *appuntati*," the man said, pointing to Strazio, "asked me if I had seen anything suspicious or someone coming in from outside…"

"And you didn't think it was suspicious that this woman had come downstairs twice?"

"Nope, that's commonplace in a hotel. Many people suffer from insomnia, need a little walk, a break from their room. Sometimes they keep themselves to themselves in the foyer, other times they come up and have a chat with me. Night concierges are rarely lonely."

"And did you chat with anybody that night?"

"Not that night. But Mr Gagliardi, for example, does most of his work sitting at one of the tables in the hall, and when he takes a break, we have a chat and a cup of coffee."

"I see," Paolo said with feeling. He needed to have a word with Strazio about how to conduct an interview. Giò would tease him mercilessly when she found out about this oversight. But for now, back to the questions – without leaving anything out this time.

"And did you see anybody else that night?"

Paolo and Strazio kept questioning the man until they were convinced they knew the exact sequence of movements in the hotel the night Margherita had died. When they had finished, they let him go.

"I'm sorry, Brigadiere," said Strazio contritely. "I should have done better when we spoke to him the first time round."

"Indeed," Paolo growled. "But never use *leading* questions during an interview. Remember, it's the basic rule."

Strazio nodded, but his mind was pondering what a *reading* question was. He'd google it as soon as he had a chance; no good would come from asking the brigadiere right now.

"I need to speak to them all again. But this time, we will leave them no room for lies."

"You don't want to speak to Giovanna Brando?"

"No, let's start with Valentina."

Strazio nodded and left the room. "Ms Valentina Valsecchi," he called into the bar a few moments later. "The brigadiere wants to speak to you."

Valentina went pale. In unison, Alberto and Vittoria asked, "Again?"

"We have new evidence," Strazio said, feeling like a TV cop. But then he smiled softly; he could never play the tough guy, and these people all looked too good to be guilty. Unless they'd done it all together, like the murderers on the Orient Express.

Già didn't even look up at Guido and shrugged him away when he tried to approach her. She'd sat as far from him as she could on purpose, she was so mad at him. He was forcing her to make a choice, disrupting her life. Why, of all places, did he have to land up in Maratea?

She was dragged from her thoughts by the sight of Valentina leaving the interview room. The woman went directly to the lifts, while Strazio came to the bar where the rest of the writers were gathered.

"Ms Vittoria Valsecchi, it's your turn. The rest of you, please don't speak to Valentina until we have completed this round of interviews."

"Are you going to interview all of us again?" Erminia asked furiously. "As if once wasn't enough!"

"Indeed we are." Strazio, as he'd been instructed by the brigadiere, didn't offer an explanation, which suited him just fine. Mrs Spilimbergo scared him quite a bit.

Despite the order, as soon as Strazio and Vittoria had disappeared, Alberto rushed over to Valentina, who was still waiting for the lift.

"What's going on? Are you OK?"

"It's too late, Alberto, too late. Forget about me," she replied, repeatedly pressing the button to call the lift. Alberto walked away with a desolate look on his face and returned to the bar, sitting at a table on his own, obviously determined not to speak to anyone. And, in fact, no one seemed to want to speak, apart from Erminia who kept trying to talk to her son.

"Mum, please be quiet," said Francesco eventually. "Things have taken a turn for the worse. They must suspect one of us."

"Suspect one of us of what?"

"Of a double murder."

"But that's ridiculous!" and she let out a loud false chuckle, but no one joined in.

ANNIKA BECKONED TO GIÒ TO ACCOMPANY HER OUTSIDE. GIÒ WAS relieved; she was getting fed up with having to ignore Guido's looks and attempts to speak to her. Getting away, even for a few minutes, would do her good.

"You know what?" said Giò as they left the hotel terrace and moved on to the walkway taking them over the rocks below the restaurant windows towards Anginarra Beach. "I can't help but wonder why Margherita decided to join your group in the first place. She was so critical of you all, and she already had a powerful network of people. I can't understand why she wanted to join if she felt you were so far beneath her."

"Can't you see?" Annika said, gazing over the white rocks towards the sea and the deep blue line of the horizon beyond. Giò shook her head. She didn't have a clue.

"There's a lot of talent in our group. You know about Guido, and there's Simone too, despite him feeling like he's anything but a successful author. Valentina will do great, and even the mother and son duo has put out a few bestsellers. I think Margherita wanted to get her hands on all that talent."

"But it seems to me she did her best to alienate the writers, not encourage them!" Giò protested.

"Her technique was more wicked than you could imagine. She'd do her best to destroy an author's confidence so she could get her hands on their work and dominate their career. As soon as I recognised the scheme for what it was, I spoke to other authors and friends in the publishing industry, and a pattern soon emerged. She'd done it before, and that's when I decided to expel her from my group."

"I see," Giò said as they continued their walk along the beach.

"Oh Giò, what's happening? This is all too much for me."

"It looks bad. I suspect this second death has cast everyone under suspicion. I really thought Margherita's death was an unfortunate accident, but it's too much of a coincidence that Mrs Galli would die of natural causes too, in the same hotel so soon after the first death."

"I see what you mean," said Annika, sitting down on the deserted beach not far from the sea. "Nonetheless, it could have happened. A terrible coincidence, I know, but possible."

"The carabinieri have to do their job," said Giò, sitting beside her. "They are the only ones who can find out the truth."

"I'm so worried."

Something in Annika's tone made Giò prick up her ears.

"Why? I mean, I know as the retreat organiser, you feel the

weight of responsibility and blah, blah, blah. But is there something more to it than that?"

"I'm afraid I told the carabinieri a lie…"

"About Mrs Galli?"

"Nope, about the night Margherita died."

"And what was it?"

"After we'd had our chat in the hall, I went to see how Simone was doing. I knew he was shocked at having to face Margherita again. During our first retreat, the woman had been dreadful to him, and as you know, he is full of self-doubt. Margherita enjoyed playing cat and mouse with him. She was awfully mean to him, criticising all his published work."

"But as you said, he's a successful author…"

"To some people, that doesn't mean anything. I mean, they're happy to have their readers, but they often wonder whether they really deserve their fame or not."

"Impostor syndrome?"

"Very much so."

"And you suspect he might have hurt Margherita?"

"Oh no, not at all." But again, Annika's voice lacked its usual determination. "When I visited him in his room, he was devastated. He had worked so hard to build a little confidence in the months that followed the first retreat, but hadn't written a single word since. All the same, he had arrived in Maratea full of hope that he'd get back to work… and then Margherita showed up and started ridiculing him again."

"I still can't understand why you're so worried." Giò looked intently at her friend. "I think everyone had their own reasons to be mad with Margherita. Simone is no exception."

"There's more to it, Giò. I tried to calm him down, we talked late into the night, and then I left. But half an hour later, I messaged him and got no reply. I thought it was weird – he'd been so upset, there was no way that he'd already have been fast asleep, so I returned to his room. When I got no answer, I went downstairs looking for him. I used the stairs as I didn't want to be seen by the concierge, but I hadn't even got to the ground floor before I bumped into him."

"The concierge?"

"No, Simone. He was shaking violently, was flustered and confused. He told me to leave him alone, so I…"

"So you what?"

"I went straight into the restaurant to confront that dreadful woman. I couldn't see Margherita at first, but when I walked across the room, I finally saw her. And Giò, she was dead."

23

LIFE PROCEEDS THROUGH
PROGRESSIVE COMPLICATIONS

"I thought you didn't want to see me," said Giò, peering into the interview room.

"I was saving the best for last," Paolo said dryly.

"You look annoyed…"

"I am."

Giò looked at him, puzzled. Unlike the maresciallo, the brigadiere usually had an even temper.

"Isn't Strazio here?" she asked to break the silence.

"This isn't an official interview, although we might have to have one later for paperwork's sake."

"I take it I'm not a suspect."

"Amazingly, you aren't," he finally smiled, "but the situation is rather complicated."

"You've decided you can trust me, even though I got things so very wrong last night?"

His face became even more serious, if that was possible. "I've always trusted you, Giò. But let's get out of here; this room is stuffy, and I need some fresh air."

"How about the garden near the swimming pool?" Giò asked. "They've put the chairs out, the sun is shining and we can find an isolated table to sit at."

Paolo nodded, and out they went. Despite the storm of the weekend, the garden was looking neat and tidy. It was too early in the year for the colourful explosion of flowers that characterised the place, but lilies at the foot of olive and palm trees were brazenly showing off their flowers, creating lively spots of white, yellow or red. The backdrop was the rocky mountains of Acquafredda and, beyond the vegetation and the beach, the Mediterranean, still streaked in a multitude of different blues and greens due to the water currents following the storm.

Giò and Paolo paused beside one of the large terracotta vases and stood there to let the sun warm their faces and bodies.

"It's gorgeous, isn't it?"

"The colours after a storm are more intense than ever, the view so clear," said Giò, waving a hand towards Mount Bulgheria enclosing the Policastro Gulf in the North. "It almost seems you can touch it. And look – I can see the houses of Scario from here."

"Please, take a seat." Paolo indicated a chair at a little table on the far side of the pool. From there, they could check any movements in the garden or on the beach. As she sat down, his hazel eyes searched hers, then he got started.

"We've been looking back over Margherita Durante's death."

Giò sighed. She realised this meant the carabinieri thought the two deaths were connected.

"So what did you find out?" she asked.

"We have a reconstruction of the night she passed away, based on what we've found out so far, but we need to take each person's statement with a grain of salt. Every one of your companions has been deliberately holding information back, if not lying the whole time."

Giò gulped, thinking of Annika and… well, Guido too. Was his situation desperate?

Paolo took out his notebook and opened it on a list of bullet points.

"Let's start from the first dinner you had at the Pellicano Hotel. You'd all left the restaurant by ten past ten, except for Gagliardi who stayed in there with Mrs Durante. In his first statement, he declared they'd just chatted generally, but in his second statement today, he admitted they talked about meeting Mr Pecoriello the next day, discussing the proposal they were going to put to him."

Giò shot him a look straight in the eyes.

"They discussed their business, and then at 10.30, Gagliardi left. At that time, according to him, Margherita was completely fine."

"What does Dr Siringa say about her death?"

"It might have been anaphylactic shock, but it could also have been cardiac arrest. The problem with the first hypothesis is that we don't know what triggered the reaction. No traces of contaminated food were found in her body, nor did anything used in the kitchen to prepare her food contain allergens, as we had believed before forensics gave us the results of their analysis."

"You mean," asked Giò, "it's more likely it was a sudden cardiac arrest, which would explain why she didn't try to reach for her EpiPen?"

"It's a possibility," but from his tone, it was easy to tell he didn't believe it.

"On the other hand, if it was an allergic reaction," she continued doggedly, "how long after contact with the substance would she show signs of suffering?"

"There's no hard and fast rule. It can be almost instantaneous, or it can be delayed, but it's rarely longer than an hour. Although there are exceptions."

"And what was the time of her death, according to Dr Siringa?"

"Between 10.30pm and midnight. But we digress. After Gagliardi had left the restaurant, he lingered for a while in the hall as he had asked the concierge to prepare him a thermos of coffee. He saw Valentina coming down the stairs and going into the restaurant. A few minutes later, it was the concierge who saw Valentina going back upstairs in the lift, a worried, angry look on her face."

"So Guido wasn't the last one to see Margherita alive. Why didn't he tell us this before?" Giò cried in surprise.

"He said he didn't want the finger of suspicion to point at Valentina until she was ready to tell us herself. I think he's the type who doesn't trust the carabinieri and won't tell us more than he has to. People like that make our jobs more difficult than they need to be."

"He's lived in countries where democracy doesn't exist," Giò wondered why she was trying to defend Guido, "or it's in its infancy. I guess he might have developed a certain mistrust for authorities there."

"Well he should know he's safe in Europe and learn to act accordingly."

"Don't preach! I hate it when you do that." Giò jumped down Paolo's throat, despite her best intentions to be calm and collected. He waved his hand as if to dismiss her and pointed his pen at the second item on his bullet list.

"Valentina went to speak to Margherita. According to her, she found her alive and left her alive."

Guido's safe! He's got an alibi, Giò thought with relief.

"That is if we can trust what anybody says about that night," Paolo added wistfully.

"Did she say why she went to see Margherita? What did they have to discuss?"

"Yes, she told us an interesting story. Apparently Margherita, amongst other things, was working on a memoir in which she'd mentioned Valentina and Vittoria's father, making it public that he'd become a renowned author using our very own Mrs Margherita Durante as a ghost writer."

"Really?"

"Valentina says that on the contrary, Margherita had stolen one of her father's manuscripts, pretending she'd shown it to some publishers and saying they'd all criticised it harshly and refused it. Her father dropped the whole project, but years after his death, Valentina and Vittoria came upon the book by chance, published under another author's name. They never found a copy of the manuscript in their father's archives to claim it as his work, but eventually discovered the name of the author was one of Margherita's pen names..."

"But that's awful! What a wicked woman she was."

"Are you trusting enough to believe everything Valentina says? There's no proof to back it up."

"Yes, I'm inclined to believe her. From all the bad things I've heard about Margherita, I think this accusation matches her profile."

"That's interesting, because if you trust Valentina's story, then you must also see it gives her a rather solid motive to kill."

Giò gulped.

"But that's not all. Valentina told us she threatened to kill the woman if she mentioned her father in her new book, but Margherita just laughed at her. She showed Valentina the manuscript she was working on and said she intended to tell the whole truth. But as I said, according to Valentina, Margherita was still alive when she left."

"And we don't know if we should trust her or not," said Giò, wondering if Valentina's story would mitigate Annika's suspicions about Simone.

"Wait – there's so much more. It was clearly destined to be an interesting night. After Valentina left, seen by the concierge, she bumped into Francesco about to go down."

"Francesco?"

"Yes, apparently Margherita enjoyed ridiculing him, saying the real author in the famous mother-son duo was Mummy and he was nothing more than a fraud."

"I witnessed Margherita laughing at him," Giò confirmed.

"He was in a real fury, determined to speak his mind to the woman. They had a heated discussion, but were interrupted by Erminia, who swears blind... guess what?"

"That Margherita was alive when they left."

"Exactly. But the concierge claims that Erminia never went into the restaurant. Instead, she only met up with Francesco when he was shutting the restaurant door behind him."

"So Erminia doesn't know if Margherita was alive or not?"

"Correct."

"But in any case, that means Valentina is innocent."

"Unless Francesco is covering for her."

"Why should he?"

"Maybe he's fallen for Valentina..."

"I don't think so," said Giò, shaking her head.

"His mother seems to believe the two have feelings for each other, and she would definitely approve of a relationship between them."

"Erminia might approve, but I don't think she understands how things are. But that would explain why she'd cover up for both Francesco and Valentina. So is it Francesco who's top of your list of suspects?"

"No, it's just one hypothesis of many," said Paolo, cocking his head sarcastically. "Difficult to establish what's true when you're dealing with such a bunch of liars!"

"Come on! It's just a bit of solidarity within the group. May I remind you that the first time you questioned us, we all thought Margherita's death was an accident – death by anaphylactic shock, as might still be the case."

He again waved dismissively. "Let me finish my crazy tale. At 11pm, Mrs Spilimbergo returned downstairs, after having accompanied her son to their room."

"She went to the restaurant?"

"No, apparently this time she came down in the lift and asked the concierge for a glass of hot brandy to help her get some sleep. The discussion with her son had made her restless. They moved to the bar, and while she drank her brandy, she chatted with the concierge. As he washed her glass, she asked him who the waiter was who had just gone out. The concierge thought she must be slightly drunk as there was no waiter in the hotel at that time of night. Or she might have seen one of the guests and confused him with the waiter, or made up the story entirely."

"So we now have a mystery man?"

"Indeed. This story has everything, and I've not finished yet." Paolo again pointed to his notes.

"More people going to speak to Margherita?" Giò pretended to be surprised, though she knew of at least one more person who had wanted to speak to the woman.

"Correct. And not necessarily all different to the first bunch. By 2am, Valentina Valsecchi, having thought over and over what had happened, saw from her room that the lights were still on in the restaurant and decided she'd have one more try at begging Margherita not to ruin her father's reputation. She went downstairs, and again the concierge didn't see her as he was engrossed in his favourite soap opera. He only spotted her when she went back to her room."

"And what happened?"

"She went in, but couldn't see Margherita sitting at her table, so she rushed forward and saw her on the floor. She didn't care whether the woman was dead or not; she just grabbed the manuscript lying on the table and left. She then called at Alberto's room and asked him to dispose of the manuscript the next day. Alberto confirmed that he threw the manuscript into the sea early the next morning. In the meantime, he'd accompanied Valentina back to her room, but as he returned to his own room, he came face to face with his neighbour, Simone, coming from the end of the corridor where the stairs are situated."

"And what did Simone say?"

"He was another of Margherita's victims. The woman had bullied him as, to use his own words, he's never been self-confident. Actually, she more or less destroyed him during the last retreat, and it came as a nasty shock to find her here on this one. He'd had trouble sleeping, seen the restaurant lights on, and decided to deal with her once and for all."

"Do you suspect he might have killed her?"

"He says he found her alive, that she drove him mad, so he spoke his mind to her, then left."

"He saw her alive? What time was this?"

"Just past 2am, say 2.10."

"But Dr Siringa said she'd died by midnight at the latest."

"Correct."

"So how's it possible that Simone saw her alive, especially as two other witnesses say Margherita was dead by then?"

"*Two* witnesses?" Paolo asked her.

Holy cow! Giò wasn't supposed to know about Annika.

"I meant Valentina and... the medical evidence," Giò stammered.

He glared at her, unconvinced. "I told him that. He was adamant that Margherita was alive."

"Oh my goodness, what'd be the point of making such a statement if it weren't true?"

Paolo shook his head. "I've no idea. But I have half an idea that you know what I'm going to say next."

"Huh?"

"Annika – your friend – was the last one to go into the restaurant that night, and she maintains that Margherita was 'very dead' when she saw her."

A long pause followed. Everything was a complete mess, and they'd only covered Margherita's death. Paolo was looking at his notes, as if trying to make sense of them.

She finally found the courage to speak. "Wow, so what are your conclusions?"

"I haven't come up with any conclusions. But Strazio made an interesting observation. He said how similar this case is to *Murder on the Orient Express*."

Giò thought it over. "You mean a conspiracy?"

"Exactly. Every guest seems to have played his or her role. At first, they were all innocent, the death an accident or natural causes. Now the investigations have pointed to murder, they all look guilty. They all have motive, they all had opportunity."

"Well, not all of them. Just Valentina, Francesco, and maybe Guido and Simone."

"That's not correct. Erminia would do anything to protect her son – what if she came down again unseen by the concierge? Alberto might have only given a heavily edited description of what really went on. I feel he's in love with Valentina and, very much like her sister, Vittoria, would do anything to protect her. Just like you're protecting Guido, and Annika is doing the same with Simone."

She ignored his dig at her. "You didn't mention Vittoria's statement at all, did you?"

"If you want to know, to start with, she said her sister slept all night through and that she would have heard her going out of the room. When I told her we knew everything, she then tried to make her evaluation of the time Valentina had been missing from the room as short as possible: the smaller the window of opportunity, the more difficult it would be to kill someone."

"About that – how was Margherita killed?"

"That we don't know yet," Paolo admitted, acknowledging it was the weakest point of his whole investigation. He got up, walked briskly along the southern side of the swimming pool, then returned and stood beside Giò, shaking his head. "If only people would tell the truth!"

"Then we come to the second death," Giò said softly. "Why did the killer strike again when he or she was so close to getting away with passing the first murder off as an accident?"

"I've only got one answer to that: Augusta Galli knew something that compromised the killer. Maybe she was a blackmailer, as Vittoria thought, and was blackmailing the killer, or maybe the killer just knew that she knew and couldn't take any risks, even if this meant raising the suspicion that Margherita's death wasn't an accident after all."

"Vittoria thought she heard Mrs Galli blackmailing someone. Maybe she was speaking to the killer – the person Erminia saw leaving the hotel that night."

"The outsider?" Paolo raised his eyebrows, his expression ironic. "That would be so convenient, wouldn't it?"

Giò didn't rise to the challenge. "What about this second death?"

"It seems much simpler, at least on the surface of it. The woman called Dr Gimondi at 6pm yesterday, saying she wasn't feeling well, and she asked him to call on her at 7.30 this morning. Apparently during the night, she gave herself one shot too many of insulin, and that proved fatal, especially as it was combined with too much alcohol."

"So maybe it was a case of suicide. Maybe she felt guilty for killing Margherita. Did you check her phone? Maybe she spoke to Mimì Pecoriello and he told her that he wasn't interested in using her to ghost write his book, plain and simple. She felt awful – she'd killed for nothing, and then…"

"And then I checked her phone. She'd had no contact whatsoever with Mr Pecoriello, apparently."

"Oh! And what time did she die?"

"Between 3.30 and 4.30."

Giò tried not to show that her heart was sinking. That was about the time she'd seen Guido wandering the corridor by torchlight. Was she deluding herself?

"But we have a few anomalies in this death, too," Paolo continued mercilessly. "Guido Gagliardi mentioned getting back to his room at midnight and seeing a waiter in the corridor, but at that time, the only member of staff in the hotel was the night concierge, who claimed that a) he never went upstairs and b) nobody came in from outside. So it again looks as if the people in your group are trying to create the idea of 'an outsider' being responsible. But both times, the concierge has contradicted their claims."

"But the night Margherita died, it seems that if the concierge wasn't dozing off, he was chatting with guests or watching his favourite soap opera. He's hardly the most reliable of witnesses…" But in reality, she knew she was just speaking to buy herself time. Would she have to tell Paolo about Guido walking the hotel corridors at the worst possible time?

"Or maybe that's what your group wants us to think!"

Giò shrugged, feeling her impatience growing. "It's always difficult to make a point when someone has already jumped to conclusions."

"That's not what I've done," Paolo said seriously. "Anyway, at 7.30 this morning, Doctor Gimondi arrived. The cleaning staff arrived after 8am, but the kitchen staff weren't here yet as they'd only planned to open the restaurant for dinner this evening, not breakfast or lunch. The chef also arrived after 8am. So apart from the mysterious waiter seen only by Gagliardi, no one else was in the hotel except the writers' group."

"So someone walked into Mrs Galli's room and killed her. Why would she open the door to one of us if she knew it was likely to be risky?"

"From what I've heard, she liked younger men. Gagliardi seems to have been the one going back to his room at the right time. Maybe he stopped by just long enough to do her in."

"The woman died at 4am, not at midnight, you said."

"An insulin overdose doesn't always cause instantaneous death. It depends on how large the overdose is and the reaction of the individual."

Oh my goodness, had Guido injected her, and then gone back later to make sure she was dead or finish her off? Impossible! Not Guido, the guy who loved nature, photography, beauty, art, travel so much…

But it was clear that Guido had not mentioned his 4am stroll to the carabinieri. And she wouldn't tell Paolo either, not before speaking to Guido. In any case, Paolo's insinuations about the writers' group were starting to get on her nerves.

"Interestingly," Paolo continued, "Gagliardi was also one of the last people to see Margherita the night she died."

"But you have at least two witnesses claiming they saw her alive after Guido had left her and gone upstairs!" Giò cried.

"I know that, but on such a hectic night, it's not difficult to believe that the concierge didn't notice everyone's movements. And you yourself said he's not the most reliable witness. Maybe Gagliardi pretended to go to his room, but as soon as he'd seen Valentina coming back upstairs the first time, or maybe Francesco, he crept back and did Margherita in."

"That sounds like wishful thinking…"

"Not so. Isn't he the very guy who, as you mentioned last night, has a tendency not to speak the whole truth?"

"But that was confidential information I shared with my friend Paolo! You can't use it against me."

Giò had such a lost look on her face that Paolo felt miserable. But his frustration didn't help his temper. As he rose from his chair, he let fly verbally.

"Please in future, no more confidences. I don't know how to deal with them as I'm supposed to be part of a murder investigation, and I'm not a priest, nor a counsellor." He paused as if in doubt. "At least, not that I know of."

They stood in silence for a long while, each one's anger simmering inside them, trying to avoid eye contact.

"Let's call it a day," he said finally. "But this time, you need to listen to me and don't even try to interrupt. Watch yourself. We have a killer on the loose and it looks very likely that he or she – or maybe *they* – is among your group of writers."

~

Giò headed for the beach, too tired to even pretend to think. She'd hardly even had three hours' sleep the previous night, and all these doubts and findings, all these confessions... How she dreamed of peace and quiet. She walked aimlessly, her eyes fixed on a small group of seagulls in flight.

"Giò," a voice called from behind her.

She started, then slowly turned to face him.

"Please, Giò, will you stop running away from me?"

"Huh?" She tilted her head, pretending not to understand. Then Guido was in front of her, resting his hands on her shoulders. She wanted to shrug him away, but stopped herself. She would act like an adult, tell him her thoughts. Actually, better to leave him to do the speaking first.

"I'm sorry, I hope you don't feel like I'm pestering you," but she could tell he wasn't embarrassed. He had the capacity she lacked to face all sorts of situations with confidence, almost a sense of impudence. "But maybe I wasn't totally clear last night when I told you about my forthcoming trip."

"Don't tell me you've got one more revelation?" She could be as sarcastic as Paolo if she wanted to, choosing her words carefully. "It might *kill* me." But he didn't react. Could he read the mess of feelings behind her angry facade? Scary thought.

"I only want to make it clear that I'd love you to join me..." He hushed her before she could interrupt. "You remember how we felt when we were up on the mountain?" He was speaking in a low, passionate voice that made the hairs on Giò's arms stand up. "And I've seen how you enjoy the way I shoot and edit my videos and all that weird sort of stuff. Giò, I'm sure you'd turn me into a more sensitive person. I've seen what you're like, and you love travelling just as much as I do. We could go to places together."

"What are you suggesting?" asked Giò, half laughing, half trembling.

"I'm suggesting you come with me for the entire trip."

He looked into her eyes so intently that she felt the abyss

open under her feet, that dreadfully charming feeling of precipitation. She had no time to recover before he gently pulled her into his strong arms and kissed her, and it was more terribly wonderful than the first time. Giò had no barriers behind which to hide. And worse than that, she didn't want any.

24

ON THE RUN!

When Angelica woke up, she was lying on a bed, a blanket covering her, sunlight filtering through a narrow slit. Her head ached, her body felt as if she had a hangover. It took her a while to remember what had happened.

Kidnapped? Was this really happening to her?

Her hands were free, so she tried to stand up – not an easy exercise. Her room, if you could call it a room, was just a few square metres, and of course the sturdy door was locked. She had just given it a shake when it opened and a man's tanned face appeared. Behind his grey beard was a soothing smile.

"Why are you keeping me here? What do you want from me?"

He replied in a language she didn't understand and pointed outside, clearly asking if she needed the toilet. She could see a square cabin – yes, she needed it. The man waited for her and was quick to seize her as soon as she emerged. Before she could even try to run away, his arm traced an arc around them as if showing her the view. She understood what he meant: there was nothing for miles, and she would probably die in the attempt or fall into a worse situation than the one she was already in. She clasped her hands together, asking for his help. The man's face was sympathetic, nothing like the boxer, whom she now thought of as Mean Eyes, but he showed her back to her prison nonetheless. When he served her a cup of hot tea, even in her panicked state, that she could not refuse.

She pleaded, she begged, but the man shook his head and locked the door, looking at the floor as he sipped his tea. Angelica realised she'd make better use of her time by thinking and observing. Although the room was small, it had the benefit of a window. Were there any roads she could spot from the hut? Any cars passing by, even in the distance?

Iran was reputed to be a relatively safe place for tourists. The crime rate was low, so why was this happening to her? Then she remembered the bazaar. Some kind of transaction had taken place between Mean Eyes and Liam there. She remembered seeing Mean Eyes pick up a package, saying the deal was closed. What had gone wrong? Liam had been satisfied with his end of the deal, and Mean Eyes seemed satisfied at that time too. Had he changed his mind? But then, if it was between the two of them, why was Mean Eyes taking it out on her?

Then a frightening thought flashed through her brain.

Mean Eyes had spotted her in the bazaar. Liam had said not to worry, it was his wife. But Karen had left by then, without Liam realising. Angelica had the same brown hair and eyes as Karen, was a similar height… a generic description could apply to either of them.

There was no doubt about it. Mean Eyes had thought she was Liam's wife.

But what had happened at the campsite? Maybe Rolando and Sajad had gone to fetch wood and the kidnappers hadn't realised that Liam wasn't in the party? She didn't even want to consider the possibility something bad had happened to them. Would they have told the police by now? How long would it take for them to pick up her trail? Iran was such a large country – would they ever find her?

She tried once more to speak to her companion. "Liam no my husband. Me no Liam's wife. Rolando! Rolando!"

The man smiled and signalled to her to settle down. "OK," he said, then went back to his tea and thoughts.

She had to speak to Mean Eyes, clarify things. But there was no way she could make herself understood by this man. She had neither pen nor paper on which to draw faces, a car – anything to help him understand her request.

She sat in quiet despair, her eyes fixed on the only bit of road she could see down in the valley. But there were no cars, no trucks, not even any shepherds. A painful thought crossed her mind: she'd felt frustrated in Maratea, but that world seemed so far away now. Her life had been happy – two affectionate children doing well, a loving husband, a pretty home, a quaint village, and yet she had felt miserable. She'd had heaven at her fingertips and she had dared to spit on it. This must be her punishment for having been so blind.

In her mind's eye, she saw their restaurant, the waitress handing her the rose and the tickets to Iran. Rolando's face, wondering if he had done the right thing. She had made him feel so inadequate. If it hadn't been for her stupidity, they would have been celebrating their anniversary in some safe place, perhaps a weekend in Prague or London, but no. She had thrown the fact that he was so dependable back in his face, and the situation she now found herself in served her right.

Memories of their happy life together popped up in her mind as if from nowhere. Their children's birthdays; the Christmases together; the day they'd bought their own house, with its lovely patch of garden. Her roses; her lemon tree; her elderly neighbour wishing her 'good things' any time they met. How stupid she'd been! She wanted to sob and scream, but she was so mad at herself that no tears came to her eyes.

Then from the window, she saw a car climbing the hill. It looked like a four by four, but bigger than Sajad's. The man with her rose and went outside, waiting.

Yes, it was Mean Eyes. He spoke English, so she could explain the mistake to him.

The man came in, looking taller and stronger than she had realised. She prayed he meant her no harm, and finally found the courage to address him.

"I assume you know you've got the wrong person. You wanted Karen, Liam's wife. I'm not..."

"We know that, now. Liam has run away, his wife too, but since we've got you, we'll see if we can use you as a bargaining tool to get back some of the money he took from us. The bastard!"

"How much has he taken from you?" she asked, her voice trembling.

"We traded some ancient Iranian jewels for modern gold. But the man gave me fool's gold, and then thought that by joining a tourist tour, he'd be able to escape from me."

"Which, in fact, he did."

Mean Eyes cried out what had to be a swear word in Iranian or Russian, beating his huge fist on the table.

"The point now is, are you worth that much?" and he scrutinised her as if to assess her value by weight. Angelica gulped, feeling more and more uneasy every time their eyes locked. His stare was just too cold and inhuman. He was going to ask for a ransom to be paid in exchange for her freedom, but would the Iranian authorities do anything? Was it their policy to pay for the release of foreign tourists? Or would they get in touch with Rolando and ask him to pay? And the poor man – what could he do from this country? He wouldn't be able to tap into his bank account without the authorities being involved. Even credit cards were just plastic here.

Mean Eyes was in front of her, ignoring the Iranian watchman, his stare fixed on her. Angelica trembled as the man got closer. Then all of a sudden, the door slammed open. Sajad pointed a gun at Mean Eyes and shouted at him in Iranian, possibly telling him to raise his arms. But the man wasn't one to be taken by surprise. He jumped on Sajad, twisted his wrist, forcing him to let go of the gun, then kicked him so hard the man curled up on the floor in pain.

A strange instinct that she'd never experienced before made Angelica jump in front of Sajad, protecting him from the gun. Mean Eyes gestured at her to move out of the way.

"Oh no, please," Angelica cried.

"Move away!" Mean Eyes yelled at her, his expression cool and detached, apart from a cruel little twitch at the corner of his mouth. Behind him, through the open door, she saw Rolando silently crawling on all fours. When he saw Angelica looking, he winked. How could that be? He was re-enacting a joke they'd played for their children when they were young.

Angelica moved towards Mean Eyes, as if begging him to spare Sajad. The man laughed at her and took a step back to train the gun on Sajad again. As Mean Eyes fell over Rolando, the man that Angelica had once thought so boring hit him on the chin, quick as lightning. When Mean Eyes tried to rise from the floor, he cried in pain and let the gun go.

But as Rolando bent to pick the weapon up, the Russian guy was on him. They rolled outside, grappling with one another, Angelica's small husband fighting against this mountain of muscles. Angelica knew what she had to do. She picked up the gun, but the two men were too close to each other for her to use it – that was assuming she'd be able to fire it at all.

Inside the room, Sajad was still lying unconscious. The watchman was standing still, as if waiting to see what would happen. He clearly wasn't intending to get involved in the fight.

Leaning against the wall outside was a shovel. That was just what she needed. Carefully, Angelica tucked the gun into her belt, hoping it wouldn't go off, then without hesitation, she took the shovel and approached the two fighters. Mean Eyes was on top of her husband, lifting his right arm to knock Rolando out with a powerful blow.

But his fist would never make contact.

With all her strength, Angelica hit Mean Eyes, hard. The man collapsed, landing next to her husband. Rolando smiled at her as she handed him the gun – it felt white hot on her.

Sajad had recovered consciousness by now, and he helped Rolando to take the man inside the hut. He seized the handcuffs Mean Eyes had used on Angelica and chained him to the bed in the small room. The watchman was told to stay inside too.

"It will take a while for them to get free," said Sajad, locking the door as the Russian slowly recovered, shouting all sorts of curses. "You take his car and follow mine to Qazvin. If we're fast, they won't catch us."

He accompanied them to Mean Eyes' jeep, took out his mobile phone, opened it and threw the battery away, keeping the rest. Then he handed the keys to Rolando before getting into his own four by four.

"Let's go," Rolando said, but before he got into the jeep, he gently took his wife's face in his hands, whispered, "Thank goodness you're safe," and kissed her passionately. Angelica felt like she was plummeting into a deep abyss. Nothing mattered but the thrill of falling freely. She wished it could last forever, but he gently pushed her away.

"We need to go, my love."

THE JOURNEY BACK TO QAZVIN WAS A MAD RUSH, THE SMALL ROAD full of bends and potholes. Angelica remembered how carefully Sajad had driven along that very road on the way up. Who would ever have imagined that either he or Rolando could drive like demons?

Before leaving the Alamut Valley, they parked Mean Eyes' car on a tiny road, concealed by a clump of trees. As they carried on with their journey in Sajad's car, they discussed their next move.

"You mean, we're not going to the police straight away?" asked Angelica in dismay.

Sajad shook his head. "I'd say it'd be better not to. You never know how they'll take it – they might suspect you were the ones smuggling Iranian treasures out of the country. I'd avoid that, if I were you."

"So what would you suggest?" asked Rolando.

"As soon as we get to my place, I will phone your flight company to see if you can get on the next flight home."

Angelica felt better at the mere thought of being back home in Maratea.

A small entry door led to a spacious, bright living room. Sajad's wife welcomed them in, offering Angelica a cup of tea and some delicious finger food as the two men went to make their calls. When they came back, Rolando explained their situation.

"Our airline company's flights are fully booked, so we tried to buy tickets from other companies, but it seems they're all booked up for the next few days."

"My advice is to take some excursions, stay on the tourist routes. I'm pretty sure the Russian gang won't be after you any longer; it's Liam and his wife they want, and they won't make the same mistake again. I can call a taxi to take you to Isfahan, which is on the other side of the country…"

Angelica waited for her husband to protest, but to her surprise, he nodded.

"Sounds like a good plan."

"A good plan?" she asked, horrified. "But what if they want their revenge? Why don't we stay in Tehran, as close as possible to the airport, and see if we can get a last-minute seat on a flight home?"

"Because there are no seats," Rolando explained. "And if they are still interested in us, they will expect us to do just that. They'll be looking for us in Tehran."

As they parted company with faithful Sajad and his pretty, good-hearted wife, Rolando promised they would keep in touch and come back one day to trek from the Alamut Fort to the

Caspian Sea. Who was this man, so bold and self-confident? Angelica wondered. For the umpteenth time since they had arrived in Iran, she asked herself, how much did she really know about her husband? The only thing she had no doubt about was that she could trust him implicitly. Even after 24 years of marriage, she was still deeply in love with him.

25

BECAUSE THE PAST MATTERS

"Granny, Agnese, what are you doing here?" Giò asked. "Gran asked me to accompany her," Agnese explained, "as she wanted to speak to you."

Granny nodded.

"But why did you ask me to meet you outside the hotel? Don't you want to say hello to my friends?"

"Maybe later," Granny replied, looking around herself. "For now, we'd be better sitting here," and she pointed to one of the benches overlooking the beach and the sea. "We can see if anyone passes by."

"You mean, my eavesdropping Granny doesn't like to be overheard herself?"

Granny shook her head, a soft, indulgent smile on her lips. She wasn't going to rise to her granddaughter's provocation; she knew better than that.

"So, any news from the carabinieri?" she asked Giò.

"None really, except they acknowledge it's likely to be a double murder."

"Likely?" Granny said incredulously. "Do they still have doubts?"

"Well, I guess they can only say for definite once they have enough evidence."

"Do you suspect anyone?"

"I don't, but to balance things out, Paolo suspects them all, and that includes a conspiracy..."

"A conspiracy?" Agnese asked.

"Yes, as they all hated Margherita. Apparently every one of them had a reason to do her in, as well as an opportunity, so they may have agreed to lure her here, and then murder her."

"I hope you're joking, Giò," Agnese said, shocked.

"Well, you know, we're a team of writers. *Murder on the Orient Express* is a classic we've all read, and it looks as if everyone lied to the carabinieri during the first round of interviews..." And Giò shared what Paolo had told her, concluding cheerfully, "The good thing is that this time, I'm not a suspect. I'm the only one who didn't know the victim, so I have no motive... except solidarity with the rest of the group."

"Then you're bound to be the villain," Agnese laughed.

"Yes, the least likely suspect is always the murderer," said Giò, nodding. But Granny had a serious expression on her face.

"I think you're concentrating too much on the present. What if this has more to do with the past?"

"Well, Paolo and I both acknowledge that the bad feelings all stemmed from the previous retreat..."

"No, too recent. I was thinking of something that happened long ago."

Giò looked at her in surprise. Granny replied in her own sweet time. She had always liked a touch of the theatrical, and acting – the pauses, the silences, building up the tension before revealing the bombshell – came naturally to her. Giò, all too familiar with her foibles, rolled her eyes. Agnese chuckled, enjoying both her granny's teasing and her sister's impatience.

Then, a split second before Giò exploded, Granny, eyes twinkling, finally spoke.

"When you told me about Margherita Durante, I started to

think. Her name, her picture in the paper after her death, reminded me of someone, but I wasn't able to place her at once. Then I realised she lived in Maratea long ago…"

"I knew that already, she told us." Giò waved her hand as if to dismiss her granny's words, but the old lady continued as if the interruption had never happened.

"I didn't realise it was her at first because at the time, we knew her by her married name: Mrs De Santis."

"But that was 30 plus years ago," Agnese said.

"I'd say more like 40 years ago, but the thing is, before taking a fancy to Margherita and marrying her, Mr De Santis had a lover here in Maratea. And he left her for Margherita."

"Do you mean," asked Giò incredulously, "you suspect the rejected lover heard that Margherita had returned and decided to take her revenge, 40 years later? That'd be some grudge."

"Love and passion have often been the motive behind murder. Also, Mr De Santis was extremely rich. I thought it could be an interesting lead."

Giò shook her head. "Honestly, I can hardly see how this could have any bearing on the present."

"Maybe it's the link with Maratea," Agnese suggested. "Why was Margherita killed, if she was murdered, here and not elsewhere?"

"Do you really think I should dig about in the past? It could take ages to do the necessary research…"

"Not that long," Granny said with a triumphant smile. "Just the time it takes to drive 3 kilometres."

"We're visiting the cemetery?"

"No, Gerardina."

Gerardina lived in the northern outskirts of Acquafredda, a few hundred metres from the local cemetery. Her evidence had proved crucial during Giò and Paolo's first investigation, when a murder had been committed on the road not far from the woman's house, but Giò could hardly see how she could help in this case.

"If I remember rightly," Granny said, meaning she remembered perfectly well, "Gerardina worked as a house cleaner at Villa degli Incanti at the time."

"Really?"

"Really."

Maratea is like an open-air library, thought Giò. *You just have to hop from home to home to find out everything that happened in the community, even decades ago.* She kissed Granny on the cheek – all of a sudden she loved this lead. It made her heart lighter, deflecting suspicion away from her writers' retreat group. After all, hadn't two people said they'd seen a mystery man in the hotel on the night of each death? How hard would it be for a woman to pass as a man if she wore a waiter's uniform? Maybe the evidence that Paolo had so readily dismissed was worthy of attention after all.

TO REACH GERARDINA'S HOUSE, AGNESE'S CAR HAD TO CLIMB ALL the way up the steep road to Acquafredda village, glide under the railway bridge, stop at the only set of traffic lights in the whole of Maratea, and pass the food store where a couple of women, who were sitting outside, waved to them, they would spend the rest of the afternoon wondering where the Brando women were heading all together.

They drove past the only church in Acquafredda, whose red-tiled bell tower stood out against the greenery. Don Peppino, the priest, moved to the upper part of the churchyard to see exactly where Agnese parked her car. He observed the Brando women greeting Gerardina who, as usual, was sitting at her window. He watched as she beckoned them in, as the three women climbed the steps leading to the house amongst Barbary fig trees and cyan agaves. Don Peppino itched to know what they were talking about, but Mrs Rosa Brando could be rather edgy if she were in a bad mood. And she was far too knowledgeable about his little passion for gambling – safer to stay away from her. With a smile, he headed towards the food store instead. He knew he'd find good company there, especially when he shared his latest news.

Unobserved by Don Peppino, Gerardina greeted her guests with sincere happiness and strangely black hands. She kept the latter behind her back as she kissed them one by one on each cheek.

"I'm afraid we'll have to go into the kitchen, I'm in the middle of making artichoke preserves. Can't leave them as they are."

"No problem," Agnese smiled, "we can help if you wish." She launched a meaningful look at Granny, silently warning her not to start quarrelling about the best recipes, favourite ingredients, family variations and modified quantities. Granny smiled back reassuringly.

"Agnese, if you don't mind," Gerardina said, "could you prepare the Moka pot? I'd better not touch anything but my artichokes with my hands in this state. I should have used rubber gloves, but I'm always afraid they'll make my hands too numb to part the hard leaves from the soft ones."

"Nothing like being able to feel them with your bare hands," said Granny, looking at everything on the large kitchen table.

"I've saved a few hard leaves for my afternoon tea and for soups, but the rest will go on the compost." Gerardina stripped one more artichoke from all its hard leaves, stopping only when she reached its soft heart. And even then, she cut away the thorny upper part, the stem. What was left wasn't much larger than her thumb. She threw it in a bowl with water and plenty of lemon to keep the artichokes from browning.

So far, Granny approved wholeheartedly. Ignoring Giò and Agnese, the two old women entered into rapid-fire conversation, updating each other on what was going on among the 5,000 inhabitants of Maratea. It was surprising how quickly they went through the long list of names, not missing any of the juicy details. By the time the large Moka pot was gurgling, they had nearly exhausted their latest gossip and Gerardina was clearing all the leftovers from the table, dropping them in a bin of compostable waste.

"The coffee cups are there, and the sugar too, Agnese," the woman said as she drained half the artichokes from the water and lemon bowl, making sure they didn't retain too much liquid, and then threw them in a pot on the cooker, from which the pungent smell of boiling white wine and vinegar was coming. She stirred them gently and set a timer for nine minutes.

"I've got some barley coffee for me and you, Rosa," she added. "It must still be warm as I had just turned it off when you arrived."

"Don't you worry, I'll serve that as well," Agnese reassured her.

"Giò, you're so silent." Gerardina smiled at her. "I expected you to be chirpy and happy – I heard there's a good-looking man in your writers' group."

Giò felt her jaw dropping and crashing to the floor; she would never get used to people in Maratea knowing every detail of her life, almost before she knew about it herself.

"How did you know?"

"Marinella told my neighbour, Sofia," Gerardina replied without hesitation.

"Who's Marinella?"

"The sister of the sous chef at the Pellicano. I think the receptionist or waiter must have told her, since she's always holed up in the kitchen."

Giò banged her forehead with her hand, amazed at the broad network of spies all around her.

"He's a very nice man – this time," said Granny, smiling. "And he has a sense of humour."

"And he knows how to deal with old biddies," growled Giò.

"He's far from perfect, mind you," Granny continued as if

she'd said nothing. "He never stays in one place more than a month..."

"That's not good – how are you meant to have a family if you keep skipping around the planet?" Gerardina asked Giò.

"At the same time," Granny continued, "I must admit that my granddaughter's not that dissimilar. She's forever dissatisfied, coming home and wishing she was elsewhere, being elsewhere and missing home, so the two might be a good match, after all."

"I can't understand why young people enjoy making their lives so miserable," Gerardina said, taking a sip of her barley coffee. "We had so much less when we were young, but how happy we were."

Giò was too flabbergasted to intervene. The two elderly ladies kept discussing her life right under her nose as if she weren't even there. Was she dreaming? Was this just another one of her recurring nightmares?

Agnese, fearing her sister's tongue might get the better of her any moment, managed to get a word in edgeways.

"To tell the truth, Gerardina, we had a reason for coming over."

"Oh yes," Granny said, putting down her coffee cup as if to indicate that from now on, their discussion was serious. "Am I right in thinking that you were working at Villa degli Incanti when Margherita met Mr De Santis?"

"Oh yes, I had just started working there. At the time, it was Angela Fiore who interviewed me. She was in a steady relationship with Mr De Santis, and after years of caring for him, she thought he was about to propose marriage to her. But all of a sudden, he arrived home with a party of friends, and amongst them was Margherita, hardly more than a child. She was incredibly charming, oh she was. Jet black hair, liquid doe eyes, long legs, tiny waist. Men were instantly enchanted by her, and Mr De Santis was no exception. It happened so quickly... I beg your pardon."

The alarm clock rang, so she gave the artichokes a final stir and drained them using a skimmer, ran them under some cold water for a few seconds and let them dry in a sieve, taking care not to squeeze or crush them. She then threw the second batch of raw artichokes into the liquid on the cooker and turned back towards her guests.

"So what happened to Angela?"

"The same as happens to many loyal women when a younger one seduces her man. As far as Mr De Santis was concerned, Angela ceased to exist from that day."

"Such an awful blow for the poor woman," Giò said. "But she was still young, surely she got over it."

"Hmm, it wasn't as simple as that." Giò and Agnese looked at Gerardina questioningly. "Angela was pregnant, but Mr De Santis never acknowledged the child as his."

"Oh my goodness, how mean of him!" Agnese cried, then doubt flashed in her mind. "But did she actually let him know she was pregnant?"

"She did, and I was there when she told him. But Margherita had already turned his head. He told Angela in no uncertain terms it wasn't his baby and that he'd had enough of her and her affairs. In short, he told her to get out of his life."

"And did she?"

"She was furious and desperate in equal measures. She threatened him, vowed to take her revenge and advised him to keep his eyes open. But in the end, by being so emotional, she made things easy for him. You know what men are like, don't you?"

Giò and Agnese glanced at each other, not having a clue, but Granny nodded.

"They're always looking for ways to justify their appalling behaviour."

"Exactly, and her temper tantrum was all he needed to absolve himself of any sense of guilt."

"Then what happened?" Giò asked.

"One day, when Angela came back to retrieve her belongings from the Villa degli Incanti, Mr De Santis had dumped them outside the gates. All the locks had been changed and there was nothing she could do. She had no rights whatsoever.

"A few months later, Mr De Santis married young Margherita in Rome, and in the early summer they arrived to spend six months in Maratea. By that time, Angela had already given birth to her baby. But I never saw her again."

Giò and Agnese hardly dared breathe as the old woman paused, wondering what she would reveal next. When Gerardina finally spoke again, her words chilled them to their very souls.

"Just a few months after giving birth, Angela Fiore took her own life."

26

WHO'S THAT CHILD?

"Oh my goodness!" cried Agnese. "The poor woman took her own life? What happened to the baby?"

Gerardina sat down at the table next to them, the smell of wine and vinegar from the pot still lingering in the air.

"I heard some of Angela's relatives in Marche were given custody of the baby. That's where Angela had gone when she realised everything was over between her and Mr De Santis, and I think she gave birth there."

"Do you remember if the baby was a boy or a girl?" Giò asked.

Gerardina gave the question some thought, then she shook her head. "No, I can't remember. You see, Angela wasn't originally from Maratea; her parents had moved to Scario from Marche after they got married. When her father died in Scario, her mother moved back to her hometown, where I believe she passed away a few years later."

"You mean her parents were no longer alive when she went back to Marche?"

"If I remember rightly, that is so. The truth is, there wasn't much news circulating around Maratea about Angela. Nobody knew her, and she was a rather discreet woman, kept herself to herself. People only saw her when she went walking with Mr De Santis in the town centre or they spotted her in a restaurant. Even at home, in Villa degli Incanti, she hardly spoke to anyone about her private life; she would just tell us what we had to do. And before Margherita appeared on the scene, we had never witnessed a real quarrel between her and Mr De Santis."

"This unsettling story," cried Giò, "shows what a cruel woman Margherita was. She had no pity whatsoever. I mean, I'd feel responsible for both Angela and the child..."

"Margherita was very young at the time," Gerardina said. "Just 18, I believe. There was a bit of a scandal here in Maratea as Mr De Santis was somewhat older, and she looked young for her age. Gossips used to refer to her as Lolita."

"So they got married," Giò thought aloud, walking nervously up and down from the balcony to the kitchen table. "But their marriage, from what Margherita said, didn't last long."

"No, Mr De Santis died after they'd been together only a few years and the young wife inherited his properties, including Villa degli Incanti in Maratea, which she sold almost immediately. She was an ambitious lass who had no intention of staying in Maratea."

"So that was her Maratea story. When Margherita mentioned something at dinner time about having lived here, none of us suspected she'd die very shortly afterwards..."

THEY WALKED TOWARDS THE CAR, STOPPING AT A BENCH IN A REST area under the shade of thick pine trees. Giò asked Agnese and Granny their thoughts about the things Gerardina had revealed.

"I'm not sure what to make of this story. Do you think Angela's child could be in our writers' group?"

"Maybe," Gran replied.

"That puts things in a totally different light." Giò sighed heavily – again her group was at the forefront of the investigation. "Francesco, Simone and Guido are around the right age, Alberto maybe a little older…"

"Are you sure?" Gran asked her. "It's quite easy to disguise one's age by a few years."

"Maybe you're right. And Francesco is here with his own mother."

"Are you sure she is his natural mother?"

"Obviously she is, she's so very maternal towards him."

"From the way you've described her," Agnese said, thinking of the things Giò had told her about the writers during their daily phone calls, "a bit too maternal for a guy who's around 40."

"I see what you mean," Giò replied. Even the loving Agnese wouldn't dare to be so maternal with Luca, who was heading for his teens and seemed to get more intolerant of too much affection from his mother on a daily basis, at least in public. "But why would someone come all the way to Maratea to kill Margherita and avenge their birth mother after almost 40 years? It sounds too incredible."

"And don't forget, we aren't sure if Angela had a boy or a girl," Agnese reminded her.

"A girl," Giò repeated. "But if the child was a girl, Vittoria or Valentina could be a suspect. What if one of them was adopted as a child? Though I can't see why Angela's child wouldn't have killed Margherita during their first retreat."

"Maybe the mean things she did and said pushed the killer over the edge," suggested Agnese. "Or maybe the killer hadn't had enough time to plan a murder then and decided to wait until the Maratea retreat, close to where his or her mother died…"

"But no one knew Margherita was coming to Maratea. They all thought she'd been kicked out of the group, and her sudden appearance took everyone by surprise."

"Well, everyone except Guido," Gran whispered. "Isn't that right?"

Giò was struck dumb. Just a couple of hours earlier, she'd

thought her conversation with Paolo had cleared Guido. And he was about the right age to be Angela's child. Was this the reason for his rebellious character?

"Yes, except him," she repeated in a half whisper. How could she tell Agnese and Gran that she was considering leaving Maratea and following this man around the world? Well, unless he'd been involved in the murder, of course. But what if the carabinieri didn't find the murderer? What if the mystery stayed unsolved? What would she do then? This trip would allow him to leave the country soon after two suspicious deaths. Wasn't that a bit too timely?

"Giò, are you still with us?" Agnese was shaking her sister's arm to snap her out of her train of thought. "We're going back to the car."

"I'll walk back to the hotel," Giò said as they strolled across the car park.

"Are you sure you don't want a lift?" Agnese asked.

Giò smiled at her. "No, I need a little thinking time on my own."

"Not too much thinking, though," Granny admonished her. "Tell your carabinieri friend he has to do his own investigations and stop the murderer before he or she does any more harm. And mostly, watch out for yourself."

Giò shivered. It wasn't usual for Gran to be so apprehensive, and Agnese was wearing the same pleading look.

"Be careful," she whispered.

Giò nodded and kissed her granny and sister goodbye. But instead of walking down towards the hotel, she continued in the opposite direction to Acquafredda graveyard. Before entering, she tried to call Paolo, but the call went straight to his voicemail. She left him a message, and then pushed open the tall iron gate, shaded by the cypresses.

Giò walked to her parents' graves, the sea glittering below her, the horizon a deep blue, the rocky mountains brooding all around. It was peaceful, it was beautiful. Maratea was a special place, but something evil was once again threatening the area. She couldn't accept that. Even if it meant digging where she didn't want to, she would get to the bottom of this mystery.

"Need to go now," she said, caressing the stone cross bearing her parents' names.

The tragic story of Angela and her baby had put things in a completely new perspective. Could this be the real reason why Margherita had to die? Nothing to do with her unpleasantness to the writers' community, but something stronger and more personal? Which of them could be the abandoned child? Guido, Valentina, Vittoria, Simone, even Francesco were all the right age. As Agnese had suggested, was Erminia so overprotective because her son had actually been adopted?

And if the child had returned to avenge his or her mother, what did Augusta Galli have to do with the whole story? Vittoria had mentioned hearing her blackmailing someone. Who? Margherita? Nope, it couldn't have been her, because now they were both dead. Had Mrs Galli known the adopted child story? Was she blackmailing him or her?

Giò's phone rang and she headed out of the graveyard, back onto the street to Acquafredda, walking briskly down towards the Pellicano Hotel. It was Paolo calling. She updated him on what she had discovered.

"Your gran is brilliant – a talent for sleuthing seems to run in the Brando family." Then he got serious. "I'll call the Scario carabinieri station and see if they can provide me with more details about Angela and her baby. It's almost 40 years ago, but in a little village, there'll always be someone who remembers. I only wish I knew how to move things faster. In the meantime, watch yourself, Giò. Don't go wandering about alone late at night."

"I won't!" Giò sighed. She was starting to feel rather uncomfortable with all these people reminding her that danger was lurking around every corner.

WHEN GIÒ ARRIVED AT THE HOTEL, VITTORIA WAS SITTING ON THE terrace outside, despite the breeze being a little too cool to be comfortable if you weren't moving around. She had a book on the table beside her, but she wasn't reading it; she was just watching the sun going to sleep beyond the horizon, throwing its last purple rays over the sea.

"All alone?" Giò asked her.

"All alone," Vittoria replied, slightly startled as she hadn't seen Giò approaching.

"Is Valentina about?"

"No, she's in our room. I suspect she's keeping out of the way on purpose to avoid any chance meeting with Alberto."

"Such a pity," Giò threw in, her tone of voice similar to Granny's when she was busy matchmaking. "They'd make a great couple."

"Yes, before it was silly Alberto fearing he wasn't worthy of her love – that's why he disappeared after our first retreat – and just as he seems to have found the courage he lacked... well, now it's my sister running away. I can no longer understand what's going on in her mind. Maybe she's just overworked; she's always been too sensitive. Mind you, two sudden deaths are not an easy dish for anyone to digest ..."

"But it seems she's taken the whole thing far too personally," continued Giò, now sounding like Agnese gaining the complete trust of her customers and friends.

"Exactly! I don't know how to explain it, but there are people that even if they are innocent..." Vittoria paused, as if wondering whether she was going to say too much. Giò wore her most innocent and empathetic look, and Vittoria continued, "Well, they tend to look like they're guilty."

Giò laughed and told Vittoria how she had once been interviewed by the carabinieri, and how each question had made her feel like she was the guilty party trying to pass herself off as innocent. Vittoria was clearly encouraged by Giò's confession.

"I understand, it happens. But in Valentina's case, it's different, like she feels a responsibility for the whole world on her shoulders. As if she was responsible for Margherita's death, even if she didn't kill her. And she didn't – I mean, she couldn't kill anything, not even a mosquito."

"On a totally different train of thought, can I ask you whether Valentina is your real sister, or if she was adopted?"

"How did you know?" Vittoria said, sounding shocked.

"I think she said something about it the other day," Giò lied.

"She really isn't herself at the moment. She never generally so much as hints at having been adopted to anyone."

"It must be tough on her." Again Giò played her empathy card.

"Not really. You see, she always considered our parents and me to be her real family."

"What about her natural family?"

"They were no longer able to support her. I don't mean just financially; the family was too unstable and volatile for a child."

"Was she the child of a single mother?"

"Not that I know of, but I can't be sure. As children, we were told that her parents had to get well, and in the meantime they wanted Mum and Dad to be Valentina's parents, so we'd be real sisters. And we always felt that way."

Vittoria paused for a long while, looking around the terrace as if to make sure her sister wasn't nearby before continuing in an unusually soft voice, her eyes shining.

"Valentina has always known she was adopted, but she has never been particularly curious to get to know her real parents. I suspect she remembered her life with them, and the memories weren't good. As time's passed, we've talked less about it because we feel like any other sisters – forever together, even more so since the death of Mum and then Dad. They were *our* parents."

For the first time, Giò wondered if she had any right to be doing what she was doing, prying into people's private lives. Was it just idle curiosity, or was she getting any closer to the truth? Not really, not at the moment.

She was glad to hear Annika's voice calling them.

"Hey, you two, we're about to go for dinner."

IT WAS A STRANGE DINNER. THE WRITERS' GROUP SHOULD HAVE BEEN delighted to be allowed into the Pellicano Restaurant again, as they had wished, but the atmosphere was weird. One or two of them tried to crack a few jokes, but none of them worked. Actually, they made the vibe even more awkward.

After dessert had been served, Annika announced that she wasn't going to be asking for a daily writing report because of what had happened that morning.

"I'm sure the carabinieri will confirm it was a sad accident, just an incredible coincidence that we should witness two sudden deaths during our retreat. But life will insist on happening while we are writing, so tonight, I want you to think about this: whatever goes on in your life, and the way you deal with things, will have an impact on your writing. Events shape us continuously, whether we're aware of it or not."

They all nodded, including Guido who had only just joined them. He had been shooting by the light of the sunset and it had taken him a while to clear away all of his equipment.

"You're doing great," he said to Annika, guessing she was speaking from the heart. "It's not easy to lead a group through all of this. But as you said, as artists we shouldn't shy away from troubled waters."

Simone clapped his hands. "You're right, Guido. Three cheers for our Writers Retreat Leader."

They raised their glasses and thanked Annika, who rubbed her hands over her suspiciously watery eyes.

"Thanks, guys, I needed that. And do you still want me to confirm the trip on the sailing boat I had planned for Friday? It's our last day in Maratea."

"Of course! We need something to take our minds off doom and gloom," said Vittoria, and Erminia nodded in approval.

"Then I'll ring them tomorrow, first thing in the morning," Annika said, her puffy face finally breaking into a smile.

Giò had given Guido a grateful look when he had encouraged Annika, but when he tried to approach her in the hall, she said she was too tired and all she wanted to do was to head back to her room. Not the most brilliant course of action for an aspiring sleuth, but she really was exhausted. Had she chosen to hang around with Guido, she could have asked him what he was doing wandering the hotel corridor at 4am, and also if he had been adopted as a child, but she couldn't cope with any more revelations that day. She would wait until tomorrow.

"Will you follow me?" His childlike question banged about in her head. She had no answer.

27

QUESTIONING IS HARD

Her phone rang while she was in the shower after another almost sleepless night. Should she let it ring? Maybe not.

Giò got out, frantically patted down her body with a towel, and then took hold of her mobile.

"Paolo, any news?"

"Yes, I spoke to Dr Siringa."

"And?"

"And he found some bruising on Mrs Galli's neck."

"You mean she was strangled?" she asked in horror.

"No, not at all."

"Then what?"

"The most likely scenario is that she was knocked out by someone holding chloroform or some other sedative over her face, but further analyses should tell us more. In the meantime, the position of the bruises on her neck and around her mouth and nose supports our hypothesis..."

"You mean," said Giò, gulping in air and having to sit on her bed – it was one thing suspecting a murder, another having it confirmed, "someone knocked on her door, she let them in, and he or she sedated Mrs Galli, then injected her with an overdose of insulin?"

"Very likely."

"So it has to be someone she knew."

"Maybe she invited the killer over, otherwise she might not have opened the door at all. I wasn't sure whether to tell you this, but I wanted to warn you, if you see what I mean."

"I see," she murmured.

"But just in case it's not completely clear, stop any sleuthing and leave the whole thing to us. We're getting there."

"Sure," Giò said, ending the call, her heart hammering furiously in her breast. The carabinieri were getting closer to the truth, but who were their suspects? She'd have to speak to Guido this morning; she couldn't postpone it any longer.

But when Giò joined the others at breakfast, one person was missing. Annika, recognising her disappointed look, told Giò what she knew.

"I met Guido early this morning – he was going to take his drone to Maratea harbour, and he said he might stay there to get some writing done."

"You shouldn't have told her until after she'd had her breakfast." Erminia smiled at Giò. "Come here, poor kitten."

Giò felt more like a wildcat than a kitten.

I should have asked him last night when I had the chance.

"How about a cappuccino?" Erminia asked her.

"And a cornetto?" Alberto added. In the few days they'd known her, the writers had become acquainted with her breakfast of choice. Giò mumbled her thanks as Erminia and Alberto returned from the buffet with a steamy cappuccino and a cornetto for her, but she simply couldn't participate in any conversation.

"Let's go to our rooms," Annika said after breakfast. "It's going to be a long writing sprint this morning. The bar is open if you need a coffee or cappuccino, otherwise let's not meet until lunch."

When the writers got up to leave, Giò was still pondering on her next course of action.

"Why don't you join him at the harbour?" Annika asked her as she picked up her bag to leave.

"Maybe." But Giò couldn't deny her sense of hurt pride. He'd gone without inviting her. True, she'd not been that friendly the night before, but still… she wasn't the one about to leave for a year-long trip. Her jaw stiffened, a sense of having been cheated – again! – taking possession of her.

She decided she would go to her room and get some writing done – her project was just as important as his. They'd talk later, but in the meantime, she'd look for a chance to speak to Francesco and Simone and enquire whether either of them had been adopted. Or was the fact that Valentina was an adopted child, coupled with the destroyed manuscript, the lead she and Paolo had been searching for?

More reluctantly than she would ever care to admit, Giò walked back to her room and opened her PC, only to fall into a deep sleep – the one she hadn't managed for the past few nights.

WHEN GIÒ WOKE UP, SHE COULDN'T BELIEVE HER EYES: 3.30PM. Not only had she skipped lunch, but she'd also not written a single word. She looked at her mobile.

"*Giò, should I be worried? Are you writing?*" Annika had been texting her repeatedly, the last time only a few minutes ago.

"*I'm fine, just had a good writing spell.*" Never mind Guido, lying was becoming second nature to Giò.

Out on the balcony, kissed by the sun, the gentle breeze and the soft spring light, she was looking blankly at the view when movement to her left caught her attention. A bright orange car was pulling into the parking area. Guido was back. It was now or never.

She grabbed her phone and downstairs she rushed. He was still busy unloading his equipment from the back of his car.

"Hello," she said.

"Hello." Guido jumped slightly in surprise, but then a happy smile lit up his face.

"I need to speak to you," she said icily.

"Now?"

"If possible."

He looked at her with his typical cheeky expression, banged the car door closed, stamped his feet and brought his right hand to his forehead in a soldier's salute.

"Yes, O captain! My captain! Here?"

She looked around. The terrace tables were all deserted; all the good writers had locked themselves in their rooms to avoid any distraction.

"Yes, here," she said. Poker faced, she showed him to a table facing the sea, today as calm as a lake.

"So, have you made your decision?" he whispered, any trace of cheekiness gone.

"It's not about that."

He smiled. "Then what is it about?"

She went straight on the offensive. "What were you doing yesterday at 4am? I saw you walking in the hotel corridor."

He was dumbfounded. His mouth half-opened and his eyes were wide.

"I went out to smoke a cigarette," he replied slowly, as if pondering every single word that left his mouth.

"You said you only smoke two fags a day."

"I told you I have an emergency third cigarette allowance." Something close to a smile flashed across his face. Not the right question.

"You could have smoked on your balcony."

"I wanted to stretch my legs too," he replied, the near smile vanishing. Time to deliver the next blow.

"The concierge said you never left the hotel."

"No, of course, I went out using the back stairs on our floor."

"Isn't the back door locked at night?"

"No, it is only locked to outsiders, but you can open it from the inside."

"Then how did you get back in after your night wanderings?"

He didn't like her tone, she could tell, not a tiny bit. His jaw contracted, his lips pressed into a thin line. He was trying to hold her gaze, but she deliberately avoided falling into the trap.

"I blocked the door. There's a heavy ashtray nearby, and I used that to hold the door ajar."

"What about the security of the other people in the hotel?"

"Not my best idea, I'll give you that."

"You'll give me that?" she repeated incredulously. "A woman has passed away, possibly murdered, and you can 'give me that' you left a door open, allowing anyone to get in?"

"Does the timing coincide with Mrs Galli's death?"

"Correct."

"Oh my goodness, and are the carabinieri convinced she was murdered?"

"Again, you're correct." She wouldn't tell him the overdose could easily have been given to Mrs Galli earlier on as it was unlikely that it would have caused an instantaneous death. But she had to let him know the basics. Maybe now he'd tell the truth.

Time for another blow.

"Were you adopted as a child?"

"How did you know?" he cried.

"Who were your natural parents?" Giò pressed.

"It was the classic story," he murmured, dropping his eyes from hers for the first time. "My father left my mother after she got pregnant."

"And then?"

"Since I was too much of a burden for her, I was left in care, until a respectable couple decided I was the puppy with the cutest face."

"You didn't like your adoptive parents?"

"Nope." He raised his head. "In fact, I'm no longer in touch with them."

"And what was your real mother called?"

"Why are you giving me the third degree about my childhood?" His lips were trembling with rage, his eyes shooting furious darts at her. "If I don't pass the test, I'm not good enough, is that it? I thought it was between me and you, Giò Brando, but if you want to know my entire history before you commit, then it's better we stop it here and now. I don't have a nice, heartwarming story to tell; it's a damn hard past, and I really don't need your pity."

He leapt to his feet, turned his back on her and stormed off, leaving Giò flabbergasted.

28

AQUARIUM THERAPY

Giò remained sitting at the table, shocked. How ironic that just as she'd been thinking Valentina might be the killer and all she had to do was provoke Guido out of his lies and omissions, he'd revealed exactly what she hadn't wanted to hear. He had been in the corridor at the time Mrs Galli had passed away. And he was not only an adopted child, but he had also clearly bottled up so much anger about his past.

She had been wrong in another assumption: not all the other writers had been writing. Erminia and Vittoria were climbing the steps from the beach to the terrace. Giò didn't want to speak to anybody right now; she looked around for a means of escape. Alberto was standing next to the main hotel door, so the entrance to the restaurant that gave directly onto the terrace seemed to be her only option.

The restaurant was empty, no one around. The tables had already been laid for dinner, the pretty arched windows overlooking the sea and the mountains, but even on such a wonderfully sunny day as today, Giò could appreciate neither the view nor the invigorating smell of the sea coming through the open windows.

What was happening to her world? She had striven to get

closer to the truth, but she had never really believed that Guido could be guilty. The case against Valentina had seemed to be building.

Giò sat on a nearby chair. She couldn't stay on her feet; the whole floor seemed to dance around her as if she was on a sailing boat riding the wild sea. Determined not to look at the view, she turned to face the aquarium next to the inner wall of the restaurant.

Valentina? To tell the truth, Giò had never thought she could be the killer either. She seemed to have a split personality: on one side, sensitive and humorous; on the other side, a single-minded woman determined to defend her father's reputation from being tainted by a monster. Valentina had loved her adoptive father, Guido had hated the couple who took him home. Two such similar yet opposite stories. But who was the real killer? Could either of them be Angela Fiore's child?

And why would Valentina or Guido kill Mrs Galli, too? Blackmailing was the answer that came immediately to her mind. As Paolo had said, the motive behind a second murder is generally that the killer feels exposed, that he or she is in danger. And the belligerent Augusta Galli wouldn't keep it quiet; she'd undoubtedly let the murderer know what she knew. Then the murderer had reacted immediately and mercilessly. But was this second murder characteristic of the two suspects?

Thinking was difficult now, keeping her emotions in check even more so. Giò found relief in the bubbles tickling the algae and rising to the surface of the aquarium. She looked at the lobster moving his tied claws slowly. Standing still in an almost meditative trance, all of a sudden she had the feeling that she was in just the right place.

The aquarium and the blackmailing. Vittoria thought she'd heard Mrs Galli blackmailing someone; Giò couldn't get that thought out of her mind. But what about the aquarium? Mrs Galli had said that looking at the aquarium soothed her. She had wanted to get into the restaurant when it should have been obvious even to her that she couldn't gain access, that it was a crime scene.

And blackmail? What if *that* had been the real blackmail, not what Vittoria had heard? And if Mrs Galli had been trying to pass on a message, Giò knew who it was for. Why had the murder occurred in Maratea and not during the previous retreat? Because the murderer had only discovered Margherita's real identity that evening in the Pellicano Hotel's restaurant. Before that, they didn't know she had any connection with Maratea. And the weapon? How stupid – *that* was the weapon. It would leave no traces. Well, it would actually leave some traces, and that's why the broken wine glass had proved so useful.

These thoughts assaulted her in a swirl, one after the other, relentlessly. Even the mysterious visitor appearing around the time of the first murder, then again in the depths of the night when Augusta Galli was killed, fitted. A black jacket and white t-shirt – if you dress up in uniform, nobody will notice you, and in fact, the two witnesses had assumed the mystery person to be a waiter.

Giò held on to the arms of her chair tightly. The truth was giving her vertigo. She had to call Paolo, soon, but she could only do this from the safety of her room. She couldn't risk being overheard, but the trouble was her legs were as soft as melted butter and she couldn't even entertain the thought of standing up.

The inner restaurant door opened and Francesco entered the room.

"Giò, what are you doing here?" he asked her in surprise, clearly having thought he'd find the place empty.

"Just looking at the aquarium."

"It's relaxing, isn't it?"

"Indeed."

They both looked at the lobster, who kept crawling from one side to the other, as if conscious of the people staring at him.

"And why are you here?" Giò asked in turn.

"Just trying to get away from Mother." He flushed, before adding quickly, "I shouldn't have said that…"

"Why not? We all love our parents, but sometimes they can be too much, especially when we're with them for too long."

"On the other hand," he murmured, "how can we leave them, especially when they're getting older and need us more than ever?"

"I'm sure you already know the answer – it's the natural order of things. We need to live our own lives."

He took a chair and sat beside her.

"I feel like algae, floating in the water, seething with rage as I long for freedom, but my roots have me stuck exactly where I am."

"Maybe it's time for you to realise you're more a fish than algae."

Giò smiled at him. The thought must have made an impression on him, because he looked at her as if considering the possibility for the first time in his life. His face contorted incredulously like he'd just had an injection of life, an overdose of adrenalin.

Right on cue, the terrace door opened and Erminia appeared. Giò felt a frisson of anxiety travelling down her spine, vertebra by vertebra.

All I need now is to be the reluctant witness to a mother-son duel. Nope, I've got better things to do.

"Hello, Erminia," she said. "Please take this seat. I'll leave the two of you to have a nice chat – this aquarium is really inspiring."

Luckily, her legs didn't betray her. She was outside the dangerous restaurant before either mother or son had time to stop her. Seconds later, she was in her room, calling Paolo.

"Hello, I was just thinking of you," he said cheerfully. "We have discovered who Angela's child is. You will never believe it…"

"And you'll never believe this – I know exactly who the

murderer is," Giò cut him short, sharing her findings, then listening to Paolo's news.

"The problem is we don't have a shred of proof," Paolo concluded.

"I thought of that. We're having a boat trip along the coast tomorrow, it's our last retreat day. I could speak to Valentina – after all, she might still have the manuscript, if you see what I mean?"

And she went into all the details.

"But we'll need the doctor," Paolo replied.

"You can always speak to Dr Siringa. Won't he sort things out?"

A few minutes later, Paolo sent her a text.

"Siringa suffers from seasickness, so he asked Gimondi to come along."

"Fine," was her laconic answer.

29

ON THE SAILING BOAT

The two-masted gulet with its rubber dinghy picked them up from the hotel beach. To start with, as they boarded, they were still slightly embarrassed, as they'd been for the past two days, as if they didn't know whether they should still laugh and make jokes after what had happened, now the carabinieri had found out that most of them hadn't told the whole truth.

As planned, Dr Gimondi joined them. On the surface of things, he had happened to visit the hotel that morning, and Giò had invited him to come along. As it was his day off, he had been glad to accept the invitation. Did the rest of the party find his presence rather melancholy? True, he was not the pathologist, but he had still been there when the victims had been found, a constant reminder of what had occurred.

For his part, Enzo, the skipper, was determined that his guests would have a good time on his boat. He started by entertaining them with a few anecdotes and legends as they left Anginarra Beach and headed north towards Punta Infreschi. The day was gorgeous and the rocky coast, seen in all its glory from the water, sent a frisson of excitement through the party. The tension slowly gave way to enjoyment and they started laughing at Enzo's jokes.

They explored grottos and little bays, and finally anchored for lunch in Baia degli Infreschi, a large rocky bay surrounded by Mediterranean bush, famous for its exotic, clear waters and white stretches of beach. It could only be reached by long hikes or boat. This time of year, unsurprisingly, the gulet passengers were the only people on the bay.

The boat docked at the jetty. When Alberto turned round in search of Valentina, she'd already gone up the hiking trail with Dr Gimondi to get a view from the top over the entire bay. Erminia and Vittoria were stretching out on the beach, ready for sunbathing, while Annika and Simone followed Giò to a little promontory she knew. Sighing, Alberto accompanied Francesco to explore the grottos, while Guido was busy flying his drone and shooting film.

Giò had barely spoken to him since their difficult conversation the previous day. It was stupid, pretending to ignore each other, but on the other hand, it was difficult to carry on as if nothing had happened. Guido hadn't even tried to catch her eye, but she couldn't help glancing at him, wondering what images he was capturing, what he had in mind, what stunning videos he would have created by the end of the day.

The horn blew, announcing to the explorers that it was time for lunch and they could get back on board.

"Enzo, the smell is simply divine!" cried Annika.

"Spaghetti with pachino tomatoes, capers, anchovies and garlic."

The writers tucked in, the only sounds for a while their murmurs of approval.

"My goodness, is there any more?" Simone asked at last, showing Enzo his empty dish.

"Of course," Enzo replied, smiling. "I made plenty, knowing too well that life at sea makes you hungry."

"But don't give it all to him," Francesco said. "There are more hungry folks here."

"There's enough for all of you," Enzo replied, scooping

second helpings into the dishes that were being held out to him, begging for more.

When lunch was over, Enzo suggested they enjoy their coffee on the sea.

"Any chance to do some sailing?" asked Guido.

"There's almost no wind, but it may be better a little further from the coast. We'll try putting the sails up on our way back."

As the gulet left the beach, Alberto offered to prepare coffee, and Dr Gimondi helped him serve it. The Moka pot gurgled and the aroma of coffee mixed with the smell of the salty water.

"The first cup to your group leader," said Dr Gimondi, serving Annika. "And then to Mrs Spilimbergo." They had all invited him to refer to them by their first names, but it seemed he felt more at ease with formality.

"Don't forget our skipper!" Giò cried.

"Of course not," Alberto replied from the kitchen. "A double for him, he needs to take us back."

"Ms Valsecchi, this is for you," Dr Gimondi said, handing Valentina one of two cups. As her hand stretched towards the wrong one, he promptly corrected her. "No, the large one is for the captain."

Valentina grinned, took the smaller one and stirred some sugar in with a loud tinkling of her spoon. She was about to lift the cup to her lips, when...

"Don't drink that coffee!" cried Giò.

Dr Gimondi snatched the cup from Valentina and, quick as lightning, threw it and all its contents into the sea.

"Why did you do that?" asked Guido, puzzled.

"I thought it was dangerous." The doctor turned towards Giò. "You said it was."

"I only told her not to drink it."

"I'm sorry, I thought there must be something wrong with it," he said, looking mortified.

"We could have analysed it," Giò continued, "and found out for sure."

"I'm sorry, I didn't think..."

"Don't you worry," Giò consoled him, walking towards the boat's galley. "We substituted the cup you were going to serve to Valentina with another."

And from the tall cupboard, Brigadiere Paolo Rossi stepped out, holding a coffee cup and wiping some of the sweat from his forehead. The first part of his trip, hidden in one of the cabins, had been fine, but when he had moved to the cupboard... well, it wasn't the most comfortable of places.

"Yes," Paolo said. "This is the original cup, but to make sure there was no margin for error, we also taped everything on a nice video." He pointed to a camera above his head.

"That's a very sharp HD camera." Guido smiled. "No blurring, all details crystal clear. We'll be able to read the name of whatever he's used, even if he has now dumped the packet in the sea."

"Who, me? I prepared the cups," Alberto said, confused.

"No, not you. Him. When Dr Gimondi put Valentina's cup on the tray," Paolo explained, "he added something to it. You'd turned your back to rinse the Moka pot out to make more coffee, so he felt safe. Was Valentina going to be your third victim, Doctor?"

Dr Gimondi's face became red with fury.

"She killed my mother! She destroyed our lives! We'd have been so happy together."

The others looked blank. Giò enlightened them.

"You're speaking of Margherita Durante, aren't you?"

"That spiteful woman!"

"Did you already know her?"

"No, I didn't."

"But that Friday night at the Pellicano Restaurant, when you heard Margherita Durante saying she had lived in Villa degli Incanti, you put two and two together. Just by chance, you had met the woman who'd stolen your father from your mother. The woman responsible for Angela's suicide."

"Exactly! I hadn't gone looking for her, but there she was. I took it as a sign. The wretched woman said her days in Maratea were the best of her life, while my mother was so heartbroken, she killed herself. I was left all alone, and she never bothered to find out what had happened to us. How dare she refer to those as fine days?"

He sat down, his face twisted by rage.

"Unluckily, that night, Margherita mentioned she had a severe allergy to fish," Giò continued at a nod from Paolo. "Severe enough to oblige her to carry her EpiPens with her, always. And just a few steps away from you, there was an aquarium containing a lobster – one of the most common and powerful allergens in the fish world."

"Exactly!" said Dr Gimondi again. "I saw my opportunity to bring my mother's killer to justice at once. When the woman said she wanted to stay in the restaurant to do some work, I made sure the outside door stayed unlocked when I left with Dr Siringa. But I only pretended to leave, returning soon after saying goodbye to my colleague."

"It was a busy night," added Giò. "After Guido Gagliardi had left, a steady stream of people came and went."

"But I was already hiding in the kitchen at that point. I would have waited for hours if necessary, but it didn't take that long. After he left," he pointed to Francesco, "I walked in, got the lobster out of the aquarium and hit Mrs Durante on the face with it. She was shocked, then she panicked as I held her bag away from her and told her who I was. She said she'd never known I existed, that she'd make up for it, if only I'd give her the EpiPen. But the attack was even faster than I'd thought it would be. I laughed in her face as her throat swelled and she started suffocating, but it was her heart that couldn't bear it any longer."

The man was standing up on the deck, laughing. He was quite clearly insane.

"And once she was dead, you wiped her face with a napkin from the table, broke a glass of red wine and made sure it was underneath her head. If during the post-mortem the pathologist saw any ecchymosis, he would have attributed it to the broken glass and wouldn't have investigated further, especially as he'd be concentrating on the contaminated food in her stomach. It was important that either the kitchen staff got the blame or it was passed off as an unexplained death. Nobody would have linked the murder to you, a chance guest in the company of the local pathologist."

"But he didn't stop there, did he?" Annika asked. "Was it he who killed Mrs Galli? And he was ready to strike again, poisoning Valentina?"

"The stupid woman tried to blackmail me." Dr Gimondi was standing on the bow of the boat, his arms and legs bent as if ready to spring. Paolo signalled to Giò to keep talking.

"Yes, I was there when you met Augusta Galli for the first time," Giò said. "She mentioned the aquarium, how soothing it was for her. But it was not a throwaway remark, as it seemed to be. No, it was a coded message for you. Possibly she had noticed something amiss with the lobster, perhaps its claw was broken, or maybe she had seen a mystery man leaving across the terrace from her window as Erminia did – the man in the black jacket – and recognised him as you."

Dr Gimondi nodded, as if explaining everything would convince them he'd had to act the way he did. "She phoned me a few days later and told me to meet her at 11pm, when the group of authors would all be asleep. She'd leave the back door of the hotel open, as I'd told her I wouldn't bring my mobile with me."

"That was a stroke of genius," Giò said admiringly. "If we were to check your movements via the GPS on your mobile, you'd appear to have been in Capitello until the next morning."

"Yes, I had to build my alibi quickly. I received a call from Mrs Galli at 6pm, which was true, and only lied about the content of the call, saying Mrs Galli had asked me to visit her the next morning. At 11pm, she let me into her room, I gave her the money she'd demanded, and while she was counting it, I knocked her out cold with chloroform. It didn't take much time nor effort, she was old and weak. In five minutes, she was sedated and I could inject a good dose of insulin into her. I had thought of an embolism, but once I saw her diabetes medication, I realised I could again pass the sudden death off as an accident. The whisky she'd been drinking would help too."

"So you stayed there…"

"For an hour or so. I left two empty vials next to her bed, but I gave her more to make sure it was enough to kill her."

Giò and Guido's eyes locked. Dr Gimondi had left around midnight, just when Guido had said he had spotted a waiter in the corridor. But they knew better than to interrupt the man.

"I knew it would be difficult to track the exact amount of insulin in the following analyses, so I took the rest of the empty vials with me. She was sweating; she was in hypoglycaemia for long enough for me to know that if, by any chance, she survived, the brain damage would be irreparable. She'd never recover enough to be a danger to me, so I left knowing the night would do the rest. At 7.30, I was back at the hotel, this time officially, and there she was, dead."

"But why would you want to kill Valentina?" Alberto cried furiously.

"That was not his… er… fault," Giò explained. "Dr Siringa phoned Dr Gimondi yesterday and told him he'd been requested to join the writers' group this morning on the sailing boat. The carabinieri were setting a trap for Valentina Valsecchi and required medical assistance on board should anything go wrong, and Dr Siringa told him how much he loathes anything moving on the water. The idea of being on so much as a canoe makes him sick, so would Dr Gimondi take his place?"

"And I imagine he was quite happy to do that?" Alberto asked.

"Even more so when Dr Siringa explained to him the carabinieri suspected Valentina had killed Margherita to protect her father's character from defamation through her memoir.

Finally, Siringa told him the manuscript hadn't been destroyed, but it was still in Valentina's hands."

"And I confirmed it was in my possession during our walk in the Baia," Valentina's jet black eyes were shining, "as Giò had instructed me."

At that moment, a desperate Gimondi jumped from the boat into the water. But miraculously, his body slipped by the propeller unharmed.

"Oh my goodness, I don't think he can swim," Giò cried, watching the doctor thrash about in a panic. Before she knew what was happening, she heard a splash from the other side of the boat.

Paolo had to swim fast to reach the man, who was flailing his arms in a desperate attempt to keep water out of his lungs. When Paolo approached him, Gimondi grabbed hold of him so violently that Paolo had to push him away and get hold of him from behind instead.

"Just stop it! I'll keep you afloat," the brigadiere cried out after a few coughs to empty his own lungs. Dr Gimondi finally calmed down as Paolo kept his head above water while the boat slowly turned back to save them. Minutes later, the two men were inside the boat's galley, drinking something hot and enveloped in warm blankets – the April sea after the storm was still far too cold for bathing. But Gimondi had now shut himself in absolute silence, refusing to answer any questions that required more than a nod or shake of the head.

"Why did you rescue him?" Guido asked Paolo that evening in the hotel.

"I'm a cop."

"Well, if he'd died, justice would have followed its natural course."

"I'm not an executioner, I need only to *bring* criminals to justice. *Administering* justice itself isn't my field," replied Paolo.

"Why was Gimondi so concerned about Margherita's manuscript? Did he think it might give him away?" Vittoria asked.

"He dreaded that. By reading it, the carabinieri would likely have been alerted to the fact that the adopted child in question wasn't Valentina at all. At the same time, he hoped Valentina's death would look like suicide and the investigations would stop there and then. We would have thought that she had poisoned herself, fearing she'd been found out, and that would buy him time. He would then try to retrieve the manuscript later. If it represented a threat to him, he would destroy it; if it would reinforce the carabinieri's opinion that Valentina had a motive to kill, he'd leave it where it was. The only important thing now was to kill her."

Valentina looked shocked, but Giò caught the lively sparkle in her eyes that had disappeared the moment Margherita had come into her life again.

"I'm alive," she whispered.

"Yes, my love," Alberto said, hugging her. "You're alive and you should never fear anything nor anybody again."

She looked at him. "Because you'll be taking care of me?" she asked with just a hint of sarcasm in her voice.

"Not at all. It's because you've learned that fearing things, being afraid, is not the way forward. And if you want, we could remind each other of that lesson in the future."

She smiled at him. This was the answer she had been hoping for – not a guide, but someone to share life's lessons with.

"And you will not run away from me again?" This time, her voice had a teasing note and she wore the expression of a jubilant kitten ready to play.

"I only feared I might be too boring a man for you. I tried to forget you, but when I saw you again, I felt... I was ready to take all the risks. And should you get fed up with my seriousness, you can always look around for someone better than me."

She smiled again, and before he could put more of his silly ideas into words, she kissed him, despite the others watching on. But as they were such good friends, they pretended to be busy chatting with one another, or reading the menu, trying to make up their minds whether or not they should indulge in dessert.

30

DEPARTURES

Annika and Giò were alone on the Pellicano terrace. Alberto had already left, and Francesco was just manoeuvring his way out of the parking space.

"Put it in reverse and pull back a couple of metres," they heard Erminia command. "Correct it, don't turn too much to the right! Watch out for that stupid tree."

"Poor Francesco, Erminia will never change," said Annika, smiling.

"So isn't it funny that he has started a relationship with Vittoria?" Giò said. "She doesn't hold back either – out of the frying pan, into the fire."

"Oh no, he needs to be bossed around," said Annika, sitting down at a table facing the sea and breathing deeply, relaxing for the first time in days. "He could only leave his mother for someone just as strong willed."

"I wouldn't want to be a fly on the wall when the two women get together," Giò blurted out.

"He'll not take sides, and who can blame him?"

"Talking of gentle men, there's something I wanted to ask you, about Simone. Why did he make his life tough by saying that he'd seen Margherita alive at 2am, at least two hours after she'd died? That convinced Paolo that he'd had a role in the murder."

"That man is a disaster!" Annika shook her head in the most tender gesture of disapproval Giò had ever witnessed. "You know, he writes of parallel universes, and he convinced himself in one of those universes he might actually have killed Margherita."

"You're kidding me?"

"Please, try to understand. He spent most of that night wishing the woman was dead, and when he finally gathered the courage to go to see her... he found her dead. No weapon nearby, just struck down by some malevolent force. So he believed it was because of the things he'd been thinking. He then thought that if he kept pretending the woman was still alive, he could somehow reverse things, turn back time..."

Giò was uncertain whether to laugh at that. It must have been torture for him.

"That's not too dissimilar to what Valentina said. She admitted that when she walked in the second time and found Margherita dead, she convinced herself she had done her in the previous time, and that her brain had wiped that traumatic memory. She couldn't come up with any other explanation."

"The worst thing is that each of us had our own theory. I was lying to protect Simone, Alberto and Vittoria wanted to help Valentina, and I've a suspicion you covered for Guido..."

This time, Giò did give a laugh – a guilty one.

"Yes, I confess I kept some information from the carabinieri. I'd seen Guido in the corridor at 4am, just at the time Mrs Galli had passed away. I didn't know whether it was a coincidence or not. Certainly the guy has a talent for making his life tougher than it needs to be."

"But how about Vittoria overhearing Mrs Galli blackmailing someone?" Annika asked. "You told me you thought she was blackmailing Margherita, didn't you?"

"That's what I thought at the time, but now I think

Margherita and Mrs Galli were simply 'discussing' their meeting with Mr Pecoriello, and Mrs Galli was trying to get a bigger cut of the money. But it was another false lead as for so long, I was concentrating on the mysterious blackmail..."

The two gassosa they had ordered arrived, a slice of lemon curled around the rim of each glass. They clinked as if it was the best champagne, then Annika continued.

"And finally, Erminia was lying to protect Francesco."

"Truth is, we were all so afraid that someone close to us was guilty, or could seem such, that we told plenty of lies and managed to confuse the carabinieri..."

"To the point that they thought Erminia and Guido had lied when they reported they'd seen 'the waiter'?"

"Yes, the carabinieri thought it was a red herring to make them believe someone outside our group was involved..."

"While that was possibly the only truth we ever told them." Annika grinned. "How could we be this awful?"

"I guess the only disappointed one will be Strazio. There was a conspiracy of sorts – a conspiracy of the innocent."

"Giò," Annika put her empty glass on the table in front of her and looked frankly at her friend, "we writers are a bad lot. You'd better stay away from us and join someone else."

"Like who?" Giò asked in alarm.

"A video maker, for example." And Annika winked at Giò as Guido made his way towards them. "I'd better go and get ready to leave my room for my new temporary home."

"AND YOU NEVER SUSPECTED ME?" GUIDO ASKED, THE FLY-AWAY RED hair on his forehead barely hiding the joyous sparkle in his hazel eyes.

"No, I never suspected you," Giò admitted.

"And why was that? I'm not a respectable guy deserving your total trust."

"Let's just say it wasn't your type of murder."

Guido threw his head back and gave one of his loud laughs. "So you don't think I'd never kill someone, only that I didn't do it in this case?"

"Not too sure about the first one, but definite about the second. You have such a temper..."

"That's true, Giò, but I don't think I could kill someone. I can get very nasty at times, though." He rose from the chair and invited her to join him by the terrace parapet to look at the only white sail on the horizon. "I do have a temper and I need to improve... Giò, would you help me?"

"Are you asking me to be your therapist?" She laughed, but her lips were quivering all of a sudden.

"Indeed." He pulled her gently into his arms. "Have you made your decision, Giò? Will you come with me?"

My goodness, am I really meant to resist this? Shouldn't I be happy just kissing him? There was a side of her that couldn't cope with too much tenderness. Again she felt like she was on the edge of an abyss – she loved the feeling and feared it at the same time. But this time, fear of the emptiness gave her the strength she needed.

"I don't think so, no." She couldn't believe she had said it.

He was surprised. It was obvious he had expected a very different answer.

"You don't have to come with me for the whole trip, just join me wherever you can..."

"No, I came over... ahem... to Maratea. I mean, to stay." The speech she had rehearsed a thousand times in her mind was falling to pieces.

"Maratea could become our home base when we're not travelling."

"You don't understand. I've lived ten years of my life trying to second guess Dorian's ambitions as well as I could."

"Is that the man you were to marry?"

"Exactly."

"The idiot!"

"Maybe, but I've realised it wasn't all his fault. There was also stupid me trying to comply with his wishes, putting my own aside."

"But we're not all Dorians."

"Not at all," but was she really that sure? No, but it was good to sound like a wise and forgiving woman. "But I need to do what *I* want. And frankly, I don't fancy packing for a world tour right now. I want to finish my travel memoir…"

"You'd have enough material for the next one, about Asia and the Silk Road."

"But that's your trip, your dream, your adventure." Was she being too dramatic? "Not mine."

"Really, Giò?"

Why wouldn't he get angry with her, say she was being selfish, so she could tell him to bugger off and have done with it? No, instead he had such an understanding expression. She felt her eyes getting watery and a thick sadness embracing her like a damp coat. Why wasn't life as simple as Granny had said it was? You'd meet a guy, marry him in your twenties, settle into a house in your own village, have a few children and be happy. Why all these choices and complications? Why Guido? And mostly, why her?

"Hey, what are you doing?" she said as his lips got closer to hers. But he wouldn't stop, despite all her protests, and in seconds she was swept into the storm. She felt her stomach drop in the vertiginous fall; she tried to resist, then had to accept the battle was in vain.

And when, thirty seconds later, he smiled at her, saying, "See you, Giò," she just about managed to walk to the bench, sit there and look at the gulf. *Her* gulf: the solid mountains behind her, Mount Bulgheria ahead, and a seagull flying above her in large circles, its wings open as it effortlessly rode the air currents.

EPILOGUE

A ngelica opened the cabinet in her bathroom, safe in her own home in Maratea, and found the red bottle of Alamut perfume she had purchased at Agnese's.

"That was all your fault," she reproached it, pointing an accusing finger. Her hand reached for the bottle and she sprayed a couple of squirts on to her pulse. Then it all came back: the amazing landscape of the Alborz Mountains, the assassins' legends, the crackling fire at night... the kidnapping. Yes, that too. By now it felt like nothing more than a thrilling adventure she'd read in a book.

Then she thought about the adrenaline of the final days in Isfahan. She had expected them to spend their days closeted in a hotel room, hardly going out, but instead Rolando had insisted they enjoy the city's charms. The sense of adventure had taken them over and they had explored the amazing city, walking around the Imam Mosque at night, visiting its glittering mosaics and enrapturing over its architecture, its colourful dome during the daytime. They'd even enjoyed the noisy bazaars that stayed open till late.

And she'd loved it all! Oh, as crazy as it sounded, she and Rolando couldn't wait to return to the country the next year.

After all, they owed their newfound happiness to Iran. And wasn't happiness the only thing that mattered?

AFTER HIS SHOWER, ROLANDO OPENED HIS CABINET. VOLEUR DE Roses – such a good perfume, and it meant so much to him. Never in almost 60 years of life had he suspected that stealing a rose, as well as a little misleading, could mean so much to a woman. He sprayed some on and got dressed, appreciating the wonderful, velvety notes.

Once in his study, Rolando browsed his email until he found the message he was looking for from Iran Cinematographic Adventures. Sajad had confirmed they had received the last chunk of Rolando's payment and hoped he and Mrs Ariosto had fully appreciated their services. John H, aka Ivan Strogoff, aka Mean Eyes, had recovered from Mrs Ariosto's blow to his head, but yes, the shovel had been padded just in case. Finally, would Mr Ariosto mind leaving them a review, even if under an alias?

Of course, Rolando was only too pleased to do that. Adjusting his glasses on his nose, he typed:

"Very reliable company. Iran Cinematographic Adventures will turn your visit into one to remember, taking you to remote and beautiful places all through the country. The actors are magnificent – a bit pricey, maybe, but totally worth it.

The Roses Thief.

DEAR READER,

I hope you enjoyed this mystery. There are three more books available featuring Giò Brando, and new ones to come.

In the meantime…

Is there any way a reader may help an author? Yes! Please **leave a review on Amazon, Goodreads** and/or **Bookbub**. It doesn't matter how long or short it is; even a single sentence can say all that needs to be said. We may live in a digital era, but **this old world of ours still revolves around word of mouth**. A review allows a book to leave the shadows of the unknown and introduces it to other passionate readers.

GRAZIE :)

GLOSSARY

ANTIPASTO – this is not properly considered a 'course', it's just something that comes before (ANTI) the meal (PASTO). In fact, the first course (usually pasta or risotto) is called PRIMO PIATTO, then you have your SECONDO PIATTO (second course), and only after that can you enjoy your longed-for dessert. An ANTIPASTO can be CALDO (warm), which means small but numerous cooked dishes, or FREDDO (cold), as in a selection of local cheeses, cured meats, or a combination of both (ANTIPASTO MISTO).

APERITIVO: this is a convivial social event, often in a bar with friends before heading home for the family lunch or dinner. Let's say it's a sort of appetiser before the real meal. It can be simple or lavish, merely a drink or a variety of finger food. In Italy, we also invite people home for an aperitivo, which is not as formal as a proper meal, but beware! Like Granny's panzerotti, it can be delicious, moreish and *very* filling.

BARLEY COFFEE – In Italy, this is an alternative to coffee that's not coffee at all, nor does it contain caffeine. The drink was popular during the Second World War when the price of real coffee rocketed, with barley and chicory being cheaper local ingredients available in the countryside. In the case of barley, the tradition continued after the war as a healthy alternative where caffeine might cause problems. The beans are roasted and ground, and a Moka pot or bar machine is used to brew it like a regular espresso.

BOCCONOTTO – plural bocconotti: a sweet typically made in Maratea, this fragrant pastry is filled with either sour cherries, sometimes with custard, or custard and chocolate. And in this at least, I agree with Giò – my favourite place to eat bocconotti is Panza in Angiporto Cavour 9.

BRIGADIERE – plural brigadieri: this can be loosely compared to a detective sergeant. In the carabinieri ranks, a brigadiere operates below a maresciallo.

CARABINIERE – plural carabinieri. In Italy, we don't only have the polizia (much like the police in most countries), we also have the carabinieri. Essentially, this is another police force, but it's part of the army and is governed by the Ministry of Defence, whereas the polizia depends on the Ministry of the Interior. The two are often in competition with one another (though they will never admit it), so never confuse one with the other (especially if you're talking with Maresciallo Mangiaboschi, he is rather touchy). For me, the only difference between the two is that we have a number of cracking jokes about the carabinieri and none about the polizia. Don't ask me why.

In Maratea, there's only the carabinieri and no polizia. But Paolo would have been a carabiniere and not a policeman in any case. By the way being a military corps carabinieri tend to wear their uniforms more than the police corps even when investigating crimes.

CORNETTO – plural cornetti. This is the equivalent of a French croissant. I have to admit it was the French who invented them, but they're very popular in Italy too.

GASSOSA – a popular non-alcoholic lemon-scented soda used mainly in Southern Italy.

HYPOBOLE – I'm sure many of you are wondering what hypobole is, and whether it's not a typo for hyperbole. Well, it's not, neither is it an Italian word. It's a word so unusual, it doesn't even appear in the Kindle Dictionary, meaning a rhetorical figure (another example of a rhetorical figure is a metaphor) where language is not used literally. In Granny's case, she is anticipating Giò's objections and refuting them one by one. I apologise for the weird word, but I could not find a better one.

LINGUINE ALLO SCOGLIO – this is one of the best and most traditional dishes from Naples and Campania (though you will find it across the whole of the southern part of the country). Its name refers to the scoglio (or sea rock), which is where these fish that can be easily found in the Mediterranean. It typically contains clams, mussels, prawns and small squid. Granny would say, "No frozen fish", but you're free to do as Giò would and defrost something – just don't tell the oldest member of the Brando family. You will need to respect the different cooking times of the fish, but they will all end up in a large frying pan with pachino tomatoes (small round tomatoes from Sicily), olive oil, garlic, and a touch of wine. Linguine is a flatter version of spaghetti, but not as large as tagliatelle.

MARESCIALLO: this rank is similar to detective inspector. A maresciallo is superior to a brigadiere, carabiniere semplice and appuntato.

MOUILLETTE: see 'TOUCHE' below.

ORECCHIETTE – literally, this means 'small ears'. This pasta is skilfully shaped with a knife, then on the tip of your thumb to look like a small ear. If you want to have fun, google 'fare le orecchiette Pugliesi' and enjoy the videos showing how skilful and fast the real pasta makers can be.

SALUTE! – or CIN CIN (pronounced chin chin)! This is the equivalent of "Cheers!" When celebrating an event with a glass of wine or prosecco, we love to accompany the word by clinking our glasses together.

TOUCHE: this is a French word that refers to paper strips onto which you can spray perfumes for people to smell. They're also called *mouillette*, again a French word.

VONGOLA – plural vongole: means clam(s), so spaghetti alle vongole means spaghetti with clams. In a real restaurant in Southern Italy, you will always find spaghetti alle vongole on the menu, but (TIP!) if it offers spaghetti Bolognese, then the place is only run for the sake of tourists. Italians do not eat spaghetti with their Bolognese sauce, which is not a common sauce in the southern part of the country anyway.

If you have found other Italian words in the story and would like to know what they mean, please let me know.

Contact me on:
   Twitter: @adrianalici
   Join the Maratea Murder Club

ABOUT THE AUTHOR

Adriana Licio lives in the Apennine Mountains in southern Italy, not far from Maratea, the seaside setting for her first cosy series, *An Italian Village Mystery*.

She loves loads of things: travelling, reading, walking, good food, small villages, and home swapping. A long time ago, she spent six years falling in love with Scotland, and she has never recovered. She now runs her family perfumery, and between a dark patchouli and a musky rose, she devours cosy mysteries.

She resisted writing as long as she could, fearing she might get carried away by her fertile imagination. But one day, she found an alluring blank page and the words flowed in the weird English she'd learned in Glasgow.

Adriana finds peace for her restless, enthusiastic soul by walking in nature with her adventurous golden retriever Frodo and her hubby Giovanni.

Do you want to know more?
Join the **Maratea Murder Club**

You can also stay in touch on:
www.adrianalicio.com

facebook.com/adrianalicio.mystery

twitter.com/adrianalici

amazon.com/author/adrianalicio

bookbub.com/authors/adriana-licio

MORE BOOKS FROM ADRIANA LICIO

And Then There Were Bones, prequel to the *An Italian Village Mystery* series, is only available by signing up to www. adrianalicio.com/murderclub – You can unsubscribe any time you like, but of course, I hope you will stay.

Murder on the Road is the first book in the series, and it lets you know how and why Giò Brando decided to come back to Maratea (and what else life has in store for her).

A Fair Time for Death is a mystery set during the Autumn Chestnut Fair in Trecchina, a mountain village near Maratea, involving a perfume with a split personality, a disappearing corpse, a disturbing secret from the past and a mischievous goat.

A Mystery Before Christmas A haunting Christmas song from a faraway land. A child with striking green eyes. A man with no past. A heartwarming mystery for those who want to breathe in the delicious scents and flavours of a Mediterranean December.

They say that…

Those well informed on Adriana's movements say she is working at **a new series that will take us through small villages**

all across Europe, starting from Castelmezzano in Basilicata. Let's wish her luck with the Muse!

JOIN THE MARATEA MURDER CLUB

You'll get exclusive content:

- **Book 0,** *And Then There Were Bones*, the prequel to the *An Italian Village Mystery* series available nowhere else
- **Giò Brando's Maratea Album** – photos of her favourite places and behind-the-scenes secrets
- **A Maratea Map** – including most places featured in the series
- **Adriana Licio's News** – new releases, news from Maratea, but no spam – Giò would loathe it!
- **Cosy Mystery Passion:** a place to share favourite books, characters, tips and tropes

Sign up to **www.adrianalicio.com/murderclub**

AND THEN THERE WERE BONES

And Then There Were Bones, prequel to the *An Italian Village Mystery* series, is only available by signing up to
www.adrianalicio.com/murderclub

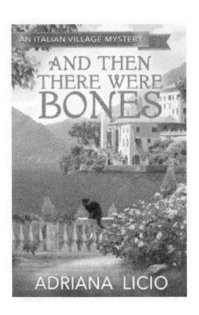

A Murder Mystery along the lines of Agatha Christie's *And Then There Were None*.

When feisty travel writer, Giò Brando, receives an invitation to join her long-time friend on an island in Calabria for a Murder Mystery weekend, she is excited by the prospect.

To run away from the grey London weather for a while; to escape her stubborn fiancé – and even better, her mother-in-law-to-be – meet her family in her Italian hometown by the sea, and enjoy the Murder weekend with some celebrity guests sounds too good to be true.

In fact, some of the guests are just as temperamental as you would expect from celebs. But when one mysteriously disappears, and strange things befall…

Gosh, what's happening?

Is a madman trying to repeat the Ten Little Indians Saga or there's a method to this madness?

As the storm ravages the island, cutting it off from the mainland,

Giò has very little time to find out what is going on and save herself as well as the surviving guests from certain death.

Made in the USA
Las Vegas, NV
11 July 2024